THE ADVENTURES OF
Santa Paws

THE ADVENTURES OF
Santa Paws

Santa Paws
The Return of Santa Paws

Nicholas Edwards

SCHOLASTIC INC.
New York Toronto London Auckland
Sydney Mexico City New Delhi Hong Kong

Santa Paws, ISBN 978-0-590-62400-8
Copyright © 1995 by Ellen Emerson White

The Return of Santa Paws, ISBN 978-0-590-94471-7
Copyright © 1996 by Ellen Emerson White

ISBN 978-0-545-22551-9

12 11 10 9 8 7 6 5 4 3 2   11 12 13 14 15/0

Printed in the U.S.A.   40
First compilation printing, October 2010

This special Christmas collection
includes these novels:

Santa Paws

1

When the dog woke up, it was very cold. On winter nights, his mother always brought him, along with his brother and sisters, to some safe place out of the wind. She would scratch up some dry leaves to make them a little nest, and they would all cuddle up together. Then, in the morning, his mother would go off and try to find food for them. Sometimes she would let them come along, although they were too small to be much help. Mostly, she would forage for food while he and his siblings would scuffle and play someplace nearby.

Once, his mother had lived in a big, nice house with a lot of college students. But then, when it got warm, they all left. She wasn't sure why they hadn't wanted her to come with them. Some of the students had even left without patting her, or saying goodbye. Her favorite, Jason, had filled up her water dish, given her some biscuits, and told her what a good dog she was. But then, he got in his car and drove away, too.

She had waited in front of the house for a long time, but none of them came back. Ever since then, she had lived on the streets. Sometimes, nice people would give her food, but more often, she was on her own. There were even times when people would be mean and throw things at her, or chase her away.

Then, when he and his siblings were born, she had to spend most of her time taking care of them. She had a special route of trash cans and other places she would check for discarded food. If she found anything, like stale bread or old doughnuts, she would drag the food back and they would all gobble it down. On special days, she might even find some meat in funny plastic packages. They would tear them open and gulp down the old hamburger or bacon or chicken. He and his siblings would always fight playfully over the last little bits, but when his mother growled at them, they would stop right away and be good. The days when she brought home meat were the best days of all. Too often though, when they went to sleep, they were all still very hungry.

He was the smallest of the four puppies, but he had the biggest appetite and slept the most, too. Lots of mornings, he would wake up and be the only one left under the abandoned porch, or in a deep gully, or wherever they had spent the night.

Lately, they had been sleeping in an old forgotten shed, behind a house where no people lived. It was safer that way. Lots of times, even if they wagged their tails, people would yell at them or act afraid. But when he saw big scary cars speed by, with happy dogs looking out the windows, he wished he knew *those* people. He also liked the people who would saunter down the street, with dogs on leashes walking proudly next to them. He really wanted to *be* one of those lucky dogs.

But, he wasn't, and he was happy, anyway. His mother always took care of them, and he loved his brother and sisters. They were a family, and as long as they were together, they were safe.

On this particular morning, he yawned a few times, and then rolled to his feet. None of the others were around, but he was sure they would be back soon with some breakfast. Maybe today they would even find some meat! Once he had stood up, he stretched a few times and yawned again. It was *really* cold, and he shivered a little. In fact, it would be nice to curl up again and get some more sleep. But he decided that he was more thirsty than he was sleepy and that it was time to go outside.

There was a hole in the back part of the old shed that they used for a door. He squirmed through it and immediately felt ice-cold snow under his paws. He shivered again, and shook the snow off each paw. It was *much* windier outside than it had been in the shed and he stepped tentatively through the fresh drifts of snow.

In the woods nearby, there was a small stream, where they would always drink. On some mornings lately, the water would be frozen, but his mother had shown him how to stamp his paw on the ice to break it. Today, there was so much snow that he couldn't even *find* the water at first. Then, when he did, he couldn't break the ice. He jumped with all four feet, slipping and sliding, but nothing happened. The ice was just too thick. Finally, he gave up and sat down in the snow, whimpering a little. Now he was going to be hungry *and* thirsty.

He swallowed a few mouthfuls of snow, but he still felt thirsty. The snow also made his insides feel cold. Where was his mother? Where were his brother and sisters? They had never left him for such a long time before. He ran back and forth in front of the frozen stream, whining anxiously. What if they were lost? What if they were hurt? What if they *never* came back? What would happen to him?

Maybe they were back at the shed, waiting for him. Maybe they had brought back food, and he and his brother could roll and play and pretend to fight over it. He should have waited for them, instead of wandering away.

He ran through the woods to the shed. Some of the snowdrifts were so tall that they were almost over his head and it took a lot of energy to bound through them. No, they would never go away and forget him. Never, ever.

But the shed was still deserted. He barked a few times, then waited for answering barks. Lately, his bark had been getting bigger and deeper, so he filled his chest with air and tried again. His bark echoed loudly through the silent backyard and woods. When there was still no answer, he whimpered and lay down to wait for them.

He rested his head on his numb front paws. They would probably come back through the big field behind the shed, and he watched the empty acres miserably. If he moved, he might miss them, so he would just stay here and wait. No matter how long it took, he would stay.

The sun was out and shining on him, which made him feel better. He waited patiently, staring at the field with his ears pricked forward alertly. He could hear birds, and squirrels, and faraway cars — but, no dogs. He lifted his nose to try and catch their scent in the air, but he couldn't smell them, either.

So, he just waited. And waited, and waited, and waited. The sun went away after a while, and dark grey clouds rolled in to cover the sky. But still, he waited.

A light snow started falling, but he didn't abandon his post. He wanted to be able to *see* his family the second they came back. Every so often he would stand up to shake off the fresh flakes of snow that had landed on his fur. Then he would shiver, stamp out a new bed for himself, and lie back down. He had never felt so cold, and lonely, and miserable in his life.

Once it began to get dark, he couldn't help whimpering some more and yelping a few times. Something very bad must have happened to his family. Maybe, instead of waiting so long, he should have tried to follow their trail. Maybe they were hurt somewhere, or trapped. But if he went to look for them, they might come back while he was gone and think *he* was lost for good. Then they might go away and he would *never* find them.

There was a street running in front of the boarded-up house and a car was cruising slowly by. A bright beam of light flashed across the house and yard. The dog cringed and tried to duck out of the way. His mother had taught them that when people came around, it was usually safer to hide, just in case.

The car braked to a stop and two big men in uniforms got out. They were both local police officers, out on their nightly patrol.

"Come on, Steve," the man who had been driving said, as he stood by the squad car. "I didn't see anything."

Steve, who was about thirty years old with thick dark hair, aimed his flashlight around the yard. "We've had three break-ins in the last

6

week," he answered. "If we have drifters in town, this is the kind of place where they might hide out."

"I know," the other cop, who was named Bill, said, sounding defensive. He was heavier than Steve was, with thinning blond hair and a neatly trimmed mustache. "I went to the academy, too, remember?"

Steve grinned at him. "Well, yeah, Bill," he agreed. "But *I* studied."

Bill laughed and snapped on his own flashlight. "Okay, fair enough," he said, and directed the beam at the boarded-up windows of the house. "But, come on. Oceanport isn't exactly a high crime area."

"Law and order," Steve said cheerfully. "That's our job, pal."

The men sounded friendly, but the dog uneasily hung back in the shadows. One of the lights passed over him, paused, and came whipping back.

"There!" Steve said, and pointed towards the shed. "I told you I saw something!"

"Whoa, a *dog*," Bill said, his voice a little sarcastic. "We'd better call for back-up."

Steve ignored that and walked further into the yard. "It must be one of those strays," he said. "I thought Charlie finally managed to round all of them up this morning." Charlie was the animal control officer in Oceanport.

Bill shrugged. "So, he missed one. We'll put a

report in, and he can come back out here tomorrow."

"It's *cold*," Steve said. "You really want to leave the poor thing out here all night? He looks like he's only a puppy."

Bill made a face. "I don't feel like chasing around after him in the snow, either. Let Charlie do it. He needs the exercise."

Steve crouched down, holding his gloved hand out. "Come here, boy! Come on, pup!"

The dog hung back. What did they want? Should he go over there, or run away and hide? His mother would know. He whined quietly and kept his distance.

"He's wild, Steve," Bill said. "This'll take all night."

Steve shook his head, still holding his hand out. "Charlie said they were just scared. He figured once the vet checked them over and they got a few decent meals, they'd be fine." He snapped his fingers. "Come here, boy. Come on."

The dog shifted his weight and stayed where he was. He had to be careful. It might be some kind of trap.

"He's pretty mangy-looking," Bill said critically.

Steve frowned at him. "Are you kidding? That dog's at least half German shepherd. Clean him up a little, and he'd be something to see. And he's young, too. He'd be easy to train."

8

Bill looked dubious. "Maybe. Give me a good retriever, any day."

Steve stood up abruptly. "Wait a minute. I've got an idea. I still have a sandwich in the car."

"I'm starved," Bill said, trailing after him. "Don't give it to the dog, give it to *me*."

Steve paid no attention to that. He dug into a brown paper bag below the front seat of the squad car and pulled out a thick, homemade sandwich wrapped in waxed paper. "If I catch him, can you take him home?" he asked.

"Are you serious? You know how tough my cat is," Bill said. "Besides, you're the one who likes him so much."

"Yeah," Steve agreed, "but I can't keep him. Not with Emily due any day now. I don't want to do anything to upset her. Besides, she's *already* bugged about me not getting the lights on the Christmas tree yet."

"You'd better get moving," Bill said, laughing. "There's only a week to go."

Steve nodded wryly. "I know, I know. I'm going to do it tomorrow, before my shift — I swear."

As he crossed the yard, carrying the sandwich, the dog shrank away from him. After all, it *could* be some kind of trick. His mother always helped him decide who they could trust, and who they couldn't. He didn't know *how* to take care of himself.

"Hey, what about your brother?" Bill suggested. "Didn't he have to have that old collie of his put to sleep recently?"

"Yeah, a few weeks ago," Steve said, and held the sandwich out in the dog's direction. "My niece and nephew are still heartbroken."

Bill shrugged. "So, bring the dog to them."

Steve thought about that, then shook his head. "I don't know, you can't force a thing like that. They might not be ready yet."

Just then, the police radio in their squad car crackled. They both straightened up and listened, as the dispatcher called in a burglar alarm in their sector.

"Looks like the dog is going to have to wait," Bill said. He hurried over to the car and picked up the radio to report in.

Steve gazed across the dark yard at the shivering little dog. "I'm sorry, pal," he said. "We'll send Charlie out after you tomorrow. Try to stay warm tonight." Gently, he set the meatloaf sandwich down in the snow. "Enjoy your supper now." Then he hustled back to the car.

The dog waited right where he was, even after the police car was gone. Then, tentatively, he took a couple of steps out of the woods. He hesitated, sniffed the air, and hesitated some more. Finally, he got up his nerve and bolted across the yard. He was so hungry that he gobbled each sandwich half in two huge bites, and then licked the surrounding snow for any crumbs he might have missed.

It was the best meal he had had for a long time.

Once he was finished, he ran back to the shed and wiggled inside through the hole in the back. If he waited all night, maybe his family would come back. No matter what, he would stay on guard until they did. He was very tired, but he would *make* himself stay awake.

The night before, he and his family had slept in a tangle of leaves and an old musty tarpaulin. The shed had felt crowded, but very warm and safe.

Tonight, all the dog felt was afraid, and very, very alone.

2

It was a long cold night, and even though he tried as hard as he could to remain on guard, the dog finally fell asleep. When he woke up in the grey dawn light, he was still alone. His family really *had* left him!

He crept over to the jagged wooden hole in the back of the shed and peeked outside. Even more snow had fallen during the night, and the whole world looked white and scary. Just as he started to put his front paws through the hole, he heard a small truck parking on the street. Instantly, he retreated.

It was Charlie Norris, who was the animal control officer for the small town of Oceanport. He climbed out of his truck, with some dog biscuits in one hand, and a specially designed nooselike leash in the other.

Inside the shed, the dog could hear the man tramping around through the snow, whistling and calling out, "Here, boy!" But the dog didn't move, afraid of what the man might do to him. The biscuits smelled good, but the leash looked dangerous. He *wanted* to go outside, but if the man tried to take him away, he would miss his family when they came back to get him.

"Don't see any footprints," the man mumbled to himself as he wandered around the snowy yard. "Guess the poor little thing took off last night." He looked around some more, then finally gave up and went back to his truck.

After the truck had driven away, the dog ventured outside. Today, he was going to go *look* for his family. No more waiting. First, he lifted his leg to mark a couple of spots near the shed. That way, if they came back, they would know that he hadn't gone far.

He stuck his muzzle in the wind, and then down in the snow. With the new drifts, it was hard to pick up a scent. But he found a faint whiff and began following it.

The trail led him through the woods, in the opposite direction from the frozen stream. A couple of times, he lost the scent and had to snuffle around in circles to pick it up again.

Then, he came to a wide road and lost the trail completely. He ran back and forth, sniffing frantically. The smells of exhaust fumes and motor oil were so strong that they covered up everything else. He whined in frustration and widened his search, but the trail was gone.

He galloped across the street, and sharp crystals of road salt and gravel cut into his paws. He limped the rest of the way and plunged into the mammoth drifts on the other side. Again, he ran in wide circles, trying to pick up the trail.

It was no use. His family was *gone*.

He was on his own.

He ran back to where he had first lost the scent, his paws stinging again from the road salt. He searched some more, but the trail just plain disappeared. Finally, he gave up and lay down in the spot where his family had last been.

He stayed there, curled into an unhappy ball, for a very long time. Cars drove by, now and then, but no one noticed him huddled up behind the huge bank of snow.

Finally, he rose stiffly to his feet. His joints felt achy and frozen from the cold. He had tried to lick the salt from his paws to stop the burning, but the terrible taste only made him more thirsty. He needed food, and water, and a warm place to sleep.

If he couldn't find his family, he was going to have to find a way to survive by himself.

He limped slowly down the side of the icy road. Cars would zip by, and each time, he did his best to duck out of the way so he wouldn't get hit. None of the cars stopped, or even slowed down. A couple of them beeped their horns at him, and the sound was so loud that he would scramble to safety, his heart pounding wildly.

By the time he got to the center of town, it was almost dark. Even though there were lots of people around, no one seemed to notice him. One building seemed to be full of good smells, and he trotted around behind it.

There was a tall dumpster back there, and the delicious smells coming from inside it made him so hungry that his stomach hurt. He jumped as high as he could, his claws scrabbling against the rusty metal. He fell far short and landed in a deep pile of snow.

Determined to get some of that food, he picked himself up, shook off the snow, and tried again. He still couldn't reach the opening, so he took a running start. This time, he made it a little higher, but he didn't even get close to the top. He fell down into the same drift, panting and frustrated.

The back door of the building opened and a skinny young man about sixteen years old came out. He was wearing a stained white apron and carrying a bulging plastic sack of trash. Just as he was about to heave it into the dumpster, he paused.

"Hey!" he said.

The dog was going to run, but he was so hungry that he just stood there and wagged his tail, instead.

"What are you doing here?" the young man asked. Then, he reached out to pat him.

The dog almost bolted, but he made himself stay and let the boy pat him. It felt so good that he wagged his tail even harder.

"Where's your collar?" the boy asked.

The dog just wagged his tail, hoping that he would get patted some more.

"Do you have a name?" the boy asked. "I'm Dominic."

The dog leaned against the boy's leg, still wagging his tail.

Dominic looked him over and then stood up. "*Stay*," he said in a firm voice.

The dog wasn't quite sure what that meant, so he wagged his tail more tentatively. He was very disappointed when he saw the boy turn to go.

Dominic went back inside the building and the door closed after him. He had left the trash bag behind and the dog eagerly sniffed it. There was *food* in there. *Lots* of food. He nosed around, looking for an opening, but the bag seemed to be sealed. He nudged at the heavy plastic with an experimental paw, but nothing happened.

He was about to use his teeth when the back door opened again.

Dominic was holding a plate of meatballs and pasta, and glancing back over his shoulder. "Shhh," he said in a low voice as he set the plate down. "My boss'll flip if he sees me doing this."

The dog tore into the meal, gobbling it down so quickly that he practically ate the Styrofoam plate, too. After licking away every last morsel, he wagged his tail at the boy.

"Good dog," Dominic said, and patted him. "Go home now, okay? Your owners must be worried about you."

Patting was *nice*. Patting was *very* nice. Dogs who got to live with people and get patted all the time were *really* lucky. Maybe this boy would bring him home. The dog wagged his tail harder, hoping that the boy liked him enough to want to keep him.

"Hey, Dominic!" a voice bellowed. "Get in here! We've got tables to bus!"

"Be right there!" Dominic called back. He gave the dog one last pat and then stood up. With one quick heave, he tossed the trash bag into the dumpster. "I have to go. Go home now. Good dog," he said, and went back inside.

The dog watched him leave and slowly lowered his tail. He waited for a while, but the boy didn't come back. He gave the already clean plate a few more licks, waited another few minutes, and then went on his way again.

Oceanport was a small town. Most of the restaurants and stores were clustered together on a few main streets. The town was always quaint, but it looked its best at Christmastime. Brightly colored lights were strung along the old-fashioned lampposts, and fresh wreaths with red ribbons hung everywhere.

The town square was a beautiful park, where the local orchestra played concerts on the bandstand in the summer. The park also held events like the annual art festival, occasional craft shows, and a yearly small carnival. During the holiday season, the various decorations in the park celebrated lots of different cultures and religions. The town council had always described the exhibit of lights and dioramas as "The Festival of Many Lands." Oceanport was the kind of town that wanted everyone to feel included.

Unfortunately, the dog felt anything *but* included. He wandered sadly through the back alley that ran behind the stores on Main Street. All of the dumpsters were too high for him to reach, and the only trash can he managed to tip over was empty. The spaghetti and meatballs had been good, but he was still hungry.

There was water dripping steadily out of a pipe behind a family-owned grocery store. The drip was too fast to freeze right away and the dog stopped to drink as much of the water as he could. The ice that had formed underneath the drip was very slippery and it was hard to keep his balance. But he managed, licking desperately at the water. Until he started drinking, he hadn't realized how thirsty he really *was*. He licked the water until his stomach was full and he was no longer panting.

Then, even though he was alone, he wagged his tail.

Now that he had eaten, and had something to drink, he felt much better. He trotted into the snowy park to look for a place to sleep. After food, naps were his favorite. The wind was blowing hard, and his short brown fur suddenly felt very thin. He lowered his head and ears as gusts of snow whipped into him.

The most likely shelter in the park was the bandstand and he forced himself through the uneven drifts towards it. The bandstand was an old wooden frame shaped in a circle, with a peaked roof built above it. The steps were buried in snow, and the floor up above them was too exposed to the wind. He could try sleeping on the side facing *away* from the wind, but that would mean curling up in deep snow. It would be much warmer and more comfortable if he could find a way in underneath it.

The bandstand was set above the ground, with latticelike boards running around the entire structure. The slats were set fairly far apart and he tried to squeeze between them. Even when he pushed with all of his might, he still couldn't fit. He circled the bandstand several times, looking for a spot where the slats might be broken, but they were in perfect repair.

He was too cold to face lying down in the snow yet, so he decided to keep moving. There was a small white church at the very edge of the park. Its walk and steps were neatly shovelled, and when he passed the building, he saw that the front door was ajar.

Heat seemed to be wafting out through the opening and the dog was drawn towards it. Shivering too much to think about being scared, he slipped through the open door.

It was *much* warmer than it had been outside. He gave himself a good, happy shake to get rid of any lingering snow. Then he looked around for a place to rest.

It was a big room, with high, arched ceilings. There were rows of hard wooden benches, separated by a long empty aisle. The church was absolutely silent, and felt very safe. Not sure where to lie down, the dog stood in the center aisle and looked around curiously. What kind of place was it? Did people *live* here? Would they chase him away, or yell at him? Should he run out now, or just take a chance and hope for the best?

He was so cold and tired that all he wanted to do was lie down. Just as he was about to go and sleep in a back corner, he sniffed the air and then stiffened. There *was* a person in here somewhere! He stood stock-still, his ears up in their full alert position. Instinctively, he lifted one paw, pointing without being sure why he was doing it.

All he knew for sure, was that he wasn't alone in here — and he might be in danger!

3

He sniffed cautiously and finally located where the scent was. A person was sitting alone in one of the front pews, staring up at the altar. Her shoulders were slouched, and she wasn't moving, or talking. She also didn't seem threatening in any way. In fact, the only thing she seemed to be was unhappy.

The dog hesitated, and then walked up the aisle to investigate. He paused nervously every few steps and sniffed again, but then he would make himself keep going.

It was a young woman in her late twenties, all bundled up in a winter hat, coat, and scarf. Her name was Margaret Saunders, and she had lived in Oceanport her whole life. She was sitting absolutely still in the pew, with her hands knotted in her lap. She wasn't making a sound, but there were tears on her cheeks.

The dog stopped at the end of her pew and waved his tail gently back and forth. She seemed very sad, and maybe he could make her feel better.

At first, Margaret didn't see him, and then she flinched.

"You scared me!" she said, with her voice shaking.

The dog wagged his tail harder. She was a nice person; he was *sure* of it.

"You shouldn't be in here," Margaret said sternly.

He cocked his head, still wagging his tail.

"Go on now, before Father Reilly comes out and sees you," she said, and waved him away. "Leave me alone. *Please.*" Then she let out a heavy sigh and stared up at the dark altar.

The dog hesitated, and then made his way clumsily into the pew. He wasn't sure how, but maybe he could help her. He rested his head on her knee, and looked up at her with worried brown eyes.

Margaret sighed again. "I thought I said to go away. Where did you come from, anyway? Your owner's probably out looking for you, worried sick."

The dog pushed his muzzle against her folded hands. Automatically, she patted him, and his tail thumped against the side of the pew.

"I hope you're not lost," she said quietly. "It's a bad time of year to feel lost."

The dog put his front paws on the pew. Then,

since she didn't seem to mind, he climbed all the way up. He curled into a ball next to her, putting his head on her lap.

"I really don't think you should be up here," she said, but she patted him anyway. She was feeling so lonely that even a scruffy little dog seemed like nice company. She had never had a pet before. In fact, she had never even *wanted* one. Dogs were noisy, and needed to be walked constantly, and shed fur all over the place. As far as she was concerned, they were just more trouble than they were worth. But this dog was so friendly and sweet that she couldn't help liking him.

So they sat there for a while. Sometimes she patted him, and when she didn't, the dog would paw her leg lightly. She would sigh, and then pat him some more. He was getting fur all over her wool coat, but maybe it didn't matter.

"I don't like dogs," she said to him. "Really, I don't. I never have."

The dog thumped his tail.

"*Really*," she insisted, but she put her arm around him. He was pretty cute. If it *was* a he. "Are you a boy dog, or a girl dog?"

The dog just wagged his tail again, looking up at her.

"You know, you have very compassionate eyes," she said, and then shook her head. "What am I, crazy? Talking to a *dog*? Like you're going to *answer* me?" She sighed again. "I don't know, though. I guess I have to talk to *someone*. It's been a long time."

The dog snuggled closer to her. He had never gotten to sit like this with a person before, but somehow, it felt very natural. Normal. Almost like cuddling with his brother and sisters.

"My husband died," the woman told him. Then she blinked a few times as her eyes filled with more tears. "We hadn't even been married for two years, and one night — " She stopped and swallowed hard. "He was in a terrible accident," she said finally. "And now — I don't know what to do. It's been almost a year, and — I just feel so alone. And *Christmas* makes it worse." She wiped one hand across her eyes. "We didn't even have time to start a family. And we wanted to have a *big* family."

The dog wanted to make her feel better, but he wasn't sure what to do. He tilted his head, listening intently to words he couldn't understand. Then, for lack of a better idea, he put his paw on her arm. She didn't seem to mind, so he left it there.

"People around here are trying to be really nice to me, especially my parents, but I just can't — I don't know," Margaret said. "I can't handle it. I feel like I can't handle *anything* anymore."

The dog cocked his head attentively.

"That's why I only come here at night," she

explained, "so I won't have to run into anyone. I used to go to church all the time, but now I don't know how to feel, or what to believe, or — everything's *so hard*. You know?"

The dog watched her with great concentration.

"I can't believe I'm talking to a dog. I must really be losing it." Tentatively, the woman touched his head, and then rubbed his ears. "Is that how I'm supposed to do it? I mean, I've never really patted a dog before."

He wagged his tail.

"What kind of dog are you, anyway?" she asked. "Sort of like one of those police dogs? Except, you're pretty little."

The dog thumped his tail cooperatively.

"Your owners shouldn't let you run around without a collar and license tag," she said. "They should be more careful."

He lifted his paw towards her, and she laughed. The laugh sounded hesitant, as though she hadn't used it for a very long time.

"Okay," she said, and shook his paw. "Why not. Like I told you, I'm not much for dogs, but — that's pretty cute. You seem *smart*."

When she dropped his paw, he lifted it again — and she laughed again.

"Hello?" a voice called from the front of the church. "Is anyone there?"

Now Margaret stiffened. She reached for her purse, getting ready to leave.

Not sure what was wrong, the dog sat up uneasily, too.

An older man wearing black pants and a black shirt with a white collar came out of a small room near the altar. He was also wearing a thick, hand-knit grey cardigan over his shirt. When he saw the woman, he looked surprised.

"I'm sorry, Margaret, I didn't realize you were here," he said. "I was going to lock up for the night."

Margaret nodded, already on her feet. "Excuse me. I was just leaving, Father."

"There's no need for that," he said, and then came partway down the aisle. He paused, leaning against the side of an empty pew. "I haven't seen you for a long time. How have you been?"

Margaret avoided his eyes as she buttoned her coat and retied her scarf. "Fine, Father Reilly. Everything's just fine. Just — super."

"I saw your parents at eleven o'clock Mass last Sunday," he said conversationally. "They looked well."

Margaret nodded, her head down.

Slowly, Father Reilly let out his breath. "This time of year can be difficult for *anyone*, Margaret. I hope you know that if you ever want to talk, my door is always open."

Margaret started to shake her head, but then she looked down at the dog and hesitated. Maybe it would be nice to talk to someone who could talk *back*. Maybe the dog had been good practice for the real thing.

"I was just going to make myself some tea," Father Reilly said, "if you'd like to come for a few minutes. Maybe we could talk about things, a little. How you're doing."

Margaret looked down at the dog, then back at Father Reilly. She had known Father Reilly since she was a child, and he had always been very sympathetic and understanding. The kind of priest who was so nice that even people who weren't Catholic would come and talk to him about their problems. "I think I'd like that," she said, her voice hesitant. "Or, anyway, I'd like to try."

"Okay, then," Father Reilly said with a kind smile. "It's a place to start, right?" Then his eyebrows went up as he noticed the dog standing in the pew. "Wait a minute. Is that a dog?"

Margaret nodded and patted him again. He wagged his tail in response, but kept his attention on Father Reilly. Was this stranger safe — or someone who was going to chase him away? Would the stranger be nice to his new friend?

"*Your* dog?" Father Reilly asked. "I don't think I've ever seen him around before."

Margaret shook her head. "Oh, no. I really don't even like dogs." Well, maybe she did *now*. A little. "He was just — here."

"Well, maybe we'd better call the police," Father Reilly suggested. "See if anyone has reported him missing. He shouldn't be running around alone in weather like this." He reached his hand out. "Come here, puppy."

Seeing the outstretched hand, the dog panicked. His mother had taught him that a raised hand usually meant something *bad*. He squirmed out of the pew and bolted down the aisle.

"No, it's okay," Margaret said, hurrying after him. "Come back, dog! You don't have to run away."

The dog stayed uncertainly by the door. Then, as Father Reilly headed down the aisle, too, he made up his mind and raced outside. The winter wind immediately bit into his skin, but he made himself keep running.

The strange man *might* be okay — but he couldn't take that chance.

He ran for what seemed like a long time. When he was exhausted, and quivering from the cold, he finally stopped. He was in an empty, plowed parking lot. There was a long, low red brick building beyond the lot and he followed a shovelled path over to the main entrance. There was some sand on the path, but it didn't hurt his paws the way the road salt had.

The wind was still whipping around and he ducked his head to avoid it. He couldn't remember *ever* being this cold. Cautiously, he circled the big building until he found a small, sheltered corner.

He climbed through a deep drift and then used his front paws to dig some of the snow away.

Once he had cleared away enough snow to make a small nest for himself, he turned around three times and then curled up in a tight ball. The icy temperature of his bed made him shiver, but gradually, his body heat began to fill the space and he felt warmer.

His snow nest wasn't the best bed he had ever had — but, for tonight, it would have to do.

It was going to be another long, lonely night.

4

He woke up when he heard children's voices. In fact, there were children *everywhere*. His joints felt frozen, and he had a hard time standing up. He had *never* been cold like this when he slept with his family. He stood there for a minute, in the snow, missing them. In fact, he missed them so much that he didn't even notice how hungry he was. Would he ever find them? Would they ever find *him*?

There were lots of children running around in the snow, yelling and throwing snowballs at each other. Some of them were playing a game with a round red rubber ball, and he *wanted* to bound over and join them.

He ventured out of the sheltered alcove a few steps, then paused. Could he play with them? Would they mind? The game looked like fun.

While he was still making up his mind, the big red ball came rolling in his direction and he barked happily. Then he galloped after it, leaping through the broken snow.

Two boys who were running after the ball stopped when they saw him.

"Where did he come from?" one of the boys, whose name was Gregory Callahan, asked.

The other boy, Oscar Wilson, laughed. "He *looks* like Rudolph!"

Gregory laughed, too. "Oh, so he came from the North Pole?"

"Yep," Oscar said solemnly. "He flew down early. Wanted to beat the holiday traffic."

Gregory laughed again. In a lot of ways, the dog *did* look like Rudolph. Since he was still a puppy, his nose and muzzle were too big for his face. His short fur had the same reddish tint a deer's coat might have, and his legs were very skinny compared to his body. If his nose was red, instead of black, it would be a perfect match.

"Hurry up, you guys!" a girl yelled from the kickball field. "Recess is almost over."

Gregory and Oscar looked at each other, and then chased after the ball.

It was too large to fit in the dog's mouth, so he was pushing it playfully with his paws. Each time the ball veered in a new direction, the dog would lope after it, barking. The whole time, he kept it under control, almost like he was playing soccer.

"Check it out," Oscar said, and pushed his

glasses up to see better. "We can put him in center field."

Gregory shook his head, watching the dog chase the ball in circles. "On Charlie Brown's team, maybe. Or, I don't know, the *Cubs*."

Gregory and Oscar were in the fifth grade, and they had been best friends since kindergarten. Although they both loved recess more than anything else, Gregory's favorite class was math, while Oscar liked reading.

Harriet, the girl who had been playing left field, ran over to join them. "While you guys were standing here, they scored all three runs," she said, with a very critical expression.

Oscar sighed, pretending to be extremely sad. "Downer," he said.

"Big-time," Gregory agreed.

"So go get the ball," Harriet said.

The boys both shrugged, and watched the dog play.

Harriet put her hands on her hips. "You guys aren't *afraid* of that dumb puppy, are you?"

"Yep," Oscar said, sadly.

Gregory nodded. "*Way* scared."

Harriet was much too caught up in the game to be amused. Instead, she ran after the dog and tried to get the ball away from him.

A game! The dog barked happily and nudged the ball just out of her reach. He would wait until she could almost touch it, and then bat it out of her range again.

Harriet stamped one of her boots in frustration. "Bad dog!" she scolded him. "You bring that ball to me right now!"

The dog barked and promptly knocked the ball further away.

"*That* worked," Gregory said.

"Good effort," Oscar agreed.

Harriet glared at them. "You could *help* me, you know."

Gregory and Oscar thought that over.

"We could," Oscar admitted.

Gregory nodded. "We most definitely could."

"Totally," Oscar said.

But then, of course, they just stayed right where they were and grinned at her. Since she lost her sense of humor pretty easily, Harriet was a lot of fun to tease.

She stamped her foot again. "You're just immature babies! *Both* of you!" Then she ran after the dog as fast as she could.

In the spirit of the game, the dog dodged out of her way. Harriet dove for the ball, missed, and dove again. Then she slipped, landing face-first in a deep mound of snow.

Oscar and Gregory clapped loudly.

"It's not funny," Harriet grumbled as she picked herself up.

Gregory reached behind his back and pretended to hold up a large card. "I don't know about you folks judging at home," he said, "but I have to give that one a nine."

Oscar shook his head and held up his own imaginary scoring card. "A seven-point-five is as high as I can go."

"But her compulsories were *beautiful*," Gregory pointed out.

"Well, that's true," Oscar conceded, "but — I'm sorry. The degree of difficulty *just wasn't there*."

"Babies," Harriet said under her breath as she brushed the snow off her down jacket and jeans. "Stupid, immature *babies*."

By now, the rest of the kickball players had given up on continuing the game and started a wild snowball fight instead. It was so rowdy that at least two teachers had already run over to try and break it up.

Gregory took his gloves off, and then put his pinkies in his mouth. It had taken his big sister, Patricia, a long time, but she had finally managed to teach him how to whistle that way. Patricia was convinced that, to have any hope of being cool in life, a person *had* to be able to let out a sharp, traffic-stopping whistle. And, hey, she was in the sixth grade — as far as Gregory was concerned, she *knew* these things.

His hands were a little cold, so his first whistle came out as a wimpy burst of air.

"That's good," Oscar said. "Patty taught you *great*."

Gregory ignored that, and tried again. This time, his whistle was strong and piercing, and half of the kids on the playground looked up from whatever they were doing.

Hearing the sound, the dog froze. His ears went up, and his tail stopped wagging.

"*Stay*," Gregory ordered, and walked over to him.

The dog tilted his head in confusion. Then he gave the ball a tiny, experimental nudge with his nose. Was this part of the game?

"*No*," Gregory said.

The dog stopped.

Gregory patted him on the head. "Good dog," he said. He picked up the ball and tossed it to Harriet.

She caught the ball, and then made a face. "Gross. There's drool all over it."

"Greg can't help it," Oscar said. "He *always* drools. They take him to doctors, but . . ."

"I almost have it licked," Gregory insisted. "All I have to do is Scotch-tape my mouth shut — and I'm fine."

"*So* immature," Harriet said in disgust, and trotted back to the kickball field.

A bell rang, signalling the end of recess. All over the playground, kids groaned and stopped whatever games they were playing. They headed for the school entrance, where they were supposed to line up by homeroom classes before going inside.

"We'd better go, Greg," Oscar said.

Gregory nodded, but he kept patting the dog. His family's collie, Marty, had died recently, and this was the first dog he had patted since then. Marty had been really old — his parents had had him since before he and Patricia were *born* — and life without him was lonely. All of them had cried about it, more than once. His parents had said that they would get another dog sometime soon, but none of them could really face the idea yet, since they still missed Marty so much.

"He doesn't have a collar," Gregory said aloud. "Do you think he's lost?"

Oscar shook his head. "I doubt it. He probably just got out of his yard or something."

Gregory nodded, but he *liked* this dog. If he thought his parents wouldn't get upset, he would bring him home.

Mr. Hastings, their teacher, strode over to them. "Come on, boys," he said sternly. "Leave the dog alone. Recess is over now."

Gregory would *much* rather have stayed and played with the dog. All afternoon, if possible. But he nodded, and gave the dog one last pat on the head.

"Good dog," he said. "Go home now, boy."

Then he and Oscar followed Mr. Hastings towards the school. The dog watched them go, very disappointed. The playground was completely empty now. Slowly, his tail drooped and he lowered his ears. He didn't know why, but for some reason, the game was over.

He was on his own again.

5

The dog waited in the playground for a while, but none of the children came back. He was *especially* waiting for the boy who had patted him for so long. He wished that he could *live* with that boy and play with him all the time.

When it was finally obvious that they had gone inside for good, he decided to move on. He walked slowly, with his head down, and his tail between his legs. He was so hungry that his stomach was growling. He ate some snow, but it only made his stomach hurt more.

There were some trash bins behind the school, overflowing with garbage bags. Smelling all sorts of wonderful food, he stopped short. He sniffed harder, then started wagging his tail in anticipation. Lunchtime!

The bins were taller than he was, but he climbed onto a pile of snow so he could reach. Then he leaned forward and grabbed onto one of the bags with his teeth. Using his legs for leverage, he was able to pull the bag free. It fell onto the ground and broke open, spilling half-eaten school lunches everywhere.

It was like a vision of dog heaven. Food, food, and *more* food!

In fact, there was so much food that he really wasn't sure where to start. Lots of sandwich crusts, carrot sticks, and apples with one bite out of them. He ate until he was full, switching from leftover peanut butter and jelly to cream cheese and olives to bologna. So far, the bologna was his favorite. He sniffed the crumpled brown paper bags, hoping to find more.

American cheese, part of a BLT, some tuna fish, pudding cups with some left inside, hard granola bars, a couple of drumsticks. He ate everything he could find, although he spit all of the lettuce out. He *definitely* didn't like lettuce. Or apples. The trash bin smelled more strongly of rotting apples than anything else, although he wasn't sure why.

Some of the milk cartons were still full, and he tore the cardboard containers open. Milk would spurt out onto the snow, and he would quickly lick it up before it drained away. Now his thirst was satisfied, too.

There was so much leftover food that even though he had been starving, he couldn't finish it all. Carefully, he used his front paws to cover the bag with snow. That way, he could come back later and eat some more. And there were other bags he hadn't even opened yet!

He trotted on his way in a much better mood, letting his tail sway jauntily. It didn't even seem as cold anymore. He didn't have anyplace special to go, so he decided to wander around town and look for his family. Could they have gone to live with some nice people? Maybe if he went down every street he could find, he would come across them.

The streets were busy with cars full of people doing last-minute holiday shopping. So, he was very cautious each time he had to cross one. Cars scared him. He would wait by the side of the road until they all seemed to be gone, take a deep breath, and dash across. When he got to the other side, his heart would be beating loudly and he could hear himself panting. No matter how many times he did it, it never got any easier.

He looked and looked, but found no signs that his family had ever existed. He even went back to the old abandoned house to check. The only thing he could find was faint whiffs of his own scent. If they hadn't come back for him by now, he knew they never would.

Tired and discouraged by his long search, it was an effort to keep walking. The sun was going down, and the temperature was dropping again. He wandered morosely through a quiet neighborhood, looking for a good place to take a nap. When in doubt, he always napped.

He could smell dogs inside some of the warmly lit houses he passed and felt very envious of them. They would bark when he went by, so they must smell him, too. A couple of dogs were outside in fenced yards, and they barked so fiercely at him that he would end up crossing to the other side of the street.

There were tantalizing smells of meat cooking and wood smoke from winter fires wafting out of many of the houses. He would stop on the sidewalk in front of the best-smelling houses and inhale over and over again. Beef, chicken, pork chops — all *kinds* of good things. He whimpered a little each time he caught a new scent, feeling very sorry for himself.

He was going by a small, unlit white house when he heard a tiny sound. A frail sound. He stopped, his ears flicking up. What was it? A bad sound. A *sad* sound.

He raised his nose into the wind to see if he smelled anything. A person, somewhere nearby. In the snow. He followed his nose — and the low moaning — around to the side of the little house.

There was a car parked in the driveway, and he could still smell gas and feel the warmth of the engine. Was it going to start up and run over him? He gave the car a wide berth, just in case, but kept tracking the sound.

41

Suddenly, he saw an old woman crumpled in the snow. She was so limp and still that he had almost stepped on her. There was a sheen of ice on the driveway, and she was lying at the bottom of a flight of steps leading to the back door. Two bags of groceries were strewn haphazardly around her.

She moaned weakly, and he went rigid. He backed away a few steps, and then circled around her a few times. Why didn't she move? When she didn't get up, he let out a small woof.

Her eyes fluttered open and she looked up at him dully. "Help," she whispered. "Please help me."

The dog put a tentative paw on her arm, and she moaned again. He jumped back, afraid. What was wrong? Why was she lying on the ground like that?

Unsure of himself, he ran up the back steps. They were covered with fresh ice and his paws skidded. He barked more loudly, standing up on his hind legs. He scratched at the door with his front paws, still barking.

"No one's there," the old woman gasped. "I live alone."

He barked some more, then ran back down the steps. Why didn't anyone come? Should he bark more?

"*Go*," she said, lifting one arm enough to give him a weak push. "Go get your owner."

He nosed at her sleeve, and she pushed him harder.

"*Go home*," she ordered, her teeth chattering from the cold. "Get some help!"

The dog didn't know what to do, and he circled her again. There *was* something wrong; he just wasn't sure exactly what it was. Should he curl up with her to keep her warm, or just run away?

At the house across the street, a station wagon was pulling into the driveway. He could hear people getting out of the car. There were at least three children, two of whom were bickering.

"Help!" the elderly woman called, but her voice was barely above a whisper. "Help me!"

There was so much urgency in her voice that the dog barked. Then he barked again and again, running back and forth in the driveway. The people noticed him, but still seemed to be going into their house.

He barked more frantically, running partway across the street and then back to the driveway. He repeated the pattern, barking the entire time.

A teenage girl, who was holding a grocery bag and a knapsack full of schoolbooks, laughed. "Whose dog is that?" she asked, pointing over at him. "He's acting like he thinks he's Lassie."

The dog barked loudly, ran up the driveway, and ran out to the street.

"He sure doesn't *look* like Lassie," one of the

girl's little brothers, Brett, scoffed. "He looks like a *mutt*."

Their mother, who was carrying her own bags of groceries, frowned. "Maybe something's wrong," she said. "Mrs. Amory usually has her lights on by now."

The teenage girl, Lori, shrugged. "Her car's in the driveway. Maybe she's just taking a nap or something."

Her mother still looked worried. "Do me a favor and go over there, will you, Lori? It can't hurt to check."

Lori shrugged, and gave her grocery bag to Brett and her knapsack to her other brother, Harold.

The dog kept barking and running back and forth as she walked over.

"Take it easy already," she said to him. "You been watching the Discovery Channel or something? Getting *dog ambitions*?"

The dog galloped over to the injured old woman and stood next to her, barking loudly.

Lori's mouth dropped open. "Oh, *whoa*," she said, and then ran over to join him. "Mom!" she yelled over her shoulder. "Call 911! Quick! Mrs. Amory's hurt!"

After that, things moved fast. Lori's mother, who was Mrs. Goldstein, dashed over to help. Brett went inside to call an ambulance and Harold hurried to get a blanket.

44

Hearing all the commotion, other neighbors on the block came outside. By the time the police and the EMS workers had arrived, a small, concerned crowd had gathered.

Since it was the northwest sector of town, two of the police officers were Steve and Bill. They worked with the other cops to move the neighbors aside so that the two EMS attendants could get through with a stretcher.

The whole time, the dog hung back nervously in the shadow of Mrs. Amory's garage, not sure if he was in trouble. There were so many people around that he might have done something bad. They all seemed very upset, and it might be his fault.

"What happened, Officer Callahan?" one of the neighbors asked Steve. "Is Mrs. Amory going to be okay?"

Steve nodded. "Looks like a broken hip, but the Goldsteins found her in time. She might have a little hypothermia, but she should be just fine."

The EMS workers shifted Mrs. Amory very gently onto the stretcher, and covered her with two more blankets. She was weak from pain, and shivering from the cold.

"Thank you," she whispered. "Thank you so much."

"Don't worry about a thing," one of the EMS workers assured her. "We'll have you over at the emergency room in a jiffy."

"He saved me," she said weakly. "I don't know where he came from, but he saved me."

"Well, don't worry, you're going to be fine," the EMS worker said comfortingly.

As she was lifted into the back of the ambulance, Steve and Bill and the other officers moved the onlookers aside.

"Let's clear away now," Bill said authoritatively. "Give them room to pull out."

The ambulance backed slowly out of the driveway, with its lights flashing and its siren beginning to wail. Everyone watched as the emergency vehicle drove away with Mrs. Amory safely inside.

"Okay, folks, show's over," Steve announced. "Thanks a lot for all of your help. You can head in for supper now."

Although there was still an eager buzz of conversation, most of the neighbors started drifting towards their houses.

Bill pulled out his notebook and went over to the Goldsteins. "We just need a few things for our report," he said to Mrs. Goldstein. "You and your daughter found her?"

"It was Lassie!" Lori's little brother Harold chirped. "He was totally cool!"

Bill looked skeptical. "What do you mean by that, son?"

Brett pointed at the dog crouching by the garage. "It was that dog!" he said, sounding just as excited as Harold. "He was barking and barking, and Lori followed him. It was just like TV!"

Bill's expression got even more doubtful. "You're saying that a *dog* came over to get help?"

"Exactly," Mrs. Goldstein answered for her sons. "I know it must sound strange — but he was very insistent, and that's when I sent Lori over. I was afraid that something might be wrong."

Bill digested that, his pen still poised over the empty notebook page. "So, wait, let me get this straight. It was *your* dog who alerted you?" he asked.

"We don't have a dog," Brett told him.

Harold nodded, looking sheepish. "On account of, I'm allergic," he said, and sniffled a little to prove it.

Bill considered all of that, and then squinted over towards the garage. "You sure the dog didn't knock her down in the first place?"

"I don't think so," Lori said doubtfully. "He was trying to help."

It was completely dark now, except for the headlights on the two remaining squad cars. Bill unclipped his flashlight from his equipment belt. He turned it on and flashed the light around the yard.

Seeing that, the dog instinctively shied away from the beam. But it was too late — Bill had already seen him.

47

"Hey!" Bill said, and nudged his partner. "It's that same stray dog you were so hot about catching the other night."

"What about him?" Steve asked, in the middle of taking a statement from one of the other neighbors.

"He's over there," Bill said, and gestured with the flashlight. "The Goldsteins say he sounded the alarm."

Steve's eyebrows went up. "Really? Hey, all right! I *told* you he was a great dog." He shoved his notebook in his jacket pocket. "Let's see if we can get him this time. Find him a good home."

All of the neighbors wanted to help capture the hero dog. So everyone fanned out and moved forward. Some of them shouted, "Here, boy!" while others whistled or snapped their fingers.

Seeing so many people coming towards him, the dog slipped deeper into the bushes. He *was* in trouble! They had taken the poor old lady away, and now they were *blaming* him. He squirmed towards the woods crouched down on all fours, trying to stay out of sight. Then, he gathered all of his energy and started running as fast as he could.

Lately, escaping to safety had become one of his best tricks!

6

The dog hid in the woods until he was *sure* that no one was coming after him anymore. It had been a very long day, and all he wanted to do now was *sleep*. He could walk back to the school and sleep in that little alcove, but it seemed too far.

There were a bunch of boulders to his right and he crept over to explore them. Most of the rocks were jammed close together and buried in snow. But a few had openings that looked like little caves. He chose the one that seemed to be the most private and wiggled inside.

He fit easily, and there was even room to stand up and turn around, if he wanted. Almost no snow had blown in, and there were lots of dry leaves to lie on. He could smell the musty, ancient odor of other animals who had used this cave for a shelter — squirrels, mostly, and maybe a skunk or two. But, as far as he could tell, no other animal had been in here for a long time.

As always, he turned around three times before

lying down. The cave was so warm, compared to being outside, that he slept for a long time.

When he woke up and poked his head out through the rock opening, it was snowing hard. He retreated back inside. He wanted to go over to the school and find some more discarded lunches to eat, but the storm was just too bad. No matter how much his stomach started growling, he would be much better off in here, out of the blizzard. The wind was howling, and he was glad to be in a place where he could avoid it.

So, he went back to sleep. Every so often, he would be startled by a noise and leap to his feet. Then, when it turned out to be nothing out of the ordinary, he would curl up again.

It snowed all day, and most of the night. He only went outside to go to the bathroom, and then he would return to his little rock cave. The snow was so deep now that his legs were completely buried when he tried to walk, and mostly he had to leap. Leaping was hard work, and made him tired after a while. He liked it better when there wasn't any snow at all. Grass and dirt were *easy* to walk on.

Once, he saw a chipmunk chattering away on a low tree branch. He was hungry, and thought about trying to catch the little animal. But before he could even *try* to lunge in that direction, the chipmunk had sensed danger and scampered further up the tree. He ducked back into his cave, not terribly disappointed. The poor little chip-munk was trying to survive the harsh winter, the same way he was. He would just go hungry today, that's all.

By the next morning, the storm had finally stopped. The temperature was higher than it had been, and the top layer of snow was already soft-ening into slush.

He hadn't eaten for such a long time that he headed straight for the school trash bins. When he got to the school, he stopped in the parking lot and shook out each front paw, since he had snow caked between his toes. Now, it was time to eat some breakfast.

He ran around behind the building, but the trash bins were empty! Now what? He had been so sure that he would find more bologna, BLTs, and other treats.

He sank back onto his haunches and whimpered a couple of times. Where had all the food gone? The trash bins were closed now and piled high with snow. All he could smell was the lingering stench of rotten apples and sour milk. They weren't very nice smells, but his stomach still rumbled.

He prowled around the back of the school for a while. Then he came to a door where he could smell food. He barked a couple of times, then sat down to see what would happen. The *last* time he had smelled food behind a door, that teenage boy had given him those great meatballs. Maybe he would get lucky again.

The door opened and a very stout woman in a big white apron looked out. She was Mrs. Gustave, the school cook.

"What?" she asked in a loud, raspy voice.

The dog barked again and held up one paw.

"Hmmm," Mrs. Gustave said, and folded her arms across her huge stomach. "Is that the best you can do?"

She seemed to be waiting for something, so he sat back and lifted both paws in the air.

"That's better," she decided, and disappeared into the kitchen.

Even though she was gone, the dog stayed in the same position. Maybe if she came back, she would like it more the second time. Then he lost his balance and fell over on his side.

"*My* dog can do much better than that," Mrs. Gustave said. She had come outside just in time to see him tumble into the snow.

He quickly scrambled up and held out one paw. One paw was *definitely* safer than two.

"You're going to have to work on that," she said. With a grunt of effort, she bent over and set a steaming plate on top of the snow.

It was crumbled hamburger with gravy, served over mashed potatoes. He wagged his tail enthusiastically and started eating.

"Now, remember," Mrs. Gustave said. "From

now on, you should eat at *home* and not go around begging like a fool." Then she closed the door so she could go back to cooking the students' hot lunch.

He enjoyed his meal very much, and licked the plate over and over when he was done. It had been a hefty serving, but he still could have eaten five or six more. Still, the one big portion made him feel much better.

Cheerfully, he wandered around to the playground. Maybe his friends from the other day would come out again! Then he might get patted some more.

He waited for a long time, and then he got bored. He scratched a little, dug a couple of holes in the snow, and then rolled over a few times.

But he was still bored. He yawned, and scratched again. Still bored. It was time for a nap.

He trudged over to the sheltered area where he had slept that one night. He dug himself a new nest, stamping down the snow with all four feet. Then he lay down and went right to sleep. He slept very soundly, and even snored a little. The day passed swiftly.

"Hey, look!" a voice said. "He *did* come back!"

The dog opened his eyes to see Gregory and his friend Oscar standing above him. He wagged his tail and sprang to his feet.

"Where've you been?" Gregory asked, patting him. "We looked all over for you yesterday."

The dog wagged his tail harder and let them take turns patting him.

"You know, he's kind of scraggly," Oscar said. "Maybe he really *is* a stray."

Gregory shrugged. "Of course he is. Why else would he sleep here?"

Oscar bent down and sniffed slightly. Then he made a face and straightened up. "I think he needs a *bath*, too."

Gregory thought about that. "My father's always home writing, so I can't sneak him into *my* house. What about your house?"

Oscar shook his head. "Not today. Delia and Todd have the flu, so Mom had to stay home with them."

The dog tried to sit up with both paws in the air again, but fell over this time, too.

Both boys laughed.

"What a goofball," Oscar said.

Gregory nodded. "He's funny, though. I really like him."

"Why don't you just say you want a dog for Christmas?" Oscar suggested. "Then you can show up with him like it's a big surprise and all."

Gregory was very tempted by that idea, but he was pretty sure it wouldn't work. "I don't know," he said doubtfully. "My parents said we could maybe go and pick one out together in a month or two."

Oscar packed together a hard snowball and

flipped it idly from one hand to the other. "What does Patricia say?" he asked.

Gregory's big sister. Her advice was advice Gregory always took seriously. Gregory sighed. "That they're still way too sad to even *look* at other dogs right now."

Oscar nodded, then threw the snowball a few feet away. The dog promptly chased after it, and brought it back.

Gregory looked pleased. "He fetches! He's really smart!"

Oscar laughed and threw the snowball even further. "How smart is a dog who fetches *snow*?" he asked as the dog returned with the snowball, his tail beating wildly from side to side.

"*Extra*-smart," Gregory said.

Oscar shrugged and tossed the snowball twenty feet away. "If you say so."

The dog galloped happily after it.

"Boys!" a sharp voice yelled. "What are you doing over there?" It was Ms. Hennessey, one of their teachers. She was always *very* strict.

Gregory and Oscar looked guilty, even though they weren't really doing anything wrong at all.

"Science," Oscar said. "We were just standing here, talking a whole lot about science."

Gregory nodded. "Like, gravity and stuff." He made his own snowball and flicked it straight up into the air.

They both watched it come down, shook their heads, and exchanged admiring glances.

"Gravity again," Oscar observed solemnly. "*Cool.*"

The dog picked up that snowball instead and offered it to Gregory.

Ms. Hennessey marched over, her face tight with concern. She was tall and extremely skinny, with lots of bright red hair. She liked to wear wide, billowy skirts, big sunglasses, and ponchos. "Don't you boys know better than to go up to a stray animal! It's *dangerous!*"

This little dog might be many things, but "dangerous" didn't seem to be one of them. Gregory and Oscar looked at each other, and shrugged.

"Get away from him right now!" Ms. Hennessey said with her hands on her hips. "He might have rabies!"

Gregory looked at the dog, who wagged his tail in a very charming way. "I don't think so, ma'am. He seems — "

"Look at him!" Ms. Hennessey interrupted, and pulled both of the boys away. "There's *foam* in his mouth!"

"That's just drool, ma'am," Oscar explained. "Because he's sort of panting."

Gregory gave him a small shove. "Saliva, Oscar. Us science types like to call it saliva."

"Well, I'm going to call the dog officer," Ms. Hennessey said grimly. "We can't have a dangerous dog roaming around near children. I just won't have it!"

For years, Gregory's parents had always explained to him that it was important to be *careful* around strange animals — but that it was *also* important to help any animal who might be in trouble. "Please don't call the dog officer, Ms. Hennessey," he said desperately. If the dog went to the pound, he would never get to see him again. "It's okay, he's — " Gregory tried to come up with a good excuse — "he's *my* dog! He just — followed me to school, that's all."

Ms. Hennessey narrowed her eyes. "Where's his collar?"

Gregory thought fast. "He lost it, when we were walking on the beach last weekend."

"A seagull probably took it," Oscar put in helpfully. "They like shiny things."

"*Raccoons* like shiny objects," Gregory told him. "Not seagulls."

"Oh." Oscar shrugged. "That's right, it was a raccoon. I heard it was a big old *family* of raccoons."

Ms. Hennessey wasn't buying any of this. "What's his name?" she asked.

Gregory and Oscar looked at each other.

"Sparky," Gregory said, just as Oscar said, "Rover."

Mrs. Hennessey nodded, her suspicions confirmed. "I see."

"His, um, his *other* nickname is Spot," Gregory said, rather lamely.

"I don't appreciate having you two tell me fibs," Ms. Hennessey said without a hint of a smile on her face. "I think you'd just better come along down to the office with me, and you can talk to Dr. Garcia about all of this."

Dr. Garcia was the vice principal — and she made Ms. Hennessey seem *laid-back*. Being sent to the office at Oceanport Middle School was always a major disaster, dreaded by one and all.

"But — " Gregory started to protest.

"Come along now," Ms. Hennessey ordered, taking each of them by the sleeve. She turned towards Ms. Keise, one of the other teachers. "Cheryl, chase this dog away from here! He's a threat to the children!"

"He's not," Gregory insisted. "He's a really *good* — "

"That will be quite enough of that," Ms. Hennessey said sharply, and led the two of them away.

The dog let the snowball fall out of his mouth. Where were his friends going? Then he saw a tall woman in a leather coat hurrying towards him. She was frowning and shaking her finger at him. Before the woman could get any closer, the dog started running.

He would much rather run away — than be *chased*.

7

The dog ended up hiding behind the trash bins. When he no longer heard any voices, he slogged back to his little alcove to sleep some more. Who knew when his friends might come back? He wanted to be here waiting when they did.

This time, though, the voice that woke him up was female. He opened one eye and saw a thin girl, with her hair tied back in a neat brown ponytail. She had the same very blue eyes Gregory had, and she was wearing a red, white, and blue New England Patriots jacket. It was Patricia, Gregory's big sister.

"So, you must be the dog my brother won't shut up about," she said aloud.

The dog cocked his head.

Patricia frowned at him. "He got *detention* because of you. So even though it's Christmas, Mom and Dad are probably going to have to ground him."

He wagged his tail tentatively. She didn't exactly sound mad, but she didn't sound friendly, either.

"Well," she said, and tossed her ponytail back. "The way he was going on and on, I figured you could *talk* or something. Tap dance and sing, maybe. But you just look regular. Even a little silly, if you want to know the truth."

Maybe she would like it if he rolled in the snow. Like *him*. So, he rolled over a couple of times.

"*A lot* silly," she corrected herself.

The dog scrambled up and shook vigorously. Snow sprayed out in all directions.

"Thanks a lot, dog," Patricia said, and wiped the soggy flakes from her face and jacket. "I enjoyed that."

He wagged his tail.

"We could still maybe talk Mom and Dad into it. I mean, it *is* almost Christmas," she said. "Although we really like *collies*." She studied him carefully. "It would be easier, if you had a limp, or your ear was chewed up, or something. Then my parents would feel sorry for you."

The dog barked. Then he sat down and held up his right paw.

Patricia nodded. "Not bad. If you could *walk* with your paw up like that, they could *never* say no. Here, try it." She clapped her hands to be sure she had his full attention. "*Come.*"

Obediently, the dog walked over to her. "Come" was an easy one.

"No, *limp*," she said, and demonstrated. "I want you to limp. Like this, see?" She hopped around on one red cowboy-booted foot. Cowboy boots might not be warm in the winter, but they *were* cool. Always. "Can you do that?"

The dog barked, and rolled over in the snow. Then he bounded to his feet and looked at her hopefully.

"Well, that's not right at all," she said, and then sighed. "If I tell you to play dead, you'll probably *sit*, right?" She shook her head in dismay. "I really don't know about this. I thought he said you were *smart*."

The dog barked and wagged his tail heartily.

"Right," Patricia said, and shook her head again. "And if I tell you to 'Speak,' you're going to look for a hoop to jump through — I can see it now."

Perplexed by all of this, the dog just sat down and looked at her blankly.

"Well, this is just a waste," Patricia said, and then straightened the tilt of her beret. "Until we can get you home and I have some serious training time with you, you're clearly *beyond* my help." She unzipped her knapsack and took out some crackers and cheese and two chicken sandwiches. "Here, we saved most of our lunches for you. The crackers are from Oscar." She placed the food down in the snow. "Don't ever say I didn't do anything for you."

The dog wagged his tail, and then gobbled up the food in several gulping bites.

"We'll bring more tomorrow, even though it's Saturday," Patricia promised. "Greg can't come back this afternoon because Dad's going to have to pick him up after detention and yell at him for a while. You know, for appearances."

The dog licked the napkin for any remaining crumbs. Then he stuck his nose underneath it, just in case. But he had polished off every last scrap.

"See you later then," she said, and jabbed her finger at him. "Stay. Okay? *Stay.*"

The dog lifted his paw.

"Ridiculous," Patricia said, and walked away, shaking her head the entire time. "Just ridiculous."

The dog hung around the school until all the lights were out, and even the janitors had gone home. Then he decided to roam around town for a while. He took what had become his regular route, heading first to the abandoned house. There was no sign of his family — which didn't surprise him, but *did* disappoint him.

Again.

After that, he wandered through the various neighborhoods, looking longingly at all of the families inside their houses. He explored the back alleys behind Main Street. The drainpipe near the pizza place was still leaking, and he had a nice, long drink.

Visiting the park was the next stop on his route. There were lots of townspeople strolling down the winding paths and admiring the holiday exhibits. He was careful to stay out of sight, but he enjoyed being around all of the activity. It was almost like being *part* of it.

There was a traditional Nativity scene, complete with a manger and plastic models of barnyard animals and the Three Wise Men. Further along, there were displays honoring Chanukah, Kwanzaa, and various other ways of celebrating the holiday season.

There was also, of course, a big, wooden sleigh. A fat model Santa Claus sat inside it, surrounded by presents, and the sleigh was being pulled by eight tiny plastic reindeer. Colored lights decorated all of the trees, and the little diorama of Main Street had been built perfectly to scale, right down to the miniature people cluttering its sidewalks.

Christmas carols and other traditional songs played from the loudspeaker above the bandstand, every night from six to ten. On Christmas Eve, live carollers would gather there and hold an early evening concert for everyone to enjoy. Oceanport took the holiday season *seriously*.

He found a nice vantage point underneath a mulberry bush, and settled down for a short nap. When he opened his eyes, the park had cleared out and all of the holiday lights had been turned off for the night. The place *seemed* to be deserted.

He wasn't sure what had woken him up, but somewhere, he heard a suspicious noise. Laughter. Low male voices. Banging and crunching sounds. He stood up, the fur slowly rising on his back. Something wasn't right. He should go and investigate the situation.

The voices were coming from over near the crèche. The dog loped silently through the snow, approaching the Nativity scene from behind. The laughter was louder and he could hear people hissing "Shhh!" to one another.

Whatever they were doing, it didn't feel right. There was a crash, and then more laughter. The dog walked around to the front of the crèche, growling low in his throat.

Inside the Nativity scene, a group of boys from the high school were moving the plastic figures around. They had always been bullies, and vandalism was one of their favorite destructive pranks. They were especially active around the holidays.

One of them was just bending down to steal the baby Jesus figure from the manger. Two other boys were walking over to the Chanukah exhibit, holding cans of spray paint. The fourth boy was knocking over the Three Wise Men, one at a time.

The dog growled the most threatening growl he knew how to make, and all of the boys froze.

"Whose dog?" one of them, Luke, asked uneasily.

The other three shrugged.

"Dunno," the biggest one, Guillermo, said. "Never seen him before."

The dog growled and took a stiff-legged step forward.

"Hey, *chill*, dog!" Michael, the leader of the group, said impatiently. "We're only fooling around." He turned to his friends. "Ignore him — it's just a dumb puppy. Let's hurry up before someone sees us."

"Hey, he looks kind of like those reindeer," another boy, Rich, said, snickering. "Let's tie him up front there."

Luke held up his can of red spray paint. "If you guys hold him, I'll spray his nose!"

They all laughed.

"Let's do it!" Michael decided.

As they crept towards him, the dog growled, his lips curling away from his teeth.

"Oh, yeah," Guillermo said. "He thinks he's *tough*."

"Let's leave *him* in the manger," Rich suggested. "That'd be pretty funny!"

As Luke and Michael lunged for him, the dog snarled and leaped forward. With his teeth bared, he slashed at Michael's jacket. The sleeve tore, and Michael stopped short. He looked down at the jagged rip and started swearing.

"That's *Gore-Tex*, man," he protested. "You stupid dog!" He aimed a kick at the dog's head, but missed. "It was really expensive! How'm I going to *explain* this?" He tried another kick, but the dog darted out of the way.

Guillermo packed together a ball of ice and snow. Then he threw it as hard as he could. The chunk hit the dog square in the ribs and he yelped.

"Yeah, all right!" Guillermo shouted, and bent down to find some more ice. "Let's get 'im!"

The dog growled at them, and then started barking as loudly as he could. He barked over and over, the sound echoing through the still night.

"If he doesn't shut up, everyone in town's going to hear him," Luke said uneasily.

"We mess up these dumb exhibits *every* year," Rich complained. "We can't let some stupid dog ruin this — it's a *tradition*."

During all of the commotion, none of them had noticed the police squad car patrolling past the park. The car stopped and Officers Kathy Bronkowski and Tommy Lee got out. They had been two of the other cops at Mrs. Amory's house the night before, when she had broken her hip on the ice.

Officer Lee turned on his flashlight, while Officer Bronkowski reached for her nightstick.

When the beam passed over them, the boys were exposed in the bright light and they all stood stock-still for a few seconds.

"Hey!" Officer Bronkowski yelled. "What do you think you're doing over there!"

The boys started running, stumbling over one another in their hurry to get away.

"Get back here, you punks!" Officer Lee shouted. "You think we don't recognize you?"

Still furious, the dog raced after them. He snapped at their heels, just to scare them a little. It *worked*. He kept chasing them all the way to the end of the park. Then he trotted back to the crèche, barely panting at all.

The two police officers were carefully reassembling the exhibit. They brushed snow off the tipped-over figures, and then set each one in its proper place.

Officer Bronkowski picked up the two discarded cans of spray paint. "Those little creeps," she said under her breath. "Who do they think they are?"

Officer Lee put the baby Jesus figure gently in the manger. "I saw Michael Smith and Guillermo Jereda. Did you get a good look at the other two?"

Officer Bronkowski shook her head. She had long blond hair, but when she was on duty, she kept it pinned up in a bun. "No, but it was probably the Crandall twins, Luke and Rich. Those four are always together."

"So let's cruise by their houses," Officer Lee

suggested. "See what their parents have to say about this."

Officer Bronkowski nodded. "Good idea. It's about time we caught them in the act."

"The dog gave them away," Officer Lee said, with a shrug. He yawned, opened a pack of gum, and offered a piece to his partner before taking one for himself. "They shouldn't have brought him along."

Officer Bronkowski started to answer, but then she noticed the dog lurking around behind the scale model of the Oceanport town hall. "You know what? I don't think they did," she said slowly.

Officer Lee glanced up from the plastic donkey he was setting upright. "What do you mean?"

She pointed at the dog. "Unless I'm crazy, that's the same dog who found Mrs. Amory yesterday."

Officer Lee looked dubious. "Oh, come on. You mean you think there's some dog *patrolling* Oceanport? You're starting to sound like Steve Callahan." Steve Callahan was, of course, the police officer who had been trying to catch the dog ever since he saw him at the abandoned house. Steve Callahan was also, as it happened, Gregory and Patricia's uncle.

Officer Bronkowski nodded. "That's exactly what I'm saying. Would we have pulled over just now if we hadn't heard him barking?"

"Well, no," Officer Lee admitted, "but — "

Officer Bronkowski cut him off. "And if Gail Amory had been out much longer last night, the doctors say she might have frozen to death. She owes her *life* to that dog."

Officer Lee grinned at her. "So let's put him on the payroll. Maybe even arrange a Christmas bonus." He gave the dog a big thumbs-up. "Good dog! Way to go!"

The dog barked once, and then trotted off.

"Wait!" Officer Bronkowski called after him. "Come back!"

The dog kept going. It was time to be on his way again.

8

Remembering how warm it had been inside, the dog went back to the church. Unfortunately, tonight, the door was already locked. He leaned his shoulder against it and pushed, but the heavy wood wouldn't even budge.

Okay. New plan. He would go back to the school, maybe. In the morning, his friends might come back. Gregory, especially, although he liked Oscar and Patricia, too. Maybe they would even have more food for him! Those chicken sandwiches were *good*.

He was cutting across a parking lot, when he heard — crying. A child, crying. It might even be a baby. He stopped to listen, lifting his paw. The sound was coming from a car parked at the farthest end of the lot.

He ran right over, stopping every few feet to sniff the air. There were several people in the car — he could smell them — but the crying was coming from a small child. A small, miserable child. A sick child.

All of the car windows were rolled up, except for the one on the driver's side, which was cracked slightly. The car was a beat-up old station wagon, and it was *crammed* with people and possessions. He could hear a soothing female voice trying to calm the crying child. The baby would cry, and then cough, and then cry some more. There were two other children in the backseat, and he could hear them coughing and sneezing, too.

He barked one little bark.

Instantly, everyone inside the car, except for the baby, was silent. They were maybe even holding their breaths.

He barked again.

One of the doors opened partway, and a tow-headed little boy peeked out.

"Mommy, it's a dog!" he said. "Can we let him in?"

"No," his mother answered, sounding very tired. "Close the door, Ned. It's cold out there."

"*Please?*" Ned asked. "He won't eat much — I promise! He can have my share."

His mother, Jane Yates, just sighed. They had been homeless since the first of the month, and she could barely afford to feed her *children*. She, personally, had been living on one tiny meal a day for almost two weeks now. For a while, after the divorce, she had been able to keep things going fine. But then, her ex-husband left the state and right after Thanksgiving, she got laid off. Since then, their lives had been a nightmare. And now, all three of the children were sick with colds. The baby, Sabrina, was running a fever, and her cough was so bad that she was probably coming down with bronchitis. They didn't have any money to pay a doctor, so the baby was just getting sicker and sicker.

"I'm sorry, Ned," Jane said. "We just can't. I'm really sorry."

Now Ned started crying, too. His sister, Brenda, joined in — and the baby, Sabrina, had yet to stop.

"Go away," Jane said to the dog, sounding pretty close to tears herself. "Please just leave us alone." She reached over the front seat and yanked the back door closed.

The door slammed in the dog's face and he jumped away, startled. Now *all* he could hear was crying and coughing. What was going on here? It was bad, whatever it was.

He pawed insistently at the door, and barked again. No matter what he did, the crying wouldn't stop.

"Bad dog! Go away!" Jane shouted from inside the car. "Stop bothering us!"

The dog backed off, his ears flattening down against his head. He circled the car a couple of times, but none of the doors opened. These people needed help! With one final bark, he trotted uncertainly back towards the church.

When he got there, Margaret Saunders, the young widow he had met earlier that week, was just coming out with her mother. If they didn't exactly look overjoyed, at least they seemed to be at peace.

"Well, hi there," Margaret said, her face lighting up when she saw him. She reached down one gloved hand to pat him. "Mom, it's the dog I was telling you about. He's pretty cute, isn't he?"

Her mother nodded.

"Maybe I should *get* a dog, sometime," Margaret mused. "To keep me company."

"Sounds like a great idea," her mother agreed. Since Saunders had been Margaret's husband's last name, her mother was Mrs. Talbot.

Margaret patted the dog again. "I think so, too. Whoever owns *this* dog is pretty lucky."

"No doubt. But I can't help wondering if maybe someone *sent* him to you that night," her mother said softly, and smiled at her daughter.

Margaret smiled back. Her mother had a point. The dog *had* appeared out of nowhere. "Stranger things have happened, I guess."

Margaret might be patting his head, but otherwise, they didn't seem to be paying much attention to him. He could still, faintly, hear the sound of crying, and he barked loudly. One thing

73

the dog had learned, was that if he barked a lot, he could get people to follow him. He just *knew* that baby shouldn't be crying like that. He dashed off a few steps, barked, and ran back to them.

Margaret grinned. She had been feeling a little happier over the last couple of days. Hopeful, for the first time in many months. "What do you think, Mom? *I* think he's telling us that Timmy fell down the mine shaft, and we're supposed to bring rope. Manila, preferably."

Her mother laughed. "It certainly looks that way." Of course, neither of them was used to dogs. But *this* one seemed to have come straight out of a movie.

The dog barked again, and ran a few steps away. He barked more urgently, trying to make them understand.

Father Reilly came outside to see what all the commotion was. "What's going on?" he asked, buttoning his cardigan to block out some of the wind.

"Look, Father," Margaret said, and gestured towards the street. "That nice dog is back."

Father Reilly nodded, and then shivered a little. "So he is. But — what's wrong with him?"

The dog barked, and ran away three more steps.

"I don't know," Margaret's mother answered. "I don't know much about animals, but he really seems to want us to follow him."

Father Reilly shrugged. "Well, he strikes me

as a pretty smart dog. Let's do it."

So, with that, they all followed him. The dog led them straight to the parking lot. He checked over his shoulder every so often to make sure that they were still behind him. If he got too far ahead, he would stop and wait. Then, when they caught up, he would set forth again.

He stopped right next to the sagging station wagon and barked. The baby was still coughing and wailing.

The driver's door flew open and Jane Yates got out.

"I told you to go away!" she shouted, clearly at the end of her rope.

Father Reilly stared at her. "Jane, is that you? What are you doing here?"

Realizing that the dog was no longer alone, Jane blushed. "Oh," she said, and avoided their eyes. She hadn't expected company. "Hi." Sabrina coughed and she automatically picked her up, wrapping a tattered blanket more tightly around her so she would be warm.

"You have the children in there with you?" Margaret's mother asked, sounding horrified.

"I couldn't help it," Jane said defensively. "We didn't have any other place to go. Not that it's anyone else's business. Besides, they're *fine*. We're all fine."

Since it was obvious to everyone that the family *wasn't* fine, nobody responded to that. Sometimes it was easy to forget that even in nice, small towns like Oceanport, people could still be homeless.

"Why didn't you come to the church?" Father Reilly asked. "Or the shelter? We would have helped you."

Jane scuffed a well-worn rubber boot against the snow. "I was too embarrassed," she muttered.

Again, no one knew what to say. The baby sneezed noisily, and clung to her mother.

Father Reilly broke the silence. "Still, you must know that you could *always* come to the church," he said. "No matter what."

"I'm not even *Catholic*," Jane reminded him.

Ned, and his sister Brenda, had climbed out of the car and were patting the dog. They got him to sit in the snow, and took turns shaking hands with him. Each time, they would laugh and the dog would wag his tail. Then, they would start the game all over again.

"It's not about religion, it's about community," Father Reilly answered. "About *neighbors*."

Jane's shoulders were slumped, but she nodded.

"Look," Margaret's mother said, sounding very matter-of-fact. "The important thing here is to get these poor children in out of the cold. And the baby needs to see a doctor, right away."

"I don't have any — " Jane started.

"We'll take her to the emergency room," Mrs. Talbot said. "Before she gets penumonia."

Father Reilly checked his watch. "We won't be

able to get into the shelter tonight, but after that, why don't I take you over to the convent and see if the sisters can put you up for the night. Then, tomorrow, we can come up with a better plan."

Jane hesitated, even though her teeth were chattering. "I'm not sure. I mean, I'd rather — "

"You have to do *something*," Margaret's mother said. "Once you're all inside, and get a hot meal, you'll be able to think more clearly."

"Come on," Father Reilly said. "I'll drive everyone in my car."

Throughout all of this, Margaret stayed quiet. Although Jane had been two years ahead of her, they had actually gone to high school together. Since then, their lives had moved in very different — if equally difficult — directions. It wouldn't have seemed possible that things could turn out this way, all those years ago, playing together on the softball team. The team had even been undefeated that year. In those days, they *all* felt undefeated. She shook her head and stuffed her hands into her pockets. Little had they known back then how easily — and quickly — things could go wrong.

Now, Jane looked at her for the first time. "Margaret, I, uh, I was really sorry to hear about what happened. I know I should have written you a note, but — I'm sorry."

Margaret nodded. When a person's husband was killed suddenly, it was hard for other people to know how to react. What to say, or do. "I guess we've both had some bad luck," she answered.

Jane managed a weak smile, and hefted Sabrina in her arms. "Looks that way, yeah."

They both nodded.

"So it's settled," Father Reilly said. "We'll lock up here, and then I'll run you all over to the hospital, and we can go to the convent from there."

Margaret's mother nodded. "Yes. I think that's the best plan, under the circumstances."

Seeing the shame and discomfort on Jane's face, Margaret felt sad. Then she thought of something. "I-I have an idea," she ventured.

They all looked at her.

Margaret turned to direct her remarks to Jane. "Dennis and I bought a big house, because — " Because they had wanted to have a *big* family. "Well, we just did," she said, and had to blink hard. "Anyway, I — " She stopped, suddenly feeling shy. "I have *lots* of room, and maybe — for a while, we could — I don't know. I'd like it if you came to stay with me, until you can get back on your feet again. What do you think?"

Jane looked shy, too. "We couldn't impose like that. It wouldn't be — "

"It *would* be," Margaret said with great confidence. "I think it would be *just* the right thing — for both of us." She bent down to smile at Ned and Brenda. "What do you think? Do you all want to come home with me and help me — deck my

78

halls?" This would give her a reason to buy a Christmas tree. Even to celebrate a little.

"Can we, Mom?" Brenda pleaded.

Jane hesitated.

"I think it's a wonderful idea," Father Reilly said, and Margaret's mother nodded.

"Please," Margaret said quietly. "You may not believe this, but it would probably help *me* out, more than it's going to help you."

Jane grinned wryly and gestured towards the possessions-stuffed station wagon. "You're right," she agreed. "I don't believe it."

Margaret grinned, too. "But you'll come?"

"If you'll have us," Jane said, looking shy.

"Actually, I think it's going to be great," Margaret said.

Standing alone, off to the side, the dog wagged his tail. Everyone seemed happy now. Even the baby wasn't really crying anymore, although she was still coughing and sneezing. He could go somewhere and get some much-needed sleep. In fact, he was *long* overdue for a nap.

"Can we bring the dog with us, too, Mommy?" Ned asked. "Please?"

"Well — " Jane glanced at Margaret, who nodded. "Sure. I think we should."

They all looked around to see where the dog was.

Margaret frowned as she scanned the empty parking lot. The dog was nowhere in sight. "That's funny," she said. "I'm sure he was here just a minute ago."

They all called and whistled, but there was no response.

The dog was gone.

9

Walking along the dark streets, the dog was just plain tuckered out. The park was much closer than the school, so he went there to find a place to sleep. He was going to go back underneath his mulberry bush, but it was a little bit too windy. So he took a couple of minutes to scout out another place, instead.

There was lots of straw piled up in the Nativity scene, but it felt scratchy against his skin. None of the other dioramas were big enough for him to squeeze inside. He was about to give up and go under the bush, when he saw the sleigh. It was stuffed tight with the Santa model and the make-believe gifts, but maybe there would be room for him, too.

Wool blankets were piled around the gifts to make it look as though they were spilling out of large sacks. He took a running start, and leaped right into Santa's lap. Then he squirmed out of sight underneath the blankets. The blankets were almost as scratchy as the hay had been, but they were much warmer. This would do just fine.

He let out a wide, squeaky yawn. Then he twisted around until he found a comfortable position. This was an even better place to sleep than his rock cave had been. Snuggling against the thick blankets was — almost — like being with his family again.

He yawned again and rested his head on his front paws. Then, almost before he had time to close his eyes, he was sound asleep.

It had been a very eventful day.

The blankets were so comfortable that he slept well into the morning. When he opened his eyes, he felt too lazy to get up. He stretched out all four paws and gave himself a little "good morning" woof.

Food would be nice. He crawled out from underneath the heavy blankets. The sun was shining and the sky was bright and clear. The ocean was only a couple of blocks away, and he could smell the fresh, salty air. Oceanport was at its best on days like this.

Instead of jumping down, he kept sitting in the sleigh for a while. Being up so high was fun. He could see lots of cars driving by, and people walking around to do their errands. He kept his nose in the wind, smelling all sorts of intriguing smells.

A sanitation worker named Joseph Robinson,

who was emptying the corner litter basket, was the first person to notice him.

"Hey, check it out!" he said to his coworker. "It's Santa Paws!"

His coworker, Maria, followed his gaze and laughed. "I wish I had a camera," she said.

The town mailman, Rasheed, who was passing by on his morning delivery route, overheard them. "Santa Paws?" he repeated, not sure if he had heard right.

Joseph and Maria pointed at the dog sitting up in the sleigh, looking remarkably like the Grinch's dog, Max.

Rasheed shook his head in amusement. "That *is* pretty goofy." He shook his head again. "Santa Paws. I like that."

Then they all went back to work, still smiling.

Unaware of that whole conversation, the dog enjoyed his high perch for a while longer before jumping down. It was time to find something good to eat.

There was a doughnut shop at the corner of Tidewater Road and Main Street. The dog nosed through the garbage cans in the back. Finally, he unearthed a box of old-fashioneds that had been discarded because they were past the freshness deadline. To him, they tasted just fine. A little dry, maybe.

From there, he went to the ever-leaking drain-pipe behind the pizza place and drank his fill.

There was so much ice now that the flow was slowing down, but he was still able to satisfy his thirst. He cut his tongue slightly on the jagged edge of the pipe and had to whimper a few times. But then, he went right back to drinking.

With breakfast out of the way, he decided to make the rounds. The middle school would be his last stop. He visited all of his usual places, neither seeing — nor smelling — anything terribly interesting. It was three days before Christmas, and everything in Oceanport seemed to be just fine.

He was ambling down Meadowlark Way when he noticed something unusual in the road. To be precise, there were cows *everywhere*. Lots and lots of *cows*.

He stopped, his ears moving straight up. He had seen cows before, but never up close. They were *big*. Their hooves looked sharp, too. Dangerous.

The cows belonged to the Jorgensens, who owned a small family farm. They sold milk, and eggs, and tomatoes, in season. The weight of all of the snow had been too much for one section of their fence, and the cows had wandered through the opening. Now they were all standing in the middle of the street, mooing pensively and looking rather lost.

The dog's first instinct was to bark, so he did. Most of the cows looked up, and then shuffled a few feet down the road. Then they all stood around some more.

Okay. If he kept barking, they would probably keep moving, but he wasn't sure if that's what he wanted them to do. Except they were in the middle of the road. They were *in his way*. And what if scary cars came? That would be bad.

He barked again, experimentally, and the cows clustered closer together. They looked at him; he looked at them.

Now what? The dog barked a very fierce bark and the cows started shuffling down the lane. The more he barked, the faster they went. In fact, it was sort of fun.

The cows seemed to know where they were going, and the dog followed along behind. If they slowed down, he would bark. Once, they sped up too much, and he had to race up ahead. Then he skidded to a stop and barked loudly at them.

The cows stopped, and turned to go back the other way. That didn't seem right at all, so the dog ran back behind them. He barked a rough, tough bark, and even threw in a couple of growls for good measure.

With a certain amount of confusion, the cows faced forward again. Relieved, the dog barked more pleasantly, and they all resumed their journey down the road. He didn't know where they were going, but at least they were making progress.

When they came to a long, plowed driveway, the cows all turned into it. The dog was a little perplexed by this, but the cows seemed pretty sure of themselves. He barked until they got to the end of the driveway where there was a sprawling old farmhouse and a big wooden barn.

The cows all clustered up by the side of the barn, and mooed plaintively. The dog ran back and forth in a semicircle around them, trying to keep all of them in place. If he barked some more, who knew *where* they might go next.

A skinny woman wearing overalls and a hooded parka came out of the barn. She stared at the scene, and then leaned inside the barn. "Mortimer," she bellowed in a voice that sounded too big for someone so slim. "Come here! Something very strange has happened."

Her husband, who had a big blond beard, appeared in the doorway, holding a pitchfork. "What is it, Yolanda?" he asked vaguely. "Did I leave the iron on again?"

"Look, Morty," she said, and pointed. *"The cows came home."*

He thought about that, and then frowned. "Weird," he said, and went back into the barn.

Yolanda rolled her eyes in annoyance. There was a fenced-in paddock outside the barn and she went over to unlatch the gate. "Come on, you silly cows," she said, swinging the gate open. "You've caused more than enough trouble for one day. Let's go."

The cows didn't budge.

"Great," she said. She turned and whistled in the direction of the barn.

After a minute, a very plump Border collie loped obediently outside.

"Good girl," Yolanda praised her. "Herd, girl!"

The Border collie snapped into action. She darted over to the cows, her body low to the ground. She barked sharply, and herded them into a compact group.

Wanting to help, the dog barked, too. The Border collie didn't seem to want any interference and even snapped at him once, but when she drove the cows towards the open gate, he ran along behind her. It was almost like being with his mother again. *She* liked him to stay out of the way when she was busy, too.

One cow veered away from the others, and the Border collie moved more swiftly than seemed to be physically possible for such a fat dog. She nipped lightly at the cow's hooves and nudged it back into the group.

Imitating her, the dog kept the cows on the other side in line. Whatever the Border collie did, he would promptly mimic. In no time, the cows were safely in the paddock.

"Good girl, Daffodil," Yolanda said, and handed

the Border collie a biscuit from her coat pocket. "That's my little buttercup."

The Border collie wagged her tail and waddled off to eat her treat.

The biscuit smelled wonderful. The dog sat down and politely lifted his paw. Maybe he would get one, too.

"Yeah, I think you've earned one," Yolanda said, and tossed him a Milk-Bone. "Whoever you are."

He had never had a Milk-Bone before, but he liked it a lot. Nice and crunchy. When he was finished, he barked.

"No, just one," Yolanda told him. "Run along now. I have work to do."

The dog barked, trotted partway down the driveway, and trotted back.

"Oh." Yolanda suddenly understood what he was trying to tell her. "The cows had to come from *somewhere*, didn't they? I bet there's a big hole in the fence." She turned towards the barn. "Mortimer! The fence is down again! We have to go fix it!"

"Okay. You do that, honey," he called back.

"It doesn't sound like he's going to *help* me, now does it," she said to the dog.

The dog cocked his head.

"Men," Yolanda pronounced with great disgust, and went to get her tools.

The dog led her down the road to the broken spot.

"Well, how about that," she said. She bent down and lifted the fallen fence post. Then she pounded it back in place. "I don't suppose you want to stay," she said conversationally. "Our Daffodil would probably like some help herding."

Stay. He had heard "Stay" before. It meant *something*, but he wasn't sure what. He rolled over a couple of times, to be cooperative, but she didn't even notice. So he just sat down to wait for her to finish. Maybe she would give him another one of those good biscuits.

Yolanda hefted the two wooden bars that had collapsed and slid them into place. "There we go!" she said, and brushed her hands off triumphantly. She reached into her pocket for another Milk-Bone and held it out. "Here's your reward."

The dog barked happily and took the biscuit. Then he headed down the road, carrying it in his mouth. He had places to go, things to do — and a school to visit!

"Well, wait a minute," Yolanda protested. "You don't have to go, you can — "

The dog had already disappeared around the curve and out of sight.

10

It was fun to walk along carrying his biscuit, like he was a *real* dog, with a *real* owner, who loved him. But soon, he couldn't resist stopping and eating it.

When he got to the middle school, the building was deserted. No cars, no buses, no teachers, no students, no Mrs. Gustave.

No Patricia, no Oscar, no *Gregory*.

Where was everyone? They should be here!

He slumped down right where he was and lay in a miserable heap. Maybe they had gone away forever, the way his family had. Why did everyone keep leaving him?

He stayed there on the icy front walk until his body was stiff from the cold. Then he got up and slunk around to the back of the building. Maybe he would be able to find some garbage to eat.

When he passed his little sleeping alcove by the playground, he caught a fresh scent. Gregory and Oscar had been here! Not too long ago! He ran into the alcove and found a big red dish full of some dark meaty food. What was it? There were lots of chunks and different flavors. It tasted soft and delicious, like a *special* food, made just for dogs. It was *great*.

Next to the red dish, there was a yellow dish full of water. The top had frozen, but he slapped his paw against it, and the ice shattered. He broke a hole big enough for his muzzle to fit through. Then he drank at least half of the water in the bowl in one fell swoop.

What a nice surprise! Food *and* water! They hadn't forgotten him, after all.

If he waited long enough, maybe they would come again. He lay down next to the dishes and watched the empty playground with his alert brown eyes.

Several hours passed, but no one came. He still lay where he was, on full-alert, without moving. A couple of birds flew by. A squirrel climbed from one tree to another, and then disappeared inside a hole. A big chunk of ice fell off the school roof, landing nearby.

That was it.

Maybe they had just come back *once*, and never would again. Maybe he was doomed to be alone forever.

Discouraged, the dog dragged himself to his feet. His back itched, but he was too sad to bother scratching. It would take too much energy.

He wandered off in a new direction, exploring a different part of town. Soon, he came upon the largest parking lot he had ever seen. There were only a few cars in it, but the smell of exhaust fumes was so strong that there must have been many other cars here, not too long ago. He marked several places, just to cover up the ugly stench of gasoline and oil.

The parking lot went on and on and on. It seemed endless. In the middle, there were a lot of low buildings. They were different sizes, but they seemed to be attached.

He walked closer, sniffing the air curiously. *Many* people had been walking around here. Recently. There were food smells, too. His feet touched a rubber mat, and to his amazement, two glass doors swung open in front of him.

Alarmed, he backed away. Why did the doors open like that? For no good reason?

Gingerly, he stepped on the mat again — and the doors opened again! Since it seemed to be all right, he walked cautiously through the doors and inside.

It was a very strange place. There was a wide open space in the center, with lots of benches scattered around. Water bubbled inside a big fountain, and the lights were very dim. He could smell the sharp odor of industrial cleaner, and hear people talking about a hundred feet away. A radio was playing somewhere, too.

He wasn't sure if he liked this place, but then he saw a sleigh. It was just like the one in the park! He wagged his tail, and happily leaped inside. Mounds of soft cloth were tucked around the cardboard presents in the back. He wiggled around until he had made enough room to sleep among the boxes. This was even *better* than the sleigh in the park!

He yawned and rolled onto his back. Sometimes he liked to sleep with his feet up in the air. It was restful.

Off to the side of the Santa Claus display, two mall custodians walked by with mops and pails. Hearing them, the dog crouched down in the sleigh. This was *such* a nice place to sleep that he didn't want them to see him. In the dark, they probably wouldn't, but he wanted to be sure.

"You two about finished?" a woman called to the two men.

"Yeah!" one of the custodians answered. "The food court was a real mess, though."

The woman, who was their supervisor, walked down the mall with a clipboard in her hand. "Well, let's lock up those last two electric doors, and get out of here. We open at nine tomorrow, and this place is going to be *packed* with all the last-minute shoppers."

The other custodian groaned. "I'm glad Christmas only comes once a year."

"Wait until the after-Christmas sales," his partner said glumly. "That's even crazier."

Their supervisor shrugged, making check marks on her clipboard. "Hey, with this economy, we should just be *glad* to have the business." She tucked the clipboard under her arm. "Come on. We'll go check in with the security people, and then you two can take off."

As they walked away, the dog relaxed. It looked like he was safe. He yawned again, shut his eyes, and went to sleep with no trouble whatsoever.

During the night, he would hear someone walk by every so often, along with the sound of keys clanking. But he just stayed low, and the guards would pass right by without noticing him. He got up a couple of times to lift his leg against a big, weird plant, but then, went back to bed each time. It was morning now, but he was happy to sleep late.

Then, a lot of people came, and he could hear metal gates sliding up all over the place. Different kinds of food started cooking somewhere nearby, and Christmas music began to play loudly.

He started to venture out, but he was afraid. What would happen if the people saw him? Maybe he *shouldn't* have come in here, after all. It might have been bad.

Suddenly, the weight of the sleigh shifted as a hefty man sat down on the wide vinyl bench in the front. He was wearing a big red suit with a broad black belt, and he smelled strongly of coffee and bacon.

The dog scrunched further back into the presents. He wanted to panic and run away, but for now, he decided to stay hidden. There were just too many people around.

"Ready for another long day of dandling tots on your lap, Chet?" a man standing next to the sleigh said.

All decked out in his Santa Claus costume, Chet looked tired already. "Oh, yeah," he said. "I *love* being one of his helpers."

"Better you than me," the man said, and moved on to open up his sporting goods store.

Soon, there were people *everywhere*. So many people that the dog quivered with fear as he hid under the soft layers of red and green felt. All of the voices, and music, and twinkling lights were too much for him to take. Too many sounds. Too many *smells*. He closed his eyes, and tried to sleep some more. For once in his life, it was *difficult*.

Tiny children kept getting in and out of the sleigh. They would talk and talk, and Chet would bounce them on his big red knee. Sometimes, they cried, and every so often, a bright light would flash.

It was *horrible*. And — he had to go to the bathroom again. Could he go on the presents, or would that be bad? He would try to wait, maybe.

Unknown to the dog, Gregory and Patricia Callahan had come to the mall with their mother. They still had some presents to buy, and the next day was Christmas Eve. Mrs. Callahan had told them that they could each bring along a friend. So Gregory invited Oscar, and Patricia called up *her* best friend, Rachel. Mrs. Callahan was going to buy all of them lunch and then, if they behaved, they would get to go to a movie later.

"I'm going to have a burrito," Gregory decided as they walked along.

His mother looked up from her lengthy Christmas list. Mrs. Callahan taught physics at the high school, so she had had to do most of her shopping on the weekends. She had been doing her best, but she was still very far behind. She was a woman of *science*, but not necessarily one of precision.

"We just had breakfast, Greg," she said. "Besides, I thought you wanted sweet and sour chicken."

"Dad said we could order in Chinese tonight," Gregory reminded her. "So he could finish his chapter, instead of cooking."

"Pizza," Patricia said flatly. "Pizza's *way* better."

Hearing that, their mother stopped walking. "If you two start fighting . . ."

They gave her angelic smiles.

"Never, *ever*, Mommy," Gregory promised, trying to sound sweet.

96

"We *love* each other," Patricia agreed.

Then, when their mother turned her back, Gregory gave his sister a shove. Patricia retaliated with a quick kick to his right shin. Gregory bit back a groan, and hopped for a few feet until it stopped hurting.

"You think the dog ever came back?" Oscar asked him, as they paused to admire the window of the computer store.

Gregory shrugged. "I sure hope so. If we keep leaving food, he'll know he can trust us. Then we'll be able to catch him."

"What did your parents say?" Rachel asked, tapping the floor just ahead of her with her cane. She had been blind since she was four, but she got around so well that they all usually forgot about it. Her eyes hadn't been physically scarred, but she still *always* wore sunglasses. If people asked, she would explain that it was "a coolness thing." No one who knew the two of them was surprised that she and Patricia had been best friends since kindergarten. "Do you think they'll let you bring him home?" she asked.

"Well — we're working on them," Patricia assured her. "They still really miss Marty, so I think they want to wait a while before we get another dog." Then she touched her friend's arm lightly. "Trash can, at nine o'clock."

Rachel nodded and moved to avoid the obstacle.

"Next year, you're old enough to get a dog,

right?" Gregory said, meaning a guide dog.

Rachel nodded. "I can't wait. Except I have to *stay* at that school for a while, to learn how. Live away from home."

Patricia shrugged. "It's not so far. We can come and visit you and all."

Rachel pretended to be disgusted by that idea. "And that would be a *good* thing?"

"For *you*," Patricia said, and they both laughed.

"Those guide dogs are really smart," Gregory said, and paused. "Although not as smart as *my* new dog is going to be. He's the best dog *ever*."

Oscar snorted. "Oh, yeah. He's a whiz, all right." He turned towards Patricia and Rachel. "Fetches *snowballs*, that dog."

The girls laughed again.

"Well, that makes him about Gregory's speed," Rachel said.

"Absolutely," Patricia agreed. "He doesn't even know how to *sit* right." She glanced a few feet ahead. "Baby carriage, two o'clock," she said, and then went on without pausing. "Rachel, you're going to have to help me train him, so he won't *embarrass* us."

Rachel grinned, tapping her cane and deftly avoiding the baby carriage. "You mean, Gregory, or the dog?"

"*Gregory*, of course," Patricia said.

"What if he never comes back?" Oscar said. "I mean, he might belong to someone, or — I don't know. He could be really far away by now."

Gregory looked worried. He was so excited about the dog that he had forgotten that he might not even see him again. Someone else might find him, or he might get hurt, or — all sorts of terrible things could happen! The worst part would be that he would never even *know* why the dog hadn't come back. He would just be — gone.

"Cheer up, Greg," Patricia said. "He's probably still hanging around the school. I mean, he didn't exactly seem like, you know, a dog with a lot of *resources*."

Gregory just looked worried.

"Are you kids coming or not?" Mrs. Callahan asked, about ten feet ahead of them. "We have a lot of stops to make."

They all nodded, and hurried to catch up.

Down in front of the Thom McAn shoe store, a young father was trying to balance a bunch of bulging shopping bags and a stroller, which held his two-year-old son, Kyle. At the same time, he was trying to keep track of his other three children, who were four, six, and seven. His wife was down in the Walden bookstore, and they were all supposed to meet in the food court in half an hour.

"Lucy, watch it," he said to his six-year-old as she bounced up and down in place, croaking. She was pretending to be a frog. His four-year-old, Marc, was singing to himself, while the seven-year-old, Wanda, was trying to peek inside the

Toys "R" Us bags. "Wanda, put that down! Marc, will you — " He stopped, realizing that the stroller was empty. "Kyle? Where's Kyle?"

The other three children stopped what they were doing.

"I haven't seen him, Daddy," Wanda said. "Honest."

The other two just looked scared.

Their father spun around, searching the crowd frantically. "Kyle?" he shouted. "Where are you? Kyle, come back here!"

His two-year-old was missing!

11

Immediately, a crowd gathered around the little family. Everyone was very concerned, and spread out to look for the lost little boy. The mall security guards showed up, and quickly ran to block off all of the exits. Children got lost at the mall all the time, and the guards just wanted to make sure that when it happened, they didn't *leave* the mall.

"What's going on?" Mrs. Callahan asked, as they came out of the Sharper Image store. One of her contact lenses had fogged up a little, and she blinked to clear it.

"Oh, no!" Patricia said, with great drama. "Maybe it's a run on the bank!"

"You mean, a run on the ATMs," Rachel corrected her.

"Maybe there's a movie star here or something," Oscar guessed. "Someone *famous*."

That idea appealed to Gregory, and he looked around in every direction. "What if it was someone like Michael Jordan," he said. "That'd be great!"

"*Shaquille*," Oscar said, and they bumped chests in the same dumb-jock way NBA players did.

Mrs. Callahan reached out to stop a woman in a pink hat who was rushing by. "Excuse me," she said. "What's going on?"

"A little boy is lost," the woman told her. "Curly hair, two years old, wearing a Red Sox jacket. They can't find him anywhere!"

"Can we look, Mom?" Gregory asked.

"We'll look *together*," Mrs. Callahan said firmly. "I don't want us to get separated in this crowd."

Up in the sleigh, the dog had heard all of the sudden chaos, too. The noise had woken him up. What was going on? Why was everyone so upset? He couldn't resist poking his head up and looking around. People were running around all over the place, and shouting, "Kyle! Kyle! Where are you, Kyle?"

The dog didn't know what to think. But, once again, he was sure that something was very wrong. Then, amidst all of the uproar, he heard a distinct little sound. A strange sound. He stood up in the sleigh and pricked his ears forward, listening intently.

It had been a *splash*. Now, he could hear a tiny *gurgle*. Where was it coming from? The fountain. Something — some*one*? — must have fallen into the huge, bubbling fountain in the middle of the mall. The dog stood there indecisively. What should he do? Run away? Run to the *fountain*? Stay here?

A man searching for Kyle right near the sleigh stared at him. It was Rasheed, the mailman, who had seen the dog in the park the day before — sitting up in Santa's sleigh. The dog that Joseph, the sanitation worker, had called Santa Paws.

Rasheed had come to the mall on his day off to buy some presents for his coworkers. This was certainly the *last* place he would have expected to see that dog.

"Look at that!" he gasped to his wife, who was standing next to him. "It's Santa Paws!"

She looked confused. "What?"

"Santa Paws!" he said, pointing up at the sleigh.

The dog had his full concentration on the distant fountain. There was something *in* there. Under the water. Movement. It was — a child! A drowning child!

He sailed off the sleigh in one great leap. Then he galloped through the crowded mall as fast as he could. The top of the fountain was very high, but he gathered his legs beneath him and sprang off the ground.

He landed in the fountain with a huge splash and water splattered everywhere. He dug frantically through the water with his paws, searching for the child.

By now, Kyle had sunk lifelessly to the bottom

of the fountain. The dog dove underneath the churning water and grabbed the boy's jacket between his teeth. Then he swam furiously to the surface, using all of his strength to pull the boy along behind him.

All at once, both of their heads popped up. Kyle started choking weakly, and the dog dragged him to the edge of the fountain. He tried to pull him over the side, but the little boy was too heavy, and the dog was too small. He tightened his jaws on the boy's jacket, and tried again. But it was no use. The edge of the fountain was just too high.

The dog used his body to keep the little boy pressed safely against the side of the fountain. Then he started barking, as he dog-paddled to try and keep them both afloat.

"I hear a dog barking," one of the security guards yelled. "Where's it coming from? Someone find that dog!"

In the meantime, Rasheed was running down the mall towards the fountain.

"In there!" he panted, gesturing towards the fountain. "The little boy's in there! Don't worry, Santa Paws has him!"

Even in the midst of all the excitement, people stared at him when they heard the name, "Santa Paws."

"Santa *Paws*?" the security guard repeated. "Well. Hmmm. I think you mean — "

Rasheed ignored him, climbing over the side of

the fountain. He plucked Kyle out of the water and lifted him to safety. Everyone nearby began to clap.

"Is he all right?" Kyle's father asked, frantic with worry. "Oh, please, tell me he's all right!"

Kyle was coughing and choking, but fully conscious. He would be just fine. Very carefully, Rasheed climbed back over the side of the fountain, holding the little boy in his arms.

Kyle's sisters and brother promptly burst into tears.

"Oh, *thank you*, sir," Kyle's father said, picking up his wet son in a big hug. Kyle started crying, too, and hung on to him tightly. "I don't know how I can ever thank you," his father went on.

"It wasn't me," Rasheed said. "It was Santa Paws."

All of the people who had gathered by the fountain to watch stared at him.

"Are you new to this country?" one of them asked tentatively. "Here, in America, we call him Santa *Claus*."

Rasheed looked irritated. "Oh, give me a break," he said, sounding impatient. "I'm *third-generation*."

Now, the dog struggled over the edge of the fountain. He jumped down to the wet pavement and shook thoroughly. Water sprayed all over the place.

"*There's* your hero," Rasheed proclaimed proudly. "It's Santa Paws!"

Everyone clapped again.

Several stores away, still trying to get through the crowd, Gregory saw the dog. Instantly, he grabbed his mother's arm.

"Mom, that's him!" he said eagerly. "My dog! Isn't he great? Can we keep him? Please?"

His mother shook her head, not sure if she could believe the coincidence. "What? Are you sure?" she asked. "Here, in the *mall*?"

"That's the dog!" Gregory insisted. "The one we want to come live with us!"

"That's no dog," a woman next to them said solemnly. "That's *Santa Paws!*"

"He just saved that little boy," one of the workers from the taco stand agreed. "He's a hero!"

Patricia looked disgusted. "*Santa Paws?*" she said. "What a *completely* dumb name."

Rachel nodded. "It's embarrassing. It's . . ." — she paused for effect — "not cool."

Patricia nodded, too. It wasn't cool *at all*.

"I have to get him!" Gregory said, and started trying to push his way through the crowd.

Down by the fountain, the dog was shrinking away from all of the people and attention. Everyone was trying to touch him and pat him at once. There were too many people. Too much noise. Too much *everything*.

So unexpectedly that everyone was startled, the dog raced away from them.

"Someone catch him!" Kyle's father shouted. "He saved my little boy!"

People started chasing the dog, but he was much too fast. He ran until he found one of the rubber mats and then jumped on it. The doors opened and he tore out of the mall. He raced through the parking lot, dodging cars and customers.

It was a scary place, and he was never going back!

Inside the mall, Gregory got to the fountain only seconds after the dog had left.

"Where's my dog?" he asked urgently. "I mean — where's Santa Paws!"

Everyone turned and pointed to the exit.

"Thanks!" Gregory said, and ran in that direction. But when he got outside, the dog was already long gone.

Disappointed, he walked slowly back inside. He had *almost* gotten him, this time. What if he never got another chance?

Oscar caught up to him. "Where'd he go? Is he still here?"

Gregory shook his head unhappily. "Lost him again. What if he disappears for good, this time?"

"I'm sorry," Oscar said. Then he threw a comforting arm around his friend's shoulders. "Don't worry. We'll find him again. Count on it."

"I sure *hope* so," Gregory said glumly.

Just then, Kyle's mother came walking up to the fountain. She was carrying lots of bags and whistling a little. She gave her husband and children a big smile.

"Well, *there* you are," she said. "I've been waiting in the food court *forever* — I was starting to worry."

Then, seeing the large crowd around her family, she frowned.

"Did I miss something?" she asked.

Everyone just groaned.

12

The name "Santa Paws" caught on, and news of the hero dog spread quickly all over Oceanport. People began coming forward with tales about *their* experiences with Santa Paws. Some of these stories were more plausible than others. There were people who thought that a stray dog on his own might be wild — and possibly dangerous. They thought that he should be caught, and taken to the pound as soon as possible. One man even claimed that Santa Paws had growled viciously at him on Hawthorne Street, but since he was a Yankees fan living in the middle of New England, nobody took him very seriously.

Most of the town was behind Santa Paws one hundred percent. Officers Bronkowski and Lee told how the dog had scared the vandals away from the Nativity scene. Mrs. Amory spoke from her hospital bed about how he had saved her life when she fell on the ice and broke her hip. Yolanda's husband Mortimer said, vaguely, "Oh, yeah, that was the weird dog who brought the cows home." One woman said that Santa Paws had magically cleared the snow from her front walk and driveway earlier that week. Another family claimed that he had been up on the roof and suddenly their television reception was much better. A little girl in the first grade was *sure* that he had come into her room while she was asleep and chased the monsters from her closet.

By now, the dog's brother and sisters and mother had all been adopted. Seeing the strong resemblance, their new owners were boasting that they owned dogs who might be *related* to the great Santa Paws. Although they had originally just gone to the pound to adopt nice stray dogs, these owners now felt very lucky, indeed.

In short, Santa Paws was the talk of the town. There was even a group who hung out at Sally's Diner & Sundries Shop taking bets on when, and where, Santa Paws might show up next. What heroic acts he would perform. Everyone who came into the diner had an enthusiastic prediction.

The newscasters on television had set up a Santa Paws hotline so people could phone in sightings. He was described as being small, and brown, and very, very wise.

In the meantime, the poor dog had barely stopped running since he had left the mall. He ran and ran and ran. He had gotten so wet from diving into the fountain that his fur froze. No matter what he did, he couldn't get warm. He ended up huddling against a tree in a vacant lot, as his body shook uncontrollably from the cold. He was glad that the little boy hadn't drowned, but it had still been a bad, scary day.

He was so tired and cold that he felt like giving up. He didn't *like* being on his own. It was too hard. He wanted a home. He wanted a family. He wanted to feel *safe*.

Instead, he sat in the vacant lot all by himself and shivered. Every few minutes, he whimpered a little, too.

He was just plain *miserable*.

The same afternoon, Mrs. Callahan let Gregory and Oscar skip going to the movies and leave the mall early. As long as they got home before dark, they had permission to go over to the school and leave some more food and water for the dog. If they could catch him, she said, Gregory could bring him home.

Gregory was overjoyed. Getting to keep the dog would be the best Christmas present he ever had! He just prayed that the dog would be there waiting for him. If not — well, he didn't want to think about the possibility of never finding him again. His parents would probably take him to the pound in a couple of weeks to get a different dog — but the *only* dog he wanted was Santa Paws. He had to be over at the school, he just *had* to be.

So, he and Oscar gathered up a bunch of supplies. Then Gregory's father left his word processor long enough to drive them over to the school. Gregory and Oscar were in such good moods that they didn't even complain when Mr. Callahan made them listen to Frank Sinatra on the radio. They also didn't laugh when Mr. Callahan sang along. Much.

Just as the chorus from "New York, New York" was over, Mr. Callahan pulled up in front of the school. When he was in the middle of a new book, he was sometimes very absentminded. Today, he still had on his bunny slippers. Gregory and Oscar were afraid that they would laugh more, so they pretended not to notice.

"Okay, guys," Mr. Callahan said, as he put the car in park. "You want me to wait, or would you rather walk home?"

Gregory and Oscar looked at each other.

"Would we have to listen to more Sinatra, Mr. Callahan?" Oscar asked politely.

Gregory's father nodded. He was tall and a little bit pudgy, with greying hair and thick horn-rimmed glasses. "I'm afraid so," he said.

"Well, then," Oscar answered, very politely, "maybe it would be very good exercise for us to walk."

"Thanks for driving us, though," Gregory added.

Mr. Callahan grinned, raised the volume on the radio, and drove away. He beeped the horn twice, waved, and then turned onto the main road to head home.

"For Christmas, you should give him a CD of *good* music," Oscar said. "So he'll know what it sounds like."

Gregory laughed. His father's idea of modern music was the Eagles. Mr. Callahan liked the Doobie Brothers, too.

He and Oscar had brought more dog food, some biscuits, a couple of thick beach towels, and a new collar and leash. Gregory was also carrying a big cardboard box the dog could use for shelter, in case they missed him again. He hoped that as long as they kept leaving things, the dog would keep coming back.

When they got to the little alcove, they saw that all of the food was gone. Most of the water was, too.

"Good!" Gregory said happily. "He found it!" He would have been very sad if the bowls hadn't been touched.

Oscar nodded, bending down to refill the water dish. "I hope so. I mean, I wouldn't want *other* dogs to be eating his food."

Now, Gregory frowned. "Whoa. I didn't even think of that."

Oscar shrugged. "Don't sweat it. It was probably him, anyway." Then he took out a big can of Alpo. To open it, he used a special little can opener his father had had in Vietnam. Oscar was very proud that his father had given it to him, and he always carried it on his key chain.

Gregory set up the cardboard box in the most protected corner. It had come from some catalog when his mother ordered new comforters, so it was pretty big. Then he packed some snow against the side, so it wouldn't blow away. Right now, the wind wasn't blowing very hard, but it might pick up later.

"On the top, too," Oscar advised. "Just in case."

Gregory considered that, and then frowned. The box was *only* made of cardboard. "Maybe a little. I don't want it to collapse."

"It might be good insulation, though," Oscar said.

That made sense, so Gregory did it. Then he folded the beach towels and put them neatly inside. One was yellow, and the other had a faded Bugs Bunny on it. He arranged them until they formed a nice, warm bed. He had also brought three dog biscuits, and he laid them out in a row on the top towel. That way, the dog could have a bedtime snack.

"Think he'll like this?" he asked.

Oscar nodded. "Totally." He put his key chain back in his pocket and dumped the Alpo into the big red dish. "I think he'll be really happy."

"Me, too," Gregory agreed. What he wanted more than anything was for the dog to feel *special*. Loved.

Once they had set everything up, they sat down in the snow to wait for a while. If they were lucky, maybe the dog would show up. If not, tomorrow was Christmas Eve, and they had a whole week of holiday vacation ahead. They could come here and wait around all day, every day, if they wanted. He would have to come back at some point — wouldn't he?

It was pretty cold, sitting there in the snow, but they stayed for over an hour. The dog was probably busy saving people somewhere. Oscar searched his jacket pockets and found a deck of cards. To pass the time, they played Hearts, and Go Fish, and Old Maid.

The sun was starting to go down, and shadows were creeping across the playground.

Gregory sighed. "We'd better go. We promised we'd get home before dark."

Oscar nodded and stood up. He put his cards in the pocket of his Bruins jacket, and brushed the snow off his jeans. "Don't worry, Greg. We'll just keep coming back until we find him."

"What if someone *else* finds him?" Gregory asked. Now that Santa Paws was famous, *everyone* was going to want him.

"*Nobody* is going to think to look here," Oscar pointed out. "Nobody."

Gregory sure hoped not.

The dog quivered against the tree in the vacant lot for a long time. The ice particles in his fur felt sharp. He couldn't remember ever feeling so uncomfortable. He was very hungry, too. He was *always* hungry.

He was also still scared from having been in the big place with all those people. He didn't like the noise, or all the unfamiliar faces staring at him. He *never* wanted to go to a place like that again.

He was very hungry. If he started walking around again, he might find some more food. Maybe it would also seem warmer, if he kept moving.

He was afraid of running into strangers, so he waited until it was dark. Then he waited until he didn't hear any cars going by. Finally, he got up enough nerve to leave the vacant lot.

He decided to travel along side roads and back alleys. It might be safer. He took a route that went along the ocean, so that he could avoid the center of town.

The dog walked very slowly along Overlook Drive. His paws hurt. He was hungry and thirsty. There was still lots of ice on his coat. Instead of carrying his tail up jauntily, the way he usually did, he let it drag behind him. He just wasn't feeling very happy right now.

He wandered unhappily off the road and down to the beach in the dark. The cold sand felt strange under his paws, but he kind of liked it. He kept slipping and sliding.

The water was very noisy. It was almost high tide, and big waves were rolling in and out. The dog trotted down to the edge of the water to drink some.

Just as he put his head down, foamy water came rushing towards him. He yelped in surprise and jumped out of the way. Why did the water *move* like that?

He waited for a minute, and then tried again. The water rushed in his direction, almost knocking him off his feet. And it was cold!

He ran back onto the dry sand and shook himself vigorously. It was like the water was *playing* with him. He decided that it would be fun to join the game. A lot more fun than feeling sad. So he chased the waves back and forth until he got tired.

A bunch of seagulls flew past him in the night sky and he barked happily at them. This was a nice place, even though the water smelled sort of funny. He tasted some and then made gagging noises. It was awful!

The taste in his mouth was so sour and salty that he lost interest in chasing the waves. It was too cold, anyway.

He trotted along the sand until he came to a big stone seawall. It took him three tries, but he finally managed to scramble over it. He landed hard on the icy sidewalk on the other side with his legs all splayed out. It hurt. But he picked himself up and only limped for about ten feet. Then he forgot that he had hurt himself at all, and went back to trotting.

Fifteen minutes later, the dog found himself at the middle school. He paused at the trash bins and lifted his nose in the air for a hopeful sniff. Even if he could have reached the garbage, what little there was smelled rotten.

Even so, his stomach churned with hunger. When had he eaten last? That nice meaty food yesterday? It had been so good that he could *still* almost taste it.

He ran behind the school to the playground. He stopped before he got to the alcove, and whined a little. If there wasn't any food there, he was going to be very disappointed. What if they had forgotten him?

He took his time walking over, pausing every few steps and whining softly. Then he caught a little whiff of that special meaty smell. There *was* food waiting for him!

He raced into the alcove so swiftly that he almost knocked the dishes over. Food and water! All for him! He *loved* Gregory and Oscar. There was another familiar smell, too. He sniffed a few more times and then barked with delight.

Milk-Bones!

The dog was very happy when he went to sleep that night.

13

The next day was Christmas Eve. The sky was overcast and the temperature was just above freezing. But the dog had been warm and comfortable inside his cardboard box. The thick towels felt very soft and clean next to his body.

He had eaten one of the biscuits right before he went to sleep. His plan was to save the other two for the morning. But they smelled so good that he woke up in the middle of the night and crunched down one more.

When he woke up just before dawn, he yawned and stretched out all four paws. He liked his box-home a whole lot! There was still one biscuit left and he held it between his front paws. It was so nice to have his own bone that he just looked at it, wagging his tail.

Then he couldn't stand it anymore, and he started crunching. It tasted just as good as the other two! He was so happy!

It was time to go outside. Feeling full of energy,

he rolled to his feet. He hit his head against the top of the box, but that was okay. He *liked* that it was cozy. He yawned again and ambled outside.

His water bowl had frozen again. He jumped on the ice with his front paws, and it broke easily. He lapped up a few mouthfuls and then licked his chops. He could still taste the Milk-Bone, a little. It still tasted delicious!

He galloped around the playground twice to stretch his legs. Because he was happy, he barked a lot, too.

Would his friends come back soon? He sat down to wait. Then he got bored. So he rolled on his back for a while. But that got boring, too.

Next, he took a little nap until the sun rose. When he woke up, Gregory and Oscar still hadn't come. He was very restless, so he decided to go for a walk. Maybe he would go back to the beach and play with the moving water some more.

After about an hour of wandering, he walked up Prospect Street, near a little strip mall. A girl was standing on the sidewalk without moving. She was holding a funny-looking stick, and she seemed worried.

It was Patricia's best friend Rachel. She was on her way to the 7-Eleven to pick up some milk and rye bread for her mother. Unfortunately, her wallet had fallen out of her pocket on the way, and now she couldn't find it.

She hated to ask people for help. So she was

retracing her steps and using her red and white cane to feel for the missing object. She could go home and tell her mother what happened, but she would rather not. It wasn't that she was afraid someone would *steal* the wallet if she left. She just liked to do things by herself.

The dog cocked his head. Why was she moving *so slowly*? Why was she swinging the little stick around? He didn't want the stick to hit him, so he kept his distance.

"Now, where is it?" Rachel muttered. She bent down and felt the snow with her gloved hands. This was so frustrating! "Why can't I find the stupid thing?" she asked aloud.

The dog woofed softly.

Rachel stiffened. "Who's there?" she said, and got ready to use her cane as a weapon. She knew that it was a dog, but how could she be sure that it was friendly? Sometimes, dogs weren't.

The dog walked closer, wagging his tail.

Rachel felt something brush against her arm. The dog? She reached out and felt a wagging tail, and then a furry back.

"Are you a dog I know?" she asked.

Naturally, the dog didn't answer.

She took off her left glove and felt for the dog's collar. Her fingertips were so sensitive from reading Braille that she could usually read the inscriptions on license tags. But this dog wasn't wearing a collar at all.

Could he be — Santa Paws? She ran her hand along his side and felt sharp ribs. He was *very* skinny. His fur felt rough and unbrushed, too. This dog had been outside for a very long time.

The dog liked the way she was patting him, so he licked her face.

"You're that dog Gregory's trying to catch, aren't you," Rachel said. "You must be."

The dog licked her face again.

It felt pretty slobbery, but Rachel didn't really mind. "Can you fetch?" she asked. "Or find? Do you know 'find'?"

The dog lifted his paw.

"I lost my wallet," she said. "I have to find it."

The dog barked and pawed at her arm.

"Okay, okay." Rachel shook her head. Patricia was right — this dog needed some *serious* training. "Stay. I have to keep looking for it."

Stay. "Stay" meant something, but right now, the dog couldn't remember what. He barked uncertainly.

"*Stay,*" she said over her shoulder.

He followed her as she kept retracing her steps. She would take a step, bend down and feel the snow, and then take another step.

Was she looking for something? The dog sniffed around. The girl was walking so slowly that he leaped over a big drift to pass her. He could cover more ground that way.

He could smell that she had already walked on

this part of the sidewalk. There were little boot-steps in the snow. He followed them until he smelled something else. He wasn't sure what it was, but the object had her scent on it. It was square and made of some kind of sturdy material.

So he picked the object up in his mouth and romped back up to the street to where she was.

"I really can't play with you now," Rachel said, pushing him away. "I have to keep searching."

He pressed his muzzle against her arm, and then dropped the object in front of her.

Rachel heard it hit the ground and reached out to feel — her wallet!

"Good dog!" she said, and picked it up. "No wonder they call you Santa Paws. Good boy!"

The dog wagged his tail and woofed again.

Rachel couldn't help wondering what he looked like. She had vague memories of things like colors and shapes. Mostly, though, she had to use her hands to picture things.

"Is it okay if I see what you look like?" she asked, surprised to find herself feeling shy. He was only a *dog*, even if he was a particularly good one.

The dog wagged his tail.

She put her hand out and felt the sharp ribs again. His fur was short and fairly dense. His winter undercoat, probably. The fur wasn't silky at all. Her family had a cocker spaniel named

Trudy and *she* was very silky. This dog's fur was much more coarse.

The dog's hips were narrow, but his chest was pretty broad. Gregory had said that he wasn't full grown yet, but he was already at least forty or fifty pounds. He felt bony and athletic, not solid and stocky. That was the way her friend Gary's Labrador retriever felt. This dog was built differently.

She ran her hand down the dog's legs. They were very thin. His paws were surprisingly *big*. That meant Gregory was right, and the dog was going to grow a lot more.

She left his head for last. His ears seemed to be pointy, although they were a little crooked right at the very tip. His head and muzzle were long and slim. His mouth was open, but he was so gentle that she knew he wouldn't bite her.

"Thank you," she said, and removed her hands. She always felt better when she could *picture* something in her mind. She had a very clear picture, now, of this dog. A nice picture.

She was almost sure that the 7-Eleven was only about half a block away. There was a pay phone there. She should call Patricia's house right away and tell them to come pick up the dog.

"Come here, Santa Paws," she said. "Just follow me down to this telephone, okay?"

There was no answering bark.

"Santa Paws?" she called. "Are you still here?"

She listened carefully, trying to hear him panting or the sound of his tail beating against the air. She could almost always sense it when any living being was near her.

The only thing she could sense right now was that the dog had gone away.

Rachel sighed. Oh, well. She could still call Patricia and tell her that the dog *had* been here. Briefly.

She wasn't sure if that would make Gregory feel better — or worse.

The dog's next stop was behind the doughnut shop. He checked the garbage cans, but all he found were coffee grounds and crumpled napkins. He was more lucky at the pizza place, because he found a box full of discarded crusts. They were a little hard, but they tasted fine.

Now it was time to go to the beach. A couple of people shouted and pointed when they saw him, but he just picked up his pace. They sounded very excited to see him, but he had no idea why. So he kept running along until he outdistanced them.

Trotting down Harbor Cove Road, he heard several dogs barking and growling. They sounded like they were just around the next corner. He could also hear an elderly man shouting, "No, no! Bad dogs!" There was definitely trouble up ahead!

More alarmed than curious, he broke into a full

run. He stretched his legs out as far as they would go, feeling the wind blow his ears back.

Just up ahead, at the base of an old oak tree, a big Irish setter, a Dalmatian, and a husky-mix were all barking viciously. They had chased a kitten up the tree and were still yapping wildly at her from the bottom.

The elderly man, Mr. Corcoran, was brandishing a stick and trying to make the dogs run away. The kitten belonged to him, and he loved her very much.

"Bad dogs!" he shouted. "Go home!"

The little kitten trembled up on the icy tree branch. Even though she was tiny, the branch was swaying under her weight and might break at any second.

The dog growled a warning, and then ran straight into the fray. He butted the Dalmatian in the side, and then shoved past the husky-mix, still growling.

At first, since he was obviously a puppy, the other dogs ignored him. They were having too much fun tormenting the kitten. The Irish setter seemed to be the leader of the pack, so the puppy confronted him with a fierce bark.

This got the Irish setter's attention, but the puppy refused to back down. He showed his teeth and the Irish setter returned the favor. The Dalmatian and the husky-mix decided to join in, and the odds were three against one.

The dog was ready to fight *all* of them! He would probably lose, but he wasn't afraid. He stood his ground, trying to keep all three dogs in sight at once and not let any of them sneak up on him from behind. It was much harder than herding cows! And this time, Daffodil wasn't here to help him!

"Bad dogs!" Mr. Corcoran yelled. "Leave him alone!"

Just as the husky-mix lunged towards the puppy, with her teeth bared, the kitten fell out of the tree with a shrieking meow. She landed in a clumsy heap in the snow, mewing pitifully.

Before the other dogs could hurt her, the puppy jumped past them, ready to protect her with his body. The other three dogs circled him slowly, planning their next moves. The puppy kept his teeth bared and growled steadily.

Swiftly and silently, the husky-mix leaped forward and bit his shoulder. The puppy yelped in pain, but snapped at one of the husky's back legs and heard the husky yelp, too.

Now the Irish setter moved in. At the last second, the puppy ducked and the setter sailed right over him. While the setter was trying to recover his balance, the puppy whirled around to face the Dalmatian.

The Dalmatian didn't like to fight, and he took one nervous step forward. Then he backed up, whining uneasily. The puppy made a short, fierce move towards him and the Dalmatian hesitated for a second. Then he tucked his tail between his legs and started running home.

Before the puppy had time to enjoy that victory, the Irish setter and the husky had already jumped on him. The puppy fought back, trying not to let them get between him and the mewing kitten.

He was ready to fight for his life — and the kitten's life!

14

The fight was fast, confusing, and brutal.

"Stop it!" Mr. Corcoran kept yelling helplessly. "Stop it right now!" He tried to break the fight up, using a stick he had found on the ground. It took a while, but he finally managed to knock the snarling husky away.

The husky growled at him, but then just limped off towards his owner's house. He had had enough fighting for one day.

Mrs. Quigley, who lived across the street, came tearing outside in her bathrobe. "Pumpkin!" she shouted. "Bad dog, Pumpkin! You come here *right now!*"

Hearing the voice of authority, the Irish setter instantly cringed. Mrs. Quigley grabbed him by the collar and hauled him away a few feet. "Bad, bad dog! You, *sit!*"

The Irish setter sat down, looking guilty.

"I'm so sorry, Carl," she said to Mr. Corcoran,

out of breath. "I don't know what could have gotten into him."

"*Eggnog*, probably," Mr. Corcoran grumbled.

Mrs. Quigley sniffed her dog's breath and then glared down at him. "Pumpkin! How could you? You bad, bad dog!" She looked up at Mr. Corcoran. "I am so sorry. Are Matilda and your puppy all right?"

Mr. Corcoran reached down and gently lifted his terrified kitten out of the snow. She was a calico cat, and her name was Matilda. He checked her all over, but except for being very frightened, she wasn't hurt.

"Oh, thank God," he said gratefully. "She's okay. I don't know what I would have done if they'd hurt her."

"I'm sorry," Mrs. Quigley said, wringing her hands. "I promise I won't let Pumpkin get out like that again."

Hearing his name — and his owner's disappointment — the Irish setter cringed lower. He was very ashamed.

In the meantime, feeling dazed, the puppy dragged himself to his feet. He hurt in a lot of places. He could feel blood on his left shoulder and his right ear was dripping blood, too. He had lots of other small cuts and slashes, but his ear and shoulder hurt the most. He shook his head from side to side, trying to clear away the dizziness.

Suddenly, Mrs. Quigley looked horrified. "That

isn't Santa Paws, is it?" she asked.

Mr. Corcoran's eyes widened. "I don't know. I guess it could be. Who else would come save Matilda?" He studied the dog more carefully. "The TV *did* say that he was small, and brown, and wise."

At that moment, the dog mainly looked *small*.

"Well, we're going to have to take him straight to the vet," Mrs. Quigley said decisively. She aimed a stern finger at her Irish setter. "You are *very bad*, Pumpkin! You're going to have to go back to obedience school!"

The Irish setter wagged his tail tentatively at the puppy. Now that the heat of the battle was over, he couldn't remember how, or why, the fight had started.

The puppy ignored him and tried to put weight on his injured shoulder. It hurt so much that he whimpered.

"Oh, you poor thing," Mrs. Quigley cooed. "You just come here, snook'ums, and I'll take you to the vet."

The puppy veered away from her. He was in so much pain that he just wanted to be alone. Mrs. Quigley and Mr. Corcoran both tried to stop him, but he staggered off down the street. Then he forced himself into a limping run.

He wanted to get as far away from Harbor Cove Road as possible!

* * *

The dog only managed to run a couple of blocks before he had to stop. He lurched over to the side of the road and into the woods. His injured leg didn't want to work at all.

He collapsed next to an old tree stump. He rested on his bad side, and the snow numbed the pain a little. But it still hurt. A lot.

The dog whimpered and tried to lick the blood away from his wounds. He had never been in a fight with other dogs before. Dog fights were terrible! Especially when it was three against one!

His ear was stinging badly. He rubbed it against the snow to try and get rid of the pain. Instead, it started bleeding even more.

The dog whimpered pitifully and then closed his eyes. Right now, he was too weak to do anything else. Then, before he had a chance to fall asleep, he passed out.

It would be a long time before he woke up again.

Gregory and Oscar met on the school playground at ten-thirty. Patricia had insisted on coming along, too. Since the food was gone and the towels in the cardboard box were rumpled, they knew that the dog had been there. But he was gone now — and they had no way of knowing if he would ever come back.

"Where does he *go* every day?" Gregory asked, frustrated. "Doesn't he want us to find him?"

Oscar shrugged as he opened a brand-new can

of Alpo stew. "He's off doing hero stuff, probably."

Patricia didn't like to see the towels looking so messy. She bent down to refold them. "You know, that was really something at the mall," she remarked. "I've never seen a dog do anything like that before."

"He's not just any dog," Gregory said proudly.

Patricia nodded. For once, her brother was right. "I have to say, it was pretty cool." She reached into the open Milk-Bone box. "How many should I leave him?"

"Three," Gregory told her. "In a nice, neat row."

"Since it's Christmas Eve, let's give him four," Oscar suggested.

"Sounds good," Patricia said, and took out four biscuits.

When they were done, they sat down on a wool blanket Oscar had brought. It was much more pleasant than sitting in the cold snow. Mrs. Callahan had packed them a picnic lunch, too.

So they spent the next couple of hours eating sandwiches, drinking out of juice boxes, and playing cards. Patricia hated Hearts, so mostly they played inept poker.

"Is this going to get any more interesting?" Patricia asked at one point.

Gregory and Oscar shook their heads.

"Great," Patricia said grumpily. Then she slouched down to deal another hand of cards.

"Aces wild, boys. Place your bets."

They waited and waited, but the dog never showed up. They had stayed so long that the batteries in Gregory's portable tape deck were running down.

"Is it okay if we go now?" Patricia asked. "I'm *really* tired of playing cards."

"Me, too," Oscar confessed.

"We might as well," Gregory said with a sigh. He was pretty sick of cards, too. "I don't think he's coming." He reached for a small plastic bag and started collecting all of their trash. "Do you think Mom and Dad would let us come here at night? Maybe we'd find him here, asleep."

"They wouldn't let us come *alone*," Patricia said. "But if we asked really nicely, they might come with us. I mean, they're the ones who are always telling us to be kind to animals, right?"

Gregory nodded. His parents had always *stressed* the importance of being kind to animals.

"You should write down what you're going to say first," Oscar advised them. He never really liked to leave things to chance. In the Cub Scouts, he had learned a lot about being prepared. "That way, you can practice how you're going to do it. Work out all the bugs."

"Let me write it," Patricia told her brother. "I have a bigger vocabulary."

Gregory just shrugged. All he wanted to do was find the dog — one way or another.

He was beginning to be afraid that the dog didn't *want* to be found.

Hours passed before the dog regained consciousness. It was well past midnight, and the woods were pitch-black. His shoulder had stiffened so much that at first, he couldn't get up. But finally, he staggered to his feet. He wanted to lie right back down, but he made himself stay up.

He stood there, swaying. He felt dizzy and sick. What he wanted right now, more than anything, was to be inside that warm cardboard box, sleeping on those soft towels that smelled so clean and fresh.

He limped out to the road, whimpering every time his bad leg hit the ground. The bleeding had stopped, but now that he was moving around, it started up again.

The only way he was going to make it back to the school was if he put one foot after the other. He limped painfully up the road, staring down at his front paws the whole way. One step. Two. Three. Four. It was hard work.

Whenever possible, he took shortcuts. He cut through alleys, and parking lots, and backyards. The lights were off all over town. People were sound asleep, dreaming about Christmas morning. The dog just staggered along, putting one foot in front of the other. Over and over.

He was plodding through someone's front yard

when he felt the hair on his back rise. Oh, now what? He was *too tired*. But — he smelled smoke! Even though he was dizzy, he lifted his head to sniff the air. Where was it coming from?

He followed the trail across several yards and up to a yellow two-story house. Smoke was billowing out through a crack in the living room window. Someone had left the Christmas tree lights on, and the tree had ignited! The lights were snapping and popping, and the ornaments were bursting into flames. He could hear the crackle of electricity, and smell the smoke getting stronger.

The house was on fire!

He lurched up the front steps and onto the porch. He was too weak to paw on the door, but he *could* still bark. He threw his head back and howled into the silent night. He barked and barked until the other dogs in the neighborhood woke up and started joining in. Soon, there were dogs howling and yapping everywhere.

After a few minutes of that, lights started going on in houses up and down the block. The dog was losing strength, but he kept barking. Why didn't the people come outside? Didn't they know that their house was burning?

The living room windows were getting black from the smoke, as the fire spread. Why wouldn't the people wake up? Maybe he was going to have to go in and *get* them. But, how?

He started throwing his body feebly against the

front door, but it wouldn't budge. Why couldn't the people hear him barking? Where were they? If they didn't wake up soon, they might die from the smoke!

The dog limped to the farthest end of the porch, trying to gather up all of his strength. Then he raced towards the living room window and threw himself into the glass at full speed. The window shattered and he landed in the middle of the burning room. He was covered with little shards of glass, but he didn't have time to shake them off. He had to go find the family! The floor was very hot, and he burned the bottom of his paws as he ran across the room. It was scary in here!

The doorway was blocked by fire, but he launched himself up into the air and soared through the flames. He could smell burned fur where his coat had been singed, but he ignored that and limped up the stairs as fast as he could. He kept barking and howling the entire way, trying to sound the alarm. A burning ember had fallen onto his back and he yelped when he felt the pain, but then he just went back to barking.

A man came stumbling out of the master bedroom in a pair of flannel pajamas. It was Mr. Brown, who lived in the house with his wife and two daughters, and he was weak from smoke inhalation.

"Wh-what's going on?" Mr. Brown mumbled. "It's the middle of the — "

The dog barked, and tugged at his pajama leg with his teeth, trying to pull him down the stairs.

Mr. Brown saw the flames downstairs and gasped. "Fire!" he yelled, and ran into his children's bedroom. "Wake up, everyone! The house is on fire!"

The dog ran into the master bedroom, barking as loudly as he could until Mrs. Brown groggily climbed out of bed. She was coughing from the smoke, and seemed very confused. The dog barked, and nudged her towards the door.

Mr. Brown rushed down the stairs with his two sleepy children and a squirming Siamese cat, and then went back for his wife. By now, she was only steps behind him, carrying a cage full of gerbils.

The dog was exhausted, but he kept barking until they were all safely outside. Once he was sure the house was empty, he staggered out to the yard, his lungs and eyes hurting from the thick smoke. He sank down in the snow, coughing and gagging and quivering from fear.

One of the neighbors had called 911, and the first fire engine was just arriving. The firefighters leaped out, carrying various pieces of equipment and grabbing lengths of hose. By now, the fire had spread from the living room to the dining room.

"Is anyone still in there?" the engine company lieutenant yelled.

"No," Mrs. Brown answered, coughing from the

smoke she had inhaled. "It's okay! We all got out."

Because they had been called only a minute or two after the fire started, the fire department was able to put the fire out quickly. Although the living room and dining room were destroyed, the rest of the house had been saved. Instead of losing everything, including their lives, the Browns would still have a place to live.

During all of this, the dog had limped over to the nearest bush. He crawled underneath it as far as he could go. Then he collapsed in exhaustion. His injured shoulder was throbbing, he was still gagging, and all he could smell was smoke. His paws hurt, and he licked at the pads, trying to get rid of the burning sensation. They hurt so much that he couldn't stop whimpering. His back was stinging from where the ember had hit it, and he had lots of new cuts from leaping through the glass. He huddled into a small ball, whimpering to himself. He had never been in so much pain in his life.

While the other firefighters checked to make sure that the fire was completely out, the chief went over to interview Mr. and Mrs. Brown. The Oceanport Fire Department was staffed by volunteers, and Fire Chief Jefferson had run the department for many years.

"How did you get out?" Chief Jefferson asked, holding an incident report form and a ballpoint pen. "Did your smoke detector wake you up?"

Mr. and Mrs. Brown exchanged embarrassed glances.

"We, um, kind of took the battery out a few days ago," Mr. Brown mumbled. "See, the remote control went dead, and . . ." His voice trailed off.

"We were going to get another battery for the smoke detector," Mrs. Brown said, coming to his defense. "But, with the holidays and all, we just — "

"Hadn't gotten around to it yet," Chief Jefferson finished the sentence for her.

The Browns nodded, and looked embarrassed.

Chief Jefferson sighed. "Well, then, all I can say is that you were very lucky. On a windy night like tonight, a fire can get out of control in no time."

Mr. and Mrs. Brown and their daughters nodded solemnly. They knew that they had had a very close call.

"So, what happened?" Chief Jefferson asked. "Did you smell the smoke?"

The Browns shook their heads.

"We were all asleep," Mrs. Brown said.

Chief Jefferson frowned. "Then I don't understand what happened. Who woke you up?"

The Browns looked at one another.

"It was Santa Paws!" they all said in unison. "Who else?"

141

15

It was Christmas morning, and the Callahans were getting ready to go to church. On Christmas Eve, they had gone over to the Oceanport Hospital maternity ward to visit their brand-new niece. Mr. Callahan's brother Steve and his wife Emily had had a beautiful baby girl named Miranda. Gregory and Patricia thought she was kind of red and wrinkly, but on the whole, pretty cute.

On the way home, they talked their parents into stopping at the middle school. But when they went to the little alcove, the food and water dishes hadn't been touched. The towels were still neatly folded, too. For some reason, the dog had never returned. Maybe he was gone for good.

Gregory knew that something terrible must have happened to him, but right now, there wasn't anything he could do about it. As far as he knew, no one had seen the dog since he had found Rachel's wallet that morning. And that was *hours* ago. Now, for all Gregory knew, the dog could be lying somewhere, alone, and scared, and *hurt*.

His father put his hand on his shoulder. "Come on, Greg," he said gently. "It'll be okay. We'll come back again tomorrow."

Gregory nodded, and followed his family back to the car.

They went home and ate cookies and listened to Christmas carols. Mrs. Callahan made popcorn. Mr. Callahan read *The Night Before Christmas* aloud. Patricia told complicated jokes, and Gregory pretended that he thought they were funny. Then they all went to bed.

Gregory didn't get much sleep. He was too upset. Deep inside, he knew that the dog was gone for good. He was sure that he would never see him again — and the thought of that made him feel like crying.

When he got up, even though it was Christmas Day, he was more sad than excited. He and his father both put on suits and ties to wear to church. His mother and Patricia wore long skirts and festive blouses. Patricia also braided red and green ribbons into her hair.

Every year, on Christmas morning, there was a special, nonreligious, interdenominational service in Oceanport. No matter what holiday they celebrated, everyone in town was invited. This year, the Mass was being held at the Catholic church, but Rabbi Gladstone was going to be the main speaker. Next year, the service would be at the Baptist church, and the Methodist minister would lead the ceremony. As Father Reilly always said, it wasn't about religion, it was about *community*. It was about *neighbors*.

"Come on, Gregory," Mrs. Callahan said as they got into the station wagon. "Cheer up. It's Christmas."

Gregory nodded, and did his best to smile. Inside, though, he was miserable.

"When we get home, we have all those presents to open," Patricia reminded him. "And I spent *a lot* of money on yours."

Gregory smiled again, feebly.

The church was very crowded. Almost the entire town had shown up. People were smiling, and waving, and shaking hands with each other. There was a definite feeling of goodwill in the air. Oceanport was *always* a friendly and tolerant town, but the holiday season was special.

Gregory sat in his family's pew with his eyes closed and his hands tightly folded. He was wishing with all of his heart that the dog was okay. No matter how hard he tried, he couldn't seem to feel *any* Christmas spirit. How could he believe in the magic of Christmas, if he couldn't even save one little stray dog?

Rabbi Gladstone stepped up to the podium in the front of the church. "Welcome, everyone," he said. "Seasons greetings to all of you!"

Then, the service began.

After the fire had been put out and the Browns had gone across the street to stay with neighbors, the dog was alone underneath his bush. He dragged himself deeper into the woods, whimpering softly. He knew he was badly hurt, and that he needed help.

He crawled through the woods until he couldn't make it any further. Then he lay down on his side in the snow. He stayed in that same position all night long. By now, he was too exhausted even to *whimper*.

In the morning, he made himself get up. If he stayed here by himself, he might die. Somehow, he had to make it back to the school. If he could do that, maybe his friends Gregory and Oscar would come and help him. He *needed* help, desperately.

Each limping step was harder than the one before, and the dog had to force himself to keep going. The town seemed to be deserted. He limped down Main Street, undisturbed.

The park was empty, too. The dog staggered across the wide expanse, falling down more than once. He was cold, he was in pain, and he was *exhausted*.

Naturally, he was also hungry.

When he tottered past the church, he paused

at the bottom of the stairs. The doors were open and welcoming, warm air rushed out at him. For days, he had been trying to *give* help. Maybe now it was time to *get* some.

He dragged himself up the steps. His shoulder throbbed and burned with pain the entire way. When he got to the top, he was panting heavily. Could he make it any further, or should he just fall down right here?

He could smell lots of people. Too many people. Too many different scents. Some of the scents were familiar, but he was too confused to sort them all out. *Walking* took up all of his energy.

He hobbled into the church, weaving from side to side. He started down the center aisle, and then his bad leg gave out under his weight. He fell on the floor and then couldn't get up again. He let his head slump forward against his front paws and then closed his eyes.

A hush fell over the church.

"I don't believe it," someone said, sounding stunned. "It's Santa Paws!"

Now that the silence had been broken, everyone started talking at once.

Hearing the name "Santa Paws," Gregory sat up straight in his pew. Then he stood up so he could see better.

"That's my dog," he whispered, so excited that he was barely able to breathe. "Look at my poor

146

dog!" Then he put his pinkies in his mouth, and let out — noisy *air*.

Sitting next to him, Patricia sighed deeply. "*Really*, Greg," she said, and shook her head with grave disappointment. "Is that the best you can do?" She sighed again. Then she stuck her fingers in her mouth, and sent out a sharp, clear, and *earsplitting* whistle.

Instantly, the dog lifted his head. His ears shot up, and his tail began to rise.

"That's my dog!" Gregory shouted. He climbed past his parents and stumbled out into the aisle.

The dog was still too weak to get up, but he waved his tail as Gregory ran over to him.

"Are you all right?" Gregory asked, fighting back tears. "Don't worry, I'll take care of you. You're safe now."

Everyone in the church started yelling at once, and trying to crowd around the injured dog.

Patricia lifted her party skirt up a few inches so that she wouldn't trip on it. Then she stepped delicately into the aisle on her bright red holiday high heels.

"Quiet, please," she said in her most commanding voice. Then she raised her hands for silence. "Is there a veterinarian in the house?"

A man and a woman sitting in different sections of the church each stood up.

"Good." Patricia motioned for them both to

come forward. "Step aside, please, everyone, and let them through."

A few people did as she said, but there was still a large, concerned group hovering around Gregory and the dog. The veterinarians were trying to get through, but the aisle was jammed.

Patricia's whistle was even more piercing this time. "I *said*," she repeated herself in a no-nonsense voice, "please step aside, in an orderly fashion."

The people standing in the aisle meekly did as they were told.

Watching all of this from their pew, Mr. Callahan leaned over to his wife.

"Do you get the sudden, sinking feeling that someday, we're going to have another cop in the family?" he asked.

Mrs. Callahan laughed. "I've had that feeling since she was *two*," she answered.

Gregory waited nervously as the two veterinarians examined the dog.

"Don't worry," the female vet announced after a couple of minutes. "He's going to be just fine."

Her colleague nodded. "Once we get him cleaned up and bandaged, and put in a few stitches, he'll be as good as new!"

Everyone in the church started clapping.

"Hooray for Santa Paws!" someone yelled.

"Merry Christmas, and God bless us everyone!" a little boy in the front row contributed.

Mr. Callahan leaned over to his wife again. "If that kid is holding a crutch, I'm *out* of here."

Mrs. Callahan grinned. "That's just Nathanial Haversham. His parents are *actors.*"

"Oh." Mr. Callahan looked relieved. "Good."

Up in the front of the church, Rabbi Gladstone tapped on the microphone to get everyone's attention. Gradually, the church quieted down.

"Thank you," he said. "I think that this week, we've all seen proof that there *can* be holiday miracles. Even when it's hard to believe in magic, wonderful, unexplained things can still happen. That dog — an ordinary dog — has been saving lives and helping people throughout this season." He smiled in the dog's direction. "Thank you, and welcome to Oceanport, Santa Paws!"

Gregory didn't want to be rude, but he had to speak up. "Um, I'm sorry, Rabbi, but that's not his name," he said shyly.

"Whew," Patricia said, and pretended to wipe her arm across her forehead. "Promise me you're not going to call him Brownie, or Muffin, or anything else *cute.*"

Gregory nodded. If he came up with a cute name, his sister would never let him live it down. Somehow, the name would have to be *cool.*

"What *is* his name, son?" Rabbi Gladstone asked kindly from the podium.

Gregory blinked a few times. His mind was a complete blank. "Well, uh, it's uh — "

"Sparky!" Oscar shouted, sitting with his family several rows away.

Everyone laughed.

"It's *not* Sparky," Gregory assured them. "It's, uh — "

"Solomon's a very nice name," Rabbi Gladstone suggested. "Isaiah has a nice ring to it, too."

Now, everyone in the church started shouting out different ideas. Names like Hero, and Rex, and Buttons.

"Oh, yeah, *Buttons*," Patricia said under her breath. "Like we wouldn't be totally humiliated to have a dog named *Buttons*."

Other names were suggested. Champ, and Sport, and Dasher, and Dancer. Frank, and Foxy, and Bud.

Bud?

Gregory looked at his dog for a long time. The dog wagged his tail and then lifted his paw into his new owner's lap. Gregory thought some more, and then, out of nowhere, it came to him. After all, what was another name for Santa Claus?

"His name's Nicholas," he told everyone. Then he smiled proudly and shook his dog's paw. "We call him *Nick*."

The dog barked and wagged his tail.

Then, Gregory stood up. "Come on, Nicky," he said. "It's time to go home."

The dog got up, too, balancing on three legs.

He wagged his tail as hard as he could, and pressed his muzzle into Gregory's hand. He had a new owner, he had a new home, and he was going to have a whole new life.

He could hardly wait to get started!

THE RETURN OF
SANTA PAWS

1

The dog was happy every day. Eating food was his very favorite thing to do, but sleeping was a lot of fun, too. More than anything else, of course, he loved his owners, the Callahans. After living on the streets for a long, lonely time, he had finally found a family who wanted to adopt him. Now he had a warm bed to sleep on every night, fresh water in a red plastic dish that was just for him, and Milk-Bones *all day long*!

The Callahans were the nicest people in the world. Mr. Callahan was a writer, and so the dog spent most of the day following him around the house. Mrs. Callahan taught physics at Oceanport High School, and the dog liked her because she was almost always the one who fed him and brushed him. Sometimes she would also take him to the vet, but he didn't really mind. The vet was a nice person, too.

But the dog *especially* loved Gregory and

Patricia, the Callahans' children. Gregory was eleven years old and in the sixth grade, while Patricia had just started junior high this year. They took him for lots of walks, taught him tricks, and fed him snacks under the dinner table. The dog *really* liked snacks.

While Gregory and Patricia were at school, the dog usually slept under Mr. Callahan's desk. Sometimes Mr. Callahan would sit down at the desk, mutter to himself, and then pound wildly on his keyboard for awhile. On other days, he would lie on the couch and watch television, or spend hours blaring music and pacing back and forth. No matter what Mr. Callahan was doing, though, he liked to talk to himself. The dog wasn't always sure what he was saying, but he would listen, anyway, and wag his tail a lot.

When Mr. Callahan was working hard and the dog got bored, he would play with Evelyn, the family's tiger cat. If she didn't feel like playing, he would chase her until she whacked him on the nose with her paw. When that happened, the dog would always yelp and whimper a little. Mr. Callahan would come out to see what was wrong and then give them each a treat. After eating his treat, the dog would be happy again. Then he and Evelyn would lie down and sleep some more.

Everyone in the family called him by a different name. His real name was Nicholas, but they almost never used that. The dog thought it was fun to have lots of nicknames, and he answered to all of them. Mr. Callahan always called him "Pumpkin," and Evelyn was "the little Pumpkin."

Mrs. Callahan referred to him as "Smart-Guy." When he tipped over the trash, she would look stern and ask, "Are you the one who did this, Smart-Guy?" If Patricia was around, she would say, "No way, Mom — it was Greg." The dog would just stand there, and wag his tail, and lift his right paw in the most charming way he could. The family always liked it when he did tricks.

Patricia had taught him to answer to "Princess" and "Sweetpea," because it made Gregory mad. Gregory usually called him "Nick" or "Nicky" or "Bud." Evelyn, the cat, didn't really talk to him much, but the dog was pretty sure she thought of him as "Hey, you!"

But the truth was, that the Callahans — along with everyone else in town — called him "Santa Paws" more than anything else. He had shown up in town the Christmas before, and somehow, the name stuck. The dog wasn't sure why he liked that name so much, but he would wag his tail extra hard whenever anyone said "Santa Paws." There was something really *friendly* about that name.

The only thing he didn't like people to say to him was "bad dog." It didn't happen very often, but whenever he heard "bad dog," he would slump down with his tail between his legs. Usually, the person who said it, would come and pat him right away and he would feel better. He tried to be good all of the time, and not chew shoes or break anything. That way, they would just say, "What a good dog!" Whenever he heard those magic words, he would jump around and bark a lot.

Sometimes, when he and the Callahans were riding in the car, people in other cars would wave and shout, "Hi, Santa Paws!" out the window. If they were taking him for a walk, people they passed would always yell, "Look, there's Santa Paws!" Then they would smile, and sometimes even clap.

Gregory thought it was really cool that everyone in Oceanport loved their dog so much, but Patricia was always embarrassed. As far as she was concerned, all of that attention wasn't dignified. Patricia *liked* to be dignified, no matter what. Gregory didn't care, one way or the other.

Every day, the dog slept until he heard Gregory and Patricia coming up the back steps. Then he would scramble to his feet and dash out of Mr. Callahan's office. By the time they opened the door, he would be standing in the kitchen to greet them. Right after they got home, they always liked to sit down at the table and have a snack. One of them would also give him a Milk-Bone, so he could keep them company.

It was almost Christmas, and Gregory and Patricia couldn't wait for their vacation to start. There were only two days of school left before they had a whole week off. The family was going to spend the holidays up at their grandparents' lake cabin in Vermont, and they were all really looking forward to the trip.

It had snowed twice in the last week, and the backyard was still covered with about five inches of soft slush. Gregory and Patricia were just coming home from school, and they had been bickering for several blocks. Their fights were never very serious, but they liked to have *lots* of them, just to keep in practice. At least, that's what Patricia always told their parents.

"It's *really* cold," Gregory said, for at least the tenth time. He was all bundled-up in three layers of clothes — a down jacket, a Red Sox cap, and thick ragg-wool mittens, but he was still freezing.

"It is not," Patricia said — *also* for the tenth time. Her New England Patriots jacket wasn't even zipped, and her black beret was *purely* a fashion statement. She was wearing an oversized pair of red mirrored sunglasses, too. "You're just a big baby."

"*You're* a big faker," Gregory responded. "If you were, like, by yourself, I bet you'd be all shivering, and running really fast so you'd get home quicker."

Patricia shook her head. "No way. I'm too cool to be cold."

Gregory thought about that. As far as he was concerned, *nobody* was that cool — not even Patricia. "You know what would be cool?" he asked reflectively. "If I put a whole bunch of snow down your back."

Patricia stopped walking long enough to scowl at him. "If you do, I'll put a whole bunch in your *bed*. Under the blankets, inside your pillow, and everything."

Gregory grinned at her. "Oh, yeah? Then I'll put snow in all your shoes. Especially your cowboy boots."

"Then *I'll* cover your computer with snow," Patricia said, grinning now, too. "Smash it onto your keyboard, send it through the printer — you name it."

This was the kind of fight that really upset their parents, who never seemed to understand that they were mostly just kidding. *Mostly*, anyway.

The two of them looked so much alike, with

dark brown hair and very blue eyes, that people were always asking if they were twins. He *wishes* he could be so lucky, Patricia would say. She's *way* uglier, Gregory would say.

They turned the corner, and the icy wind coming up from the ocean whipped toward them. Their house was at the end of the block, and they both walked more quickly.

"I bet the windchill's about thirty-five below," Gregory guessed.

"Give me a break, Greg. It's probably twenty *above*," Patricia said.

Gregory looked over at her dubiously. "Are you really not cold?"

"Well, maybe a little," Patricia admitted, and she zipped her jacket halfway.

Gregory laughed. "I knew you were faking."

Patricia shrugged self-consciously. "So I'm faking, so what?"

Gregory just laughed.

The weekend before, the whole family had put up their Christmas decorations, and the house looked really pretty. There were wreaths on the front and back doors, and Mr. Callahan had hung lights on the pine tree in the side yard. Their Christmas tree was in the living room, right in front of the bay windows. That way, at night, everyone who drove by the house could look inside and see it.

"Did you spend all your Christmas money?" Gregory asked.

Patricia nodded. "Most of it. Why?"

"I spent all mine, and I didn't get a present for the baby yet," Gregory said.

The baby was Miranda, their cousin. She was almost exactly a year old now, and had just started talking. Miranda's parents were their Uncle Steve, and Aunt Emily. Uncle Steve was their father's little brother, and he was a police officer in the Oceanport department. Their Aunt Emily was an advertising executive at a big firm in Boston. After the baby was born, she had arranged it so that she could work at home two days a week, and commute into the city on the other three days.

"I've only got about eight-fifty left," Patricia said, "but you can borrow it, if you want."

Patricia might tease him a lot, but she was actually really, really nice, when no one was looking. "Thanks. What did you get her?" Gregory asked.

Patricia shrugged. "Sunglasses. What else?"

As they started down the shoveled walk to the back door, they could hear delighted barking from inside the house.

"It's the Princess!" Patricia said cheerfully. "She's waiting for us!"

Gregory was not amused. "Don't call him that — it's dumb."

162

Patricia laughed. "Oh, what, and *Santa Paws* isn't? Come on, Greg. Get serious."

"Call him Nick," Gregory said. "He likes Nick."

"He likes *everything*, Greg," Patricia pointed out.

That was actually true, so Gregory just opened the back door instead of arguing. Whenever he was at school, he spent a lot of time thinking about his dog and wondering how he was. It was always a relief to get home and be able to play with him. Lots of people had nice dogs — but their dog was *special*.

Gregory poked his head around the edge of the door without going inside. "Where's my pal?" he asked.

The dog barked and pawed eagerly at the door.

"He waits here the whole time for me to come home, just like Lassie," Gregory told Patricia.

Patricia shook her head. "No way, he just gets up when he hears us coming. I think he takes naps all day."

"No, he waits," Gregory insisted. "Kind of like a sentry."

"Yeah," Patricia said. "Sure."

As they came inside, the dog kept barking. He wagged his tail back and forth, and jumped up on his hind legs to greet them. He had finally stopped growing, but he was a *big* dog. Patricia was small for her age and weighed about the same, so sometimes he knocked her down by accident.

Gregory, on the other hand, was pretty tall, and outweighed both of them. He only had an advantage of about seven pounds, but he figured that it still counted. His parents had given him some light barbells for his birthday, and he did thirty repetitions every morning when he got up, and then again before he went to bed. He and his best friend Oscar did lots of endurance exercises, too, so that when they got to high school, they would be able to make the football team.

Naturally, Patricia's reaction to this was, "Yeah. You *wish*." Sometimes, she and *her* best friend Rachel did a few abdominal crunches, but that was about it. The rest of the time, they just ate Doritos and drank Cokes.

The dog had lifted his front paws up onto Gregory's shoulders, so Gregory danced him around the kitchen a little.

"What a good dog," he said proudly. "You're the *best* dog, Nicky."

The dog barked and wagged his tail.

"Are you going to have a Milk-Bone?" Gregory asked.

The dog barked more loudly.

"Okay." Gregory stopped dancing with him, and then took off his jacket. "Let's get you a Milk-Bone."

The dog wagged his tail so hard that his whole body shook. He loved Gregory! He loved Patricia! He loved his life! He loved *Milk-Bones*!

What a great day!

2

Gregory and Patricia hung up their coats on the hooks behind the door, and dropped their knapsacks on the kitchen table. In the meantime, the dog ran around in circles, barking every so often. Since he was a German shepherd and collie mix, he had a very deep and commanding bark.

"Are you hungry, Greg?" Patricia asked.

"I'm *starved*," Gregory said.

Patricia nodded. "Me, too," she said, and opened the refrigerator.

Gregory picked up the plastic dish on the floor and carried it over to the sink. He dumped out the old water and filled it with fresh water.

The dog wagged his tail cooperatively and drank some right away. It tasted *really* good. Nice and cold.

While Gregory took out the box of Milk-Bones, Patricia studied the food inside the refrigerator.

"There's a whole lot of carrot sticks, and yogurt, and stuff," she said without much enthusiasm.

"Well, you know, you're a girl, so you like, need lots of calcium," Gregory said. He'd read in magazines that women were supposed to get more calcium than men. "So your bones don't get weird."

Patricia shook her head. "No, what I need right now, is *candy*. Or — fudge, maybe. Fudge would be good."

She opened a plastic container and looked inside. Beef stew. She closed the container, and checked another. This one had leftover macaroni and cheese, and she set it out on the counter, along with some butterscotch pudding their mother had fixed the night before.

"We could make popcorn?" Gregory suggested.

"Yeah, that'd be all right," Patricia agreed. "And maybe some hot chocolate."

They could hear music playing loudly in the den, and they both stopped to listen for a minute.

"Frank," Patricia said grimly.

Gregory nodded. As usual, their father was listening to Frank Sinatra. Sometimes, he would put on Billie Holiday or Ella Fitzgerald, but mostly it was Frank, Frank, *Frank*. Endless hours of *Frank*. "Is he singing?" he asked.

They listened again. If their father was singing along, that generally meant that he wasn't getting any work done.

"No," Patricia decided. "Just listening."

"Good," Gregory said, relieved. When their father's writing was going well, they could do whatever they wanted and never get in trouble. When he had writer's block, he was much more strict.

Patricia started fixing dishes of macaroni and cheese to put in the microwave, and then stopped. "Hey, I know!" she said. "Let's go see what he's wearing!"

Gregory's eyes lit up. "Yeah!" he agreed.

When they left for school in the morning, their father would usually be wearing pajama bottoms and an old college T-shirt. Then sometimes, during the day, he would change into outfits that he thought might help him get in the mood to write better.

"Be really quiet," Patricia said softly, as they crept through the living room. "So he doesn't hear us coming."

The music was so loud there was no *way* he would hear them, but Gregory nodded anyway. If their father knew they were sneaking up on him, he would have time to whip off any goofy hats or other silly things he might be wearing.

The dog barked and galloped ahead of them. He ran so fast that he slipped on a small braided rug and skidded into a nearby wall.

"Santa Paws, shhh!" Patricia said, and then

frowned. "Did I just forget and call him Santa Paws?"

Gregory nodded.

"Hit me next time," Patricia said.

He wasn't about to pass *that* up. "Absolutely!" Gregory promised.

When they got to the den door, they could see their father sitting at his computer with his back to them. His posture was very straight and he was holding his hands motionless above the keyboard, as though he *might* start writing at any second.

Gregory and Patricia tried not to laugh when they saw that he had on a top hat and a black bow tie. Once they had caught him wearing a bright green sombrero, because he was writing a scene set in Mexico. Right now, he also had on gray sweatpants and a T-shirt with a picture of the Grinch on it.

"Bunny slippers?" Patricia whispered.

Gregory peered underneath the desk. "No, *Snoopy* slippers," he whispered back, and they both snickered. Lots of times, Mr. Callahan forgot and went out in public with his slippers on. People in Oceanport seemed to think that this was — quaint.

They waited to see if he was going to type anything, and when he didn't, they started singing, "You Make Me Feel So Young" along with Frank. Over the years, completely by accident, they had learned all of the words to an astonishing number of old songs. Their mother mostly played musicals, so they were pretty strong on those, too. When Patricia's science teacher had asked her recently to explain the concept of "osmosis," she had used their uncanny knowledge of song lyrics as an example. Her teacher had found this to be a very clever comparison, and gave her an *A* for the day.

The dog started barking again, because he *liked* singing. Singing was funny.

Mr. Callahan turned around to look at them. "You two are home early," he said, sounding surprised.

Actually, they were *late*, because Patricia had forgotten her global studies book and they had to go back to get it.

"You want to hear 'Moonlight in Vermont?' " Gregory asked. "We're good at that one, too."

Mr. Callahan smiled, saved whatever he was writing on a disk, and then stood up. Their cat, Evelyn, who had been sleeping soundly on his lap, was quite annoyed by this. She flounced over to the couch, and curled up again.

"How was school?" Mr. Callahan asked. "Are you kids hungry?"

"Fine," Patricia said, just as Gregory said, "*Yes*."

Realizing that he was still wearing his top hat,

Mr. Callahan frowned and took it off. "Ballroom scene," he explained.

Patricia and Gregory shrugged politely, doing their best not to laugh again. However, they failed miserably.

"Dad, does Nicholas wait all day for me by the door?" Gregory asked as they walked to the kitchen. "Because he misses me so much?"

"Hmmm?" Mr. Callahan said vaguely. "Oh." He paused, and then didn't quite make eye contact. "Well, sure. I mean, yes. No question about it. Sits there nonstop. Never moves."

"That means no," Patricia said to Gregory.

Mr. Callahan examined the plastic containers on the kitchen counter. He was over six feet tall, with graying hair that was almost always rumpled. He wore thick brown glasses, and usually slouched when he walked.

"This looks good," he said, taking down a plate for himself and spooning out some cold macaroni and cheese. "But try not to spoil your appetites, okay? We're meeting your aunt and uncle for dinner at six-thirty."

"Italian?" Gregory asked. Italian food was his favorite.

"How about Mexican?" Patricia suggested. "We haven't had Mexican for a while."

"Rumor has it, it's going to be Chinese," their father answered.

It was a safe bet that that rumor had come straight from their *mother*.

They had finished the macaroni and cheese, and were halfway through the beef stew, when Mrs. Callahan got home. She was carrying an oversized canvas briefcase and several bulging shopping bags.

"Hi, Mom. Are those Christmas presents?" Gregory asked.

Quickly, Mrs. Callahan held the bags behind her back. "No," she said, and grinned at them. "Whatever gave you that idea?"

The dog had been sitting alertly next to Gregory, in case a piece of beef from the stew fell on the floor by accident. Smelling something familiar, he got up and went over to sniff the bags. A rawhide chew bone! He was almost *sure* that he smelled a rawhide chew bone.

"No, it's a surprise, Santa Paws," Mrs. Callahan said, and lifted the bag up out of his reach. "Go lie down."

Lie down. He knew what "lie down" meant, but right now, he wanted to sit. If he went over to lie down on his special rug, he might forget about the beef stew and fall asleep. So he sat down next to Gregory's chair and lifted his paw, instead.

"That's good," Mrs. Callahan told him. "You're a very good dog."

She thought he was good. Yay! The dog

wagged his tail, and then returned his attention to the beef stew. So far, he had managed to catch a piece of potato Mr. Callahan dropped, and he had snapped up two chunks of meat Gregory had slipped under the table.

Mrs. Callahan glanced up at the kitchen clock, and then at her husband. "We're supposed to meet Steve and Emily and the baby in about an hour and a half," she reminded him. "Maybe you all should save some room for supper."

"It's just a snack, Mom," Patricia said.

Mr. Callahan looked a little sheepish. "A *hearty* snack," he admitted.

"Whatever you say." Mrs. Callahan started out of the room with her bags, then paused. "Did anyone feed the dog?"

The dog leaped enthusiastically to his feet again. "Feed the dog" was another one of the magic phrases, right up there with "ride in the car."

"We were about to," Gregory said.

Evelyn came ambling out from the direction of the living room. She jumped up on the side counter where her small green dish was kept and meowed loudly — and sadly.

"I'll bet you were about to feed her, too," Mrs. Callahan said. "And maybe even clean up these dishes, while you're at it."

Gregory nodded. "Yep."

"Right away," Patricia promised.

Mr. Callahan was already on his feet and heading for the sink. "Count on it."

"I thought so," Mrs. Callahan said, and then she disappeared up the stairs with her many mysterious shopping bags.

When it was time to leave for dinner, the dog watched with worried eyes as the Callahans put on their hats, coats, and gloves. Where were they going? Was he going to be left alone? Would they be back soon? This was *horrible*. He slumped down on the floor and rested his muzzle miserably on his front paws.

"Can Nicholas come?" Gregory asked. He really hated to go *anywhere* without his dog.

Hearing his name — *one* of his names, anyway — the dog's ears pricked forward.

"I don't know, Greg," his mother answered. "It's pretty cold out there, and it might not be a good idea for him to wait in the car."

"But he always comes," Patricia reminded her.

Mrs. Callahan nodded. "Okay. Bring one of the beach towels, though, so he has someplace to curl up."

When the dog saw Gregory open the cupboard and take out a thick blue towel, he stood up tentatively. Was the towel for him? Was he going to have a bath, maybe?

"Want to come for a ride in the car?" Gregory asked.

A ride in the car! His favorite! The dog barked, and then chased his tail for a minute to show how happy he was.

Next to eating — and sleeping — riding in the car was the best thing in the whole world!

3

The best part of being in the car was when one of the Callahans would roll down the window, and he could smell lots of exciting scents. But he also liked just sitting and watching objects flash by. Usually they drove to interesting places, like the beach or the city, and there was always something new to see.

When they were at stores and the dog was waiting for them to come back, he liked to sneak up into the front seat. It was fun to sit in the driver's seat and gaze out through the windshield. Then, when he saw them coming back, he would quickly jump into the back again. Most of the time, he got caught, but no one ever really got mad at him, so he figured it was okay.

Oceanport always looked very pretty during Christmas. It was a small town, and the streets twinkled with bright strings of lights. All of the stores and restaurants and office buildings would put up festive decorations, and every year, there was a contest to decide who had done the most beautiful job.

During the holiday season, the municipal park had lots of special exhibits, which were called "The Festival of Many Lands." The exhibits were devoted to all kinds of different cultures, religions, and other traditions. Oceanport was proud of being a very democratic and multicultural town.

When the dog had been a lonely stray the year before, he had slept in Santa's sleigh in the park. Some of the local townspeople had noticed him there, and they had given him the name "Santa Paws." That was before he had an owner, and he was always cold and sad and hungry. He ran into a lot of people who were in trouble, and he did his best to help them, so the name "Santa Paws" seemed perfect for him. The dog was just glad when he met Gregory and Patricia, and got to go live with them. He was *still* always hungry, though!

The Chinese restaurant was right on Main Street, and Mr. Callahan found a parking place a few doors away.

"Can we walk down to the park for a minute?" Gregory asked, as they got out of the car.

"*May* you," Mrs. Callahan corrected him automatically. "Why don't we go after supper and look at the decorations?"

Gregory nodded, and carefully unrolled one of

177

the back windows a couple of inches so that Santa Paws would have plenty of fresh air. Then he patted him, and started to close the door.

Suddenly sensing that something was wrong, the dog stood up on the seat to look outside. The fur rose on his back and he sniffed the air uneasily, trying to figure out what was happening. He knew that there was trouble brewing somewhere — he just wasn't sure what it was.

"What is it, boy?" Gregory asked.

Across the street, Mrs. Lowell had just come out of Mabel's Five-and-Dime, carrying lots of bundles. Her four-year-old daughter Bethany was skipping along next to her, bouncing a miniature Shaquille O'Neal basketball.

The sidewalk was a little bit icy, and Mrs. Lowell slipped. She dropped most of her packages and had to bend over to pick them up. As she did, Bethany's ball bounced off a chunk of snow and rolled right into the busy street!

Bethany gasped and ran after her beloved basketball, without looking both ways first.

Seeing this, the dog leaped out of the car. Barking loudly, he raced across the street, dodging traffic. Horns beeped, and cars skidded on the ice, as people tried to steer out of the way.

"Hey!" Gregory yelled. "Look out!" He started

to chase after his dog, but there were too many cars.

The man driving the car closest to Bethany jammed on his brakes, but the car spun out of control, and headed directly toward her! Everyone on the sidewalks was frozen with shock.

The dog grabbed Bethany's hood with his teeth, and dragged her out of the way at the last second. He pulled her safely between two parked cars and then gently released her hood and nudged her to her feet.

With that accomplished, he bolted back into the street to fetch the basketball. The ball was too big to fit in his mouth, so he used his nose to roll it in front of him. He deposited the ball at Bethany's feet, and then stood there, wagging his tail.

All around them, people were running across the street and jumping out of their cars to see what had happened. Everyone was very upset, and expecting the worst.

Mrs. Lowell and Gregory reached the pair first.

"Oh, thank God," Mrs. Lowell breathed, and she hugged her little daughter tightly.

Bethany smiled up at her, not even bruised by her narrow escape. "Santa Paws saved me!" she said happily. "He's Santa's best helper!"

Mrs. Lowell hugged her closer, so relieved that she couldn't even speak.

"You all right, boy?" Gregory asked the dog. Then he swiftly checked him over, running his hands over the dog's back and legs to make sure he hadn't been injured.

The dog barked once, and wagged his tail. He really liked being patted.

Patricia and their parents rushed over to join them.

"Are they okay?" Patricia asked.

Gregory nodded. "Everybody's fine."

Hearing that, most of the people who had gathered nearby began to applaud.

"Hooray for Santa Paws!" Mabel from the Five-and-Dime store hollered, and a few people cheered.

"I don't know how to thank all of you," Mrs. Lowell said to the Callahans. "If it weren't for your wonderful dog — " She stopped, overcome again.

Gregory always carried extra biscuits in his pockets, and he took one out.

The dog barked and joyfully accepted it. He crunched up the biscuit right away, his tail thumping against one of the parked cars. No matter how many Milk-Bones he ate, he was still always surprised by how delicious they were!

"You know," Mr. Callahan said thoughtfully to his wife, "he really *is* a good dog."

It was hard to disagree with that, so Mrs. Callahan just nodded.

Mr. Callahan's brother Steve had come out of the Chinese restaurant to see what all of the excitement was about. As far as he was concerned, a police officer was *never* really off-duty, and so he liked to keep an eye on things.

"What's going on?" he asked, sounding both curious and authoritative. "Everyone all right?" Uncle Steve wasn't quite as tall as Mr. Callahan, but he was a lot more muscular. He was only thirty-two and unlike Mr. Callahan, his hair hadn't started turning gray yet. Even so, it was easy to see that they were related.

"Thanks to Santa Paws!" someone shouted.

"Oh." Uncle Steve looked around and saw that everything seemed to be fine. "Okay. Good."

Patricia moved to stand next to him, folding her arms decisively across her chest. She was pretty sure that she wanted to be a police officer, too, when she grew up — that is, unless she could be a member of the Supreme Court. "Should we tell them to move along, and go about their business, Uncle Steve?" she asked.

Uncle Steve laughed, and reached out to give her ponytail a little flip. "No, it's okay, Patty. I think they'll figure out that one for themselves."

The family who owned the Chinese restaurant had come outside, too. Their last name was Lee, and their son Tom was also a member of the Oceanport Police Department. Because of that, most of the police officers in town ate at their restaurant regularly. Of course, it didn't hurt that the food was *really* good.

"Was it Santa Paws again?" Mr. Lee asked the crowd in general.

Most of the bystanders nodded, and some of them started clapping again.

Mrs. Lee smiled at the Callahans. "We would be delighted to have the hero dine in our restaurant tonight."

Gregory looked surprised. "Wait, you mean, inside? *With* us?"

Mrs. Lee nodded, and held the door open with a flourish. "Please. We would be very honored."

"Whoa," Patricia said, impressed. "That is like, *so* European."

"We will prepare our finest meat dish for him," Mr. Lee proclaimed grandly. "Please, follow me."

As they walked inside, Mr. Callahan leaned over to his wife again. "If it's their very finest dish, think a certain dog will be willing to *share* it with us?" he asked in a low voice.

Mrs. Callahan laughed. "Well, maybe if you ask nicely. . . ."

The dog couldn't believe that he was being allowed to go inside the restaurant, instead of waiting in the car like always. How fun! He trotted happily next to Gregory, waving his tail back and forth.

Mr. Lee led them over to the best table in the restaurant. Gregory and Patricia's aunt Emily was already sitting there with her baby, Miranda. Miranda was wearing a red velvet holiday dress, with black patent leather shoes, and she looked even more adorable than usual.

The Lees' teenage daughter, Nancy, brought out a special rug from the back room, which Santa Paws immediately sat on. He knew that small rugs were almost always meant just for him. This one was very soft and comfortable, with nice fancy patterns, and he woofed once before settling down.

Mr. Lee distributed menus, while Mrs. Lee filled their water glasses.

"Tonight, everything is on the house!" Mr. Lee announced. "Out of respect for the heroic Santa Paws!"

"Oh, no," Mrs. Callahan protested. "We couldn't — "

"We *insist*," Mrs. Lee said. "Consider it our holiday gesture."

Gregory nudged Patricia's arm. "So, should we order lobster, and shrimp, and all?" he whispered, since those were the most expensive items on the menu.

"Don't be a jerk," she whispered back. "Besides, Mom and Dad'll leave a *really* big tip, so it'll work out pretty much the same."

Gregory nodded and looked down at his menu. His favorites were Hunan flower steak and General Tso's chicken, anyway. Patricia almost always ordered broccoli with garlic sauce, because, she would explain, of the considerable health benefits. Mr. and Mrs. Callahan always laughed when she said things like that. Gregory and Patricia were never exactly sure what was so funny, and they would write it off to parental foolishness.

"So," Aunt Emily said, once they had all been served tea, and soda, and other drinks. "What should we toast to?"

"Santa Paws," Gregory said. "Who else?"

They all raised their cups and glasses. Miranda giggled and imitated them by holding up her bottle.

"Okay, Mr. Writer," Uncle Steve said to Mr. Callahan. "Let's see how profound you are."

Mr. Callahan frowned. Sometimes, under pressure, he lapsed into writer's block. "To Santa Paws," he said finally. "The best dog in Oceanport!"

"The best dog on the Eastern seaboard," Patricia corrected him.

"The best dog in the *world*," Gregory said.

They all drank to that, and then started in on their scallion pancakes and other appetizers.

The dog wagged his tail when Patricia gave him some pork strips on a small white plate. He had no idea why they were celebrating tonight, but he was certainly having a very nice time!

4

Over dinner, they all talked about their Christmas plans. Patricia and Gregory's grandparents lived in Montpelier, Vermont, but they also had a lake cabin in the Northeast Kingdom of Vermont, up near the Canadian border. It was winterized, and so this year, they were going to spend the holidays there. The drive from Boston was pretty long, but the cabin was right on a beautiful lake. There was skiing nearby, and plenty of other winter sports available.

"When are you all heading up?" Mrs. Callahan asked Uncle Steve and Aunt Emily.

Steve shook his head. "Emily's going to drive up with the baby, and take the week up there, but I have to work on Christmas, so I'm going to fly."

Hearing that, Gregory and Patricia perked up. They loved flying in their uncle's plane. He was a private pilot, and he shared a little Cessna Skyhawk with an old friend of his from the Army. Uncle Steve really loved baseball, and during the summer, he would fly all over New England and upstate New York to go to minor league games in tiny little towns. Lots of times, Gregory and Patricia would get to go along. As a result, they had seen all sorts of obscure teams play and had a large collection of souvenir caps.

"Why are they making you work on Christmas?" Mr. Callahan was asking him. "You worked on Thanksgiving."

"Well, they're giving me the twenty-third and Christmas Eve off, so at least I'll be able to spend a little time with all of you before I fly back," Uncle Steve said. "As long as I fly out early Christmas morning, I can make my shift."

"Can we go with you?" Gregory asked. "Please?" The last time they had gotten to fly in the plane had been way back in *October*.

"Yeah," Patricia agreed. "We could keep you company."

Mrs. Callahan looked up from her wonton soup. "You don't want to ride up with us?"

"Well — sure," Gregory said lamely, "but — " He stopped, and looked at Patricia.

"Planes are more fun than station wagons," she said.

Mr. and Mrs. Callahan exchanged glances.

"It seems to me that nice, loving children *like*

to ride with their parents," Mrs. Callahan said.

"While singing holiday tunes," Mr. Callahan added.

Patricia winced at the thought of that, and ate some of her broccoli instead of answering.

"Well, we'd be driving *home* with you," Gregory pointed out. "That counts, right?"

"Hey, if it's okay with all of you, it's fine with me," Uncle Steve said with a shrug.

"All right," Mrs. Callahan decided. "As long as I don't hear either of you arguing between now and Friday."

Gregory and Patricia looked at each other. "I would *never* fight with my best sister in the world," Gregory said.

"Your *only* sister," Patricia reminded him.

Gregory grinned at her. "Okay, but even if I had lots of others, *you'd* be the very best one."

"If I had nine brothers, you'd be in the top ten," Patricia retorted.

Gregory frowned, pretty sure that there was an insult in there somewhere. But his father was serving him some more rice and pork with garlic sauce, so he decided to pretend he hadn't heard her.

Then Patricia remembered something. "Oh," she said, and turned to Uncle Steve. "Is it okay if Santa Paws comes, too?"

Gregory promptly punched her in the arm. Patricia flinched and then socked him right back.

"Hey!" Mr. Callahan said sharply. "What did your mother just tell you two about fighting?"

"Patricia asked me to hit her the next time she said, 'Santa Paws,' " Gregory explained.

"Right, I forgot." Patricia tapped his shoulder where she had slugged him. "I withdraw my punch."

"Withdrawal accepted," Gregory said graciously, even though he was pretty sure he had a bruise.

"That wasn't a fight, he was just doing me a favor," Patricia told their parents. She was pretty sure *she* had a bruise, too.

Mr. and Mrs. Callahan looked suspicious, but they let it pass.

"Anyway," Uncle Steve said, "Santa Paws can come, as long as you bring his seat belt."

Gregory nodded. His mother had bought a special dog seat belt at the pet store. Santa Paws never wore it in the car, but he always wore it in Uncle Steve's plane. That way, there was no chance that he would jump around in the middle of the flight.

Then, just to make Patricia mad, Gregory reached over with his chopsticks and stole the last piece of sweet and sour pineapple from her plate.

"Greg!" she protested. "I was *saving* that."

Gregory ate the pineapple before she could steal it back. Then he plucked away a piece of her chicken, which he flipped to Santa Paws.

The dog caught the food with one quick lunge to his right, wagged his tail, and then sat politely on his rug again.

"Check your room *very carefully* before you go to sleep tonight," Patricia said in her most threatening voice.

Gregory shrugged. "Hey, no problem. When we get home, I'm going to spread all kinds of rumors about you on the Internet."

Patricia put her chopsticks down. "Oh, yeah? Well, *I'm* going to — "

Their mother frowned at them. "That sounds almost *exactly* like bickering to me."

Remembering that their plane trip hung in the balance, Gregory and Patricia instantly put on very sweet and innocent smiles.

"Never happen," Gregory assured her.

Patricia nodded. "Not us."

"*No way*," Gregory said.

Two whole days of not arguing was going to be a challenge!

On Friday, school was only in session for a half-day and everyone was dismissed at eleven-thirty. Mrs. Callahan came to pick up Gregory and Patricia, and they went home to eat a quick lunch. Uncle Steve wanted to take off in the early afternoon, so that they would land before it got dark.

He kept his plane at a small airfield just over the New Hampshire border, and Mrs. Callahan drove them up there to meet him. Gregory and Patricia had each packed a small knapsack, and Gregory was also holding a picnic basket on his lap. Their parents would bring the rest of their stuff up to Vermont in the car. The plane was too small to carry bulky things like skis and heavy suitcases.

"I can't *wait* to go skiing," Gregory said, as they zipped along Route 95. "When're we going to go, Mom?"

Mrs. Callahan shrugged, and glanced in her rearview mirror. "I don't know. Monday or Tuesday, maybe?"

"*Cool,*" Gregory said. He had asked for a new pair of ski goggles for Christmas, and he really hoped that he would get them. Either way, skiing was one of his favorite things to do.

"Can we go skating, too, Mom?" Patricia asked from the back. It had been so cold that the lake by the cabin was probably frozen by now.

"Sure," Mrs. Callahan promised. "If we're lucky, maybe we'll even be able to blast your father out of the house."

Gregory and Patricia laughed.

"Not likely," Patricia said.

"Never happen," Gregory agreed.

Feeling the holiday excitement in the air, the dog had trouble sitting still in the backseat. Gregory had given him a bath the night before, so his fur was nice and fluffy. Then Patricia had braided two red and green ribbons together and tied them around his neck in a big bow.

When they got to the airfield, Uncle Steve was busy filing his flight plan and running through a preflight checklist. It was really cold outside, so Gregory and Patricia waited in the car with their mother. Right before takeoff, they would give Santa Paws one last walk.

The runway had been plowed, of course, since the last snowstorm, and there was a huge pile of snow at the end of the tarmac. The small air-traffic control building had been shoveled out, but a lot of the small parked planes still had several inches of snow on their wing covers.

"Are you sure you two are dressed warmly enough?" Mrs. Callahan asked, looking worried. "You know how cold it gets up there."

"I have on like, *five* layers, Mom," Gregory said. With long underwear, a fleece turtleneck, and a hooded sweatshirt, plus a down vest under his ski jacket, he figured he was pretty well covered. He was also wearing a blue hat, a plaid wool scarf, his ski mittens, and a pair of heavy Gore-Tex lined hiking boots.

Mrs. Callahan turned around in her seat to

check on Patricia. "What about you? Are you going to be warm enough?"

Patricia was listening to her Walkman, and she lifted one of the headphones to one side. "What?"

"She wants to know if you're going to show off, and not zip your jacket and all," Gregory said.

Since they *were* going to Vermont, Patricia was wearing her Sorel winter boots, along with her Patriots jacket and ski gloves. She had also selected a pair of neon-yellow sunglasses to complete her ensemble. Other than that, she just had on a turtleneck and ragg wool sweater with her jeans.

"Where's your hat?" her mother asked.

Patricia looked down at herself. "I'm fine, Mom," she said. "I'm not cold."

Mrs. Callahan took off her own scarf. "Here, put this on. Where's your hat?"

Patricia checked the backseat, and then shrugged. "I don't know. I think I forgot it."

Mrs. Callahan sighed, and held out her own homemade knitted hat next.

"It's, um, nice and all," Patricia said politely. "But, um, well — it has a *pom-pom* on it."

Mrs. Callahan sighed again. "Humor me, Patricia. Okay? It's Christmas."

Reluctantly, Patricia tugged the hat on over her headphones. Pom-poms were *completely* not cool. Just in case they passed someone she knew, she slouched down in her seat so that her head was below the window.

Thinking that it might be the beginning of a game, the dog pawed her arm playfully.

"No, Santa Paws," Patricia said, and brushed his paw off. "*Sit.*"

The dog sat.

"Good boy," she said, and then turned up the volume on her Walkman.

"Think you'll have enough to eat?" Mrs. Callahan asked.

Gregory grinned, and patted the heavy picnic basket. It was full of sandwiches, carrot sticks, homemade brownies, sodas, and juice boxes. There was also, of course, a small plastic bag full of Milk-Bones. "This'll hold us for *at least* an hour," he said.

Mrs. Callahan smiled, too. "All right, all right. I just can't help worrying." Then she pointed out through the windshield. "Okay, let's get ready. Here comes your uncle."

Before getting out of the car, Gregory reached for Santa Paws' harness. It snapped on around his chest and front legs, and then Gregory would adjust it to fit him just right. Once they were in the plane, he could thread the seat belt through the loop on the back of the harness. When that was done, Santa Paws would be safe in his seat for the rest of the flight.

"Extra large," Gregory said to him as he put on his leash. "Because you are a good, *big* dog."

The dog wagged his tail. Gregory thought he was good! He really didn't like the way the harness felt, but if Gregory wanted him to wear it, he would.

"Okay if I take him for a quick walk before we go?" Gregory asked his uncle.

Uncle Steve nodded, and checked his watch automatically. "Sure thing," he answered. He was wearing old army jungle fatigue pants, black work boots, an Oceanport PD cap, and a heavy-weight flight jacket. For warmth, he had added leather gloves, and a long striped scarf.

"Aren't you supposed to have on a bomber jacket and a white silk scarf?" Patricia asked.

Uncle Steve winked at her. "Fashion, I leave to *you*, my friend," he said. Then he lifted the picnic basket out of the front seat. "Weather looks great all the way up," he said to Mrs. Callahan.

Mrs. Callahan nodded. "That's good. We should get there by about nine tonight."

After walking along a stretch of bushes, Gregory brought Santa Paws back.

"Okay," he said cheerfully. "We're ready."

Mrs. Callahan hugged Patricia first, then Gregory, and finally, Santa Paws. "Okay, now be good," she said to all three of them. "Make sure you do everything your uncle tells you to do."

195

"Drop and give me twenty!" Uncle Steve said without missing a beat.

Gregory and Patricia both laughed, but didn't move.

Recognizing the *sound* of a command, if not the actual words, the dog sat down obediently and lifted his front paws in the air.

Uncle Steve bent down to pat him. "Good boy. At least someone's paying attention."

The dog barked. Uncle Steve thought he was good, too!

After saying one more good-bye to their mother, Gregory and Patricia crossed the airfield to the waiting plane. The Cessna was very snug, with just four seats inside. The outside of the plane was painted white, with red markings. There was a single propeller on the front, and the wings were attached to the top of the plane, instead of coming out from the sides. The landing gear was two fat rubber wheels at the bottom of the plane.

"Whose turn to sit up front?" Uncle Steve asked.

"Me!" Patricia said eagerly. Whoever sat up front would get the extra benefit of a little flying lesson. Uncle Steve always showed them how to use the rudder pedals to control the plane and let them steer for a minute. When they were old enough, he had promised that he would give them *real* lessons, and maybe they would be able to get pilot's licenses of their own.

Uncle Steve loaded their knapsacks and the picnic basket aboard and tied them down with rope. Then Gregory let Santa Paws into the back, and climbed in after him.

"Here you go, boy," he said, patting the seat on the right.

The dog woofed once, and bounced up onto the chair. Being in a plane was like riding in the car, but lots bumpier. He had flown with Gregory and Patricia before, and he knew what he was supposed to do. So he sat quietly, until Gregory attached his harness to the seat belt.

"Okay, good dog," he said. "Stay."

The dog wagged his tail, and then lounged back against the seat. Since they were still on the ground, he couldn't see much out through the window, but he could pretend.

Gregory reached into his jacket pocket. "Want a Milk-Bone?"

The dog tried to get up, but the seat belt kept him where he was. So he settled down and let Gregory hand the biscuit to him, instead.

Up front, Patricia was belting herself into the copilot's seat. In the meantime, Uncle Steve had put on his headset and was going through his final preflight check.

Gregory's favorite part of flying was when the

engine first started. The small cockpit would be filled with noise, and he could feel the whole plane seem to shake with excitement. It was usually too loud to talk when they were flying, but he enjoyed looking out the window so much that it didn't really matter.

Flying up to the lake cabin was always especially great, because the view of the mountains was *amazing* from the air. On a clear winter day like today, they would be able to take some really pretty pictures.

"Got plenty of gas?" Patricia asked.

Uncle Steve smiled and indicated the gas gauge. Then he twisted in his seat to check on Gregory and Santa Paws. "Everyone all set?" he asked.

Gregory and Patricia nodded, and the dog panted.

"Okay," Uncle Steve said. He gave them all a thumbs-up, and started the engine.

At first, the thundering noise always seemed deafening. But after a while, Gregory and Patricia would get used to it. The rumbling of the engine was so loud that they could feel it echoing inside their own chests. The propeller started off by spinning very slowly, but soon, it was whipping around so fast they almost couldn't see it anymore.

Once they were cleared for takeoff, Uncle

Steve taxied into position. They had to wait for a Piper Cub to take off, first.

When it was their turn to go, Uncle Steve gave them one final thumbs-up. Gregory and Patricia returned the signal enthusiastically.

Then they roared down the runway, picking up speed, until suddenly, they lifted off!

They were flying!

5

Gregory and Patricia peered out the windows as the plane banked to the right and climbed high into the sky. They watched all of the cars and buildings gradually get smaller and smaller, until even the broad stripes of interstate highways looked tiny.

After climbing up to their cruising altitude of about five thousand feet, Uncle Steve leveled the plane off.

"Do *not* feel free to move about the cabin!" he yelled over the noise of the engine.

Gregory and Patricia knew he was kidding, so they just grinned. Even if they had *wanted* to move around, there wasn't exactly much room.

Gregory reached over to pat Santa Paws and make sure he was all right. The dog licked his hand once, and then went back to gazing out the window at the clouds and bright blue sky.

"Do you think he likes it?" Gregory shouted to Patricia. "I can never tell!"

"He seems to, yeah!" she shouted back.

The dog looked alertly out the window, even though there wasn't much to see out there. But he wanted to be ready, just in case.

The flight was very smooth now, and Gregory opened the picnic basket to get them some snacks. There was a thermos of hot coffee, and he carefully poured out a cup and handed it up front to his uncle.

Uncle Steve nodded his thanks, but didn't say anything because he was busy talking into his headset.

Gregory passed Patricia a juice box and a tuna fish sandwich. Then he took a meat loaf sandwich and another juice box for himself.

Smelling the meat, the dog perked up. Gregory broke off part of his sandwich and fed it to him.

Soon, each of them — including Santa Paws — was eating a butterscotch brownie for dessert.

"These are *great*!" Uncle Steve yelled. "Remind me to tell your mother that!"

Gregory and Patricia nodded. They both really liked chocolate chip cookies, but these brownies were their favorite. On the other hand, even the *worst* cookies they had ever eaten had still been pretty good.

They were flying over the mountains now, and the wind had picked up. The turbulence made the plane jounce a little in the air, and Patricia grabbed the arm of her seat for a second before remembering that it wasn't cool to do things like that. She glanced back to see if Gregory had noticed. He was laughing, so she knew that he had.

For a while, they could see lots of small cities like Concord and Laconia, as well as wide, smooth highways. The mountains were covered with snow, and there were pine trees everywhere. If they had been on the ground, they would have been able to see other kinds of trees, but from the air, the mountains looked like one big Christmas tree farm.

As they flew further north, the landscape below them grew more beautiful and deserted. There were a few little towns in the White Mountain National Forest, but there were also miles and miles of wilderness.

The previous summer, they had hiked up Mount Monadnock in southern New Hampshire with their parents. It had been fun, but they got pretty tired. Other than that, the only time they ever made it to the tops of mountains was when they rode up on ski lifts. The Blue Hills in Massachusetts probably didn't count.

The White Mountains were really something, though. Tall, and craggy, and rugged. There were more clouds than there had been before, and they made the snow-covered mountains seem dark and mysterious.

"This is great!" Patricia yelled to Gregory.

"Yeah, I wish I remembered my camera!" he yelled back to her.

Then, all of a sudden, Uncle Steve tensed in his seat.

Patricia was the first one to notice. "Is anything wrong?" she asked.

He didn't answer, which *was* an answer.

The engine was beginning to cough and sputter, which got Gregory's attention. Before he could ask what was happening, the plane abruptly lost altitude and Uncle Steve had to fight the sluggish controls to keep them aloft.

They dropped again, and Gregory felt his stomach swooping down, too. There was a strong smell of burning electricity, and wisps of smoke floated out through the instrument panel.

Sensing the anxiety around him, the dog whined softly next to him. He wanted to stand up, but the seat belt held him in place.

Just as Uncle Steve started to call the emergency in, the engine died. In the sudden, shocking silence, they all stared at each other for a second.

"Okay, okay," Uncle Steve said. His face was pale, but he sounded very calm. "Okay." He stared at the instrument panel, and then made a few adjustments. "Okay." He tried to get the radio to work, but they were below the level of the mountains now, so it was mostly just static.

Seeing Patricia tighten her seat belt, Gregory quickly did the same. He also leaned over to make sure that Santa Paws was securely hooked up.

Uncle Steve did his best to smile at them. "I think we've got a little problem here, guys."

Gregory and Patricia looked at him with wide eyes. Santa Paws whined again, and Gregory put his hand out instinctively to pat him.

The plane sailed soundlessly through the air, but they were losing altitude very fast. Below them, there was nothing but mountains and endless forests.

"Are we crashing?" Gregory asked.

Patricia glared at him.

"I'm sorry," he said defensively. "I just wanted to know."

"Take the positions I taught you, okay?" Uncle Steve ordered, as he struggled to keep the plane in the air. "Keep your eyes closed, and don't look up until we come to a stop!"

There didn't seem to be any place to land, as the trees rushed closer and closer. One of the mountains had a small bald spot near the top, and Uncle Steve guided the unresponsive plane toward it.

They were falling, more than dropping, now.

Gregory and Patricia both bent forward in their seats, and covered their heads with their arms, trying not to scream in terror.

"Lie down, Santa Paws!" Gregory yelled without lifting his head. "*Lie down*, boy!"

They smashed down into the snowy clearing, but there wasn't enough room to stop. The landing gear collapsed on one side, and sent them sliding wildly out of control. The right wing slammed into a tree, and the force of the collision tore it right off the plane! They flipped over, and then spun backward across the snow. They spun around and around, crashing through bushes and snapping through small trees.

Finally, the plane came to a stop, and it was very, very still.

The dog was the first one to react. Hanging upside down made him feel panicky, and he yelped as he struggled frantically to get out of his harness.

Gregory opened his eyes, completely confused. Freezing cold air was rushing toward him from somewhere and a flailing paw scratched his face.

"Hey!" he protested, not sure where he was or why sharp claws had just raked across his cheek.

He couldn't understand why everything looked so strange, but then he realized that he was suspended upside down, that the plane had crashed, and — Patricia!

"Patty!" he shouted. "Uncle Steve! Are you okay?"

Neither of them were moving, and he could see that the windshield and instrument panel had been crushed. Were they all right? They *had* to be all right! Gregory gulped, feeling frantic tears fill his eyes.

"Patricia!" he shouted more loudly. "Uncle Steve! Wake up!"

Swinging helplessly next to him, the dog barked and yelped in a total frenzy of fear. What was happening? Why had they fallen out of the sky like that? He had mashed his side against the window, and it hurt a lot, so he yelped even more loudly.

"Santa Paws, no!" Gregory said. The terror was contagious, and he tried to fight it off. *"Shhh!* No! Good dog! *No!"*

Up in the front, Patricia groaned quietly.

"Patty, are you all right?" Gregory asked, trying not to cry. He could see that there was blood on her face, so she must be hurt. "Patty, wake up!"

He tore at his seat belt until he finally managed to unsnap the clasp. He landed hard on what would once have been the ceiling, and the plane lurched precariously to one side. Gregory was disoriented, but he made himself roll over until he was sitting upright.

Patricia's eyes opened partway, and she blinked a few times. Then she frowned at him.

"Why are you upside down?" she asked.

"*You're* upside down," Gregory said.

"Oh." She blinked again, her voice sounding strange and sluggish. "Why?"

Gregory started crying for real now, and it was hard to think. He rubbed his jacket sleeve across his eyes, and then forced himself to take a couple of deep breaths.

The skin of the plane had been torn open when the wing sheared off, and it was bitterly cold. Most of the fuselage — which was the metal body of the plane — on the right side was gone and the passenger's door was crumpled in.

"I-I don't — " Patricia was still blinking. "I'm not — " Suddenly, she figured out what was going on and her eyes flew open. "Greg! Are you okay?"

"I'm fine," he said shakily. Okay, she sounded like herself now. This wasn't as scary when she sounded like herself. "I'm coming up there to help you."

Patricia looked around, her expression much more alert now. "Wait. Calm the dog down first, he seems really upset."

The dog yelped and dug at the back of her seat with his paws. His side hurt! It hurt a whole lot! He was still caught in the seat belt and he desperately squirmed around, trying to get free.

"Come on, take it easy, boy," Gregory said, doing his best to stop him from struggling.

Patricia turned to check on Uncle Steve, who was unconscious. It was hard to tell exactly where he was injured, but blood was spreading down the front of his flight jacket. "Uncle Steve?" She put a trembling hand out to touch his shoulder. Then she gave it a gentle shake. "Are you okay? Uncle Steve?"

"Is he breathing?" Gregory asked.

"I don't know! I mean — " Patricia stopped for a second, so that she could calm down. "Yeah. I see his chest moving. I think he's really hurt, though."

Gregory got scratched on the face again, but then he wrapped his arms around Santa Paws to hold him still.

"It's okay, I've got you," he said soothingly. "Take it easy." He held his dog tightly, feeling both of their hearts pounding. Then he unhooked the seat belt and pulled it free of the harness.

Santa Paws fell on the roof of the plane with a loud thud and the plane lurched again. Landing that way made his shoulder hurt, too. He whimpered once, but then scrambled to his feet, and the plane swayed in response.

"Why's the plane moving?" Patricia asked uneasily.

Gregory shrugged. "I don't know. Maybe we're on some ice. Can you open your door?"

Patricia tried to pull the handle, and then made a tiny sound somewhere between a gasp and a moan.

"What?" Gregory asked, alarmed.

"I, uh, I must have banged my arm a little," she said, but her voice was so weak that Gregory knew she wasn't telling the whole truth.

"You're hurt," he said, "right?"

"I'm fine." Patricia gritted her teeth against the pain, and then bent to check the badly dented door. "I don't think it'll open, anyway. It's all smashed in."

The only thing Gregory knew for sure was that Patricia needed his help. "Good dog, stay," he said to Santa Paws. "I'm going to come up front now, Patty, okay?"

As he crawled toward her, the plane unexpectedly slid a few feet. He stopped, not sure why the plane was tilted on its side now, instead of being upside down. Then he lifted one hand to start forward again.

Patricia caught on first.

"Greg, don't move!" she shouted. "We're going to fall!"

He froze right where he was. "What?"

"I don't know where we landed," she said, "but — it's not good."

Well, no *kidding*. Their plane had crashed; of *course* it wasn't *good*. *None* of this was good.

"Don't anybody move!" Patricia said, her voice extremely crisp with authority. "Don't let Santa Paws move, either. I have to figure out what's going on here."

Outside, there was a distinct creaking sound, and the plane pitched forward again.

"What was that?" Gregory asked nervously.

"I don't know," Patricia said. "Just don't move."

She turned her head cautiously, looking in every direction. The plane seemed to be bobbing up and down, and she couldn't figure out why. When she squinted through what was left of the shattered windshield, she could see swaying tree branches and then — nothing at all. Empty air. Looking out through the cracked window in her door, she could see broken pine branches, snow — and more empty air.

"I think we're on top of a tree," she said slowly.

Gregory shook his head. "No, we're on the ground. We hit *way* too hard for it just to be a tree."

"Well, only the back part of it is on the ground then, because — " Then she sucked in her breath. "Oh, no."

They could hear more creaking, and what sounded like wood splintering. The plane bobbed more, as though either the tail or the remaining wing was caught on something.

"What is it?" Gregory asked, his heart thumping in his ears.

Patricia took a deep breath, trying not to panic. "I think we're right on the edge of a mountain," she said.

6

Peering outside from his angle, Gregory saw that she was right, and that the front of the plane was suspended in midair. The only thing keeping them from falling over the cliff was a small fir tree. The tree was bent over from the weight of the plane, and he realized that the creaking sound was the trunk gradually breaking in half.

"It's okay, I can get you out," he said quickly. "I'm just going to reach over and — " As he leaned toward her, the plane lurched down another foot over the side of the mountain.

"Don't!" Patricia said.

Gregory edged back to where he had been, but the plane kept teetering.

"Just stay really still," Patricia said, her voice trembling. "If any weight shifts, we might — "

The dog stood up to see what was going on, and the plane teetered even more precariously.

"Don't!" Patricia said. "Make him sit!"

"*Sit*, Santa Paws," Gregory ordered, and then pressed down on his hindquarters.

Hearing the tension in his voice, Santa Paws quickly sat down. What was happening here? Gregory *never* got angry at him.

For the next minute, the only sounds were the wind whipping through what was left of the plane and the tree trunk creaking. Gregory and Patricia were both holding their breaths, too scared to budge.

"How high up are we?" he whispered.

Patricia was afraid to look again, so she didn't answer right away. "I don't know," she said finally. "Um, *high*, I think."

The plane swayed. The tree trunk creaked.

"Look," Gregory started. "If I — "

"Is the hole in the side big enough to crawl through?" Patricia asked.

The shell of the plane had been torn apart, so there was plenty of room. Most of the fuselage along the right side had been ripped away.

Gregory glanced over his shoulder. "Yeah. No problem. We can all fit."

There was more splintering, and the plane abruptly plunged down another foot. Patricia and Gregory gasped, and held their breaths again, as Santa Paws whimpered anxiously.

"Okay," Patricia said finally. "You and the dog get out."

Gregory stared at her. "What?!"

"Get out," she said, sounding very sure of herself. "Move as fast as you can."

"But — " Gregory stopped, and thought about it. Was that a good plan? Something didn't sound right to him. "No. That's a really bad idea."

The plane bobbed up and down. The tree trunk creaked. They might have minutes of safety left — or they might only have *seconds*.

"Just do it," Patricia said, so quietly that he could barely hear her. "Okay?"

Gregory shook his head. "*No.* If we do, there'll be way too much weight up front, and you'll fall."

"If you *don't*, *all* of us are going to fall," Patricia said through her teeth. "Just go, already!"

They stared at each other, Patricia still hanging awkwardly from her seat belt.

"You got a better idea?" she asked.

Suddenly, Gregory *did*.

"Yeah," he said, nodding. "How much does Uncle Steve weigh? Like, two hundred maybe?"

Patricia considered that. "Probably, yeah."

"And you weigh the least of any of us. So if we could get *him* out of the front, there'd be a whole lot more weight in the *back*, and we might be okay," Gregory said. "At least long enough to get us all out."

They stared at each other again.

"Well, I guess we can tell *your* mother's a physics teacher," Patricia said finally.

It was silent for a second, and then they both

laughed. *Feeble* laughs, but at least they were laughing.

"See if you can get your seat belt off, while I do his," Gregory suggested.

Patricia nodded, and fumbled awkwardly with the cold metal clasp. "He's going to be really heavy. Are you strong enough to pull him out?"

"*Santa Paws* is," Gregory said.

Hearing his name, the dog's ears pricked up.

Patricia nodded again. "You're right. Get some of the rope he used to tie our stuff down."

"Yeah." Then Gregory frowned. "Is it okay to move him? Maybe we're not supposed to. What if he hurt his back, or neck, or something? We could make it worse."

"It's okay," Patricia said. "I kind of think this counts as an emergency."

Well, that was true. If this wasn't an emergency, what *would* be? Gregory was having trouble unfastening their uncle's seat belt, and he finally realized that the metal part had been badly bent in the crash.

"What do I do? I can't open it, Patty," he said, hearing his voice shake. "We're going to fall, I *know* we are."

The plane kept bobbing up and down, and the tree kept creaking. Still too anxious to bark, the dog whined softly. First, he would sit, then he would get up, then he would sit down again. He knew that there were bad things happening here, and he wasn't sure how to help. So he just moved around skittishly in the back of the plane.

Patricia thought fast. "Go through his jacket pockets. Doesn't he have a Swiss Army knife?"

Gregory's hands were trembling so much that it was hard to make them work right. But he found the knife in the right side pocket and tugged it out. He chose the biggest blade and began hacking away at the thick seat belt.

He worked for a minute, but didn't make much progress. So he switched to one of the saw blades, yanking it back and forth as quickly as he could. He had expected Patricia to crawl over and help him once she got her seat belt off, but for some reason, she hadn't.

"You all right?" he asked over his shoulder.

"Unh-hunh," Patricia said without much expression in her voice. "Hurry up."

Was there something else wrong? She sounded like something else had gone wrong. *Everything* had gone wrong so far. But Gregory nodded and sawed even harder. When he had cut almost all the way through the seat belt, he paused.

"When I break through this, the weight's going to shift a bunch," he said tentatively.

"Unh-hunh," Patricia answered.

They both knew what might happen next, but there wasn't much they could do about it.

Gregory ripped through the last frayed

strands of the seat belt and Uncle Steve's body sagged limply into his arms. The unexpected weight was too much for him, and they both fell heavily onto what had been the ceiling.

In response, the plane swung violently to one side and then slipped forward another foot. More branches snapped off, and plummeted over the side of the cliff.

"Whatever we're going to do, we have to do *fast!*" Patricia yelled.

With his uncle's full weight crushing him, Gregory wasn't even sure if he could get up. Plus, he was so scared that —

"Don't think about it, Greg!" Patricia shouted from the front. "*Move!*"

A cold nose pressed against his cheek, and Gregory looked up at Santa Paws. The dog wagged his tail encouragingly, and then licked his face.

Okay, they all needed him to be brave right now — even Santa Paws. Gregory stretched his arm up toward what had been the floor of the plane and yanked on the first rope he saw.

The cargo underneath came tumbling down and the plane pitched forward again. There was the sound of more wood splintering, and then, a distinct *snap*. The plane sagged lower.

"Hurry!" Patricia said.

Gregory kicked the stuff out through the

shredded fuselage and shifted around until he could sit up. "Once I get him back here, you start climbing over, too, okay?" he said.

"Unh-hunh." Patricia gulped. "I mean, I'll try."

Gregory wrapped one end of the rope around Uncle Steve's chest and tied it tightly in a square knot, which was the only kind of knot he knew how to make.

"He's bleeding a lot, Patty," he said unsteadily.

"Go on!" she ordered.

Gregory nodded and pulled the rest of the rope through his hands until he got to the other end.

"Santa Paws?" he asked, looking around. "Come here, boy."

The dog wagged his tail gratefully and tried to climb onto his lap. He wasn't really sure what was going on, but they had never acted like this before. It was scaring him.

Gregory threaded the rope through the harness and tied another knot.

"Okay, Santa Paws," he said. "Go!"

The dog cocked his head to one side.

Gregory pushed him toward the hole in the fuselage. "Go on!"

The dog cocked his head the other way, perplexed.

Gregory yanked the rope, pretending that they were going to play tug-of-war. "Pull!"

Now, the dog understood. He knew the word

"pull." He grabbed the rope in his teeth and tugged as hard as he could. His legs were rigid, and he strained backward with all of his strength. His ribs were throbbing, but he just tugged harder.

"Good boy!" Gregory praised him. "Keep pulling!"

With the two of them working together, they were able to drag Uncle Steve over to the torn fuselage. Uncle Steve still wasn't conscious, but he was mumbling something Gregory couldn't quite hear. He thought he caught the words "call backup," but he wasn't sure.

"Pull, boy!" Gregory said again. "Good dog!"

The plane was still swaying back and forth, and more branches were snapping off.

When Uncle Steve was halfway outside to safety, Gregory turned to help his sister.

"Come on," he said, holding out his hand. "I'll pull you over."

She looked up at him, and he was shocked to see that she was crying. Patricia *never* cried.

"What?" he asked, afraid to hear the answer.

"I'm sorry," she said, crying harder. "My leg's stuck. I can't get it loose."

They were never going to get out. Never, never, never. Pretty much out of both courage and ideas, Gregory just stared back at her. Then he saw that from the knee down, her right leg was trapped underneath the smashed instrument panel. She was struggling to get free, but her leg was jammed there.

"Is it broken?" he asked.

Patricia shook her head, and rubbed some of the tears away with the side of her glove. "I don't think so. I'm just stuck."

Not sure what else to do, Gregory put his arms around her and pulled with all of his might.

Suddenly, the load in the back of the plane lightened and they pitched forward again. From his position, Gregory could see that there was a huge rocky ravine down below them. It went down at least two hundred feet, and — there was *no way* that they would survive, if they fell. And any second now, they might — he closed his eyes tightly and kept tugging.

"I'm sorry," Patricia kept saying, mainly to herself. "I'm really sorry."

"What if I get another rope?" Gregory asked. "Okay? I'll tie it around the back of the plane, and — "

There was a loud crack, and the plane plunged forward another couple of feet. Without looking, Gregory could tell that *most* of the plane was now hanging precariously over the edge of the cliff.

There was no time to lose!

"Santa Paws!" he bellowed.

Hearing his name, the dog sprang obediently

back inside the plane. Did they need his help? Whatever they wanted him to do, he was ready! Having his weight there made the nose of the plane rise a few inches.

"Okay, good dog. Stay," Gregory said, and crawled forward far enough to yank at the bottom of the instrument panel with his hands. "Maybe I can pry it up, and — "

Patricia shook her head. "I tried, it won't work. I don't think we can — " Then she stopped, her eyes brightening. "Oil! Get me some oil."

Gregory nodded and dug underneath the pilot's seat until he found a small plastic bottle of motor oil. He twisted the cap off, and handed it up to her.

Patricia shook the oil onto her jeans leg, forcing as much of the slippery liquid as she could below the instrument panel. Then she twisted back and forth, trying to get loose.

A few more branches broke, and they slid down another foot.

"It's not working," she said weakly. "I can't — "

No more time to fool around here — it was now, or never. "Close your eyes!" Gregory yelled. He snatched up the fire extinguisher that was also underneath the pilot's seat and sprayed the full contents at her leg. Then he threw the canister down and wrapped one arm around her. "Santa Paws! Come here!"

Instantly, the dog bounded over and Gregory grabbed onto his harness with his free hand.

"Pull, boy!" he shouted. "Go!"

The dog strained toward the torn fuselage, whimpering in frustration.

"Harder!" Gregory shouted, using his own legs to try and get them started. "Pull!"

Patricia gasped in pain, but then suddenly, her leg popped free and they all sprawled down in a heap.

"Come on!" Gregory said.

All three of them dove for the hole in the fuselage, scrambling out just as the fir tree finally gave way. The plane whipped past them, gathering speed until suddenly, it disappeared over the side of the mountain.

They had barely made it!

7

Gregory and Patricia lay in the snow, too exhausted to speak. After a minute, Patricia lifted herself up enough to look over the edge of the cliff, and then she sank back down. It was a *very* long drop.

"Is Uncle Steve okay?" she mumbled.

Gregory turned his head and saw their uncle's chest rising and falling as he breathed. He still seemed to be unconscious, though. "I think so," he answered. "He's breathing and everything."

They lay there for a few more seconds, in total silence, trying to catch their breaths. The snow was about a foot deep, and if they'd had enough energy, they would have been shivering. As it was, breathing in and out took all of their attention. Patricia didn't even have enough strength to worry about how badly her right arm hurt.

"We should have just driven up with Mom and Dad," Gregory said finally.

Patricia nodded. "Too bad we're not nice, loving children."

That broke the tension, and they snickered a little. Then they slumped back into the snow to rest some more.

Worried, the dog came over to check on them. They had never acted like this before! Why wouldn't they get up? Were they sick? This was scary! He sniffed Patricia's face, and then nudged Gregory's shoulder with his paw.

Gregory opened his eyes and lifted his hand to pat him. "It's okay," he said. "You're a good boy, Santa Paws."

That was more like it! Feeling better, the dog promptly turned in two circles and curled up between them in the snow. He rested his muzzle on Gregory's chest, and Gregory kept patting him. Patting his dog made it seem as though everything was going to be okay.

"If Santa Paws hadn't helped me pull, we wouldn't have gotten out in time," he said aloud.

"Yeah," Patricia agreed, and then paused. "You should give him a Milk-Bone."

The dog's ears flew up, and he looked at them hopefully.

It wasn't much of a reward, but Gregory fished around inside his jacket pocket until he found one. He gave it to Santa Paws, who wagged his tail and began crunching. Then Gregory stood up and looked around to see where they were.

There were craggy, tree-covered mountains in every direction. Mountains, mountains, and *more* mountains.

"Can you see any houses or anything?" Patricia asked.

Gregory shook his head. There were no signs of civilization at all. "I don't even see *roads*. We're in the like, *total* forest."

There had to be a town *someplace* nearby. It wasn't as though they'd crashed in the Yukon, right? "How about streetlights?" Patricia asked. "Or — I don't know — telephone poles, maybe."

Gregory looked and looked, but all he could see were mountains and trees. Hundreds and thousands and millions of *trees*. Dark, overcast sky. What might be a frozen lake off in the distance. Wherever they were, it looked as though they were on their own.

As though they were in *very* serious trouble.

Behind them, Uncle Steve started moving restlessly and saying something that sounded like "eltee." It didn't make any sense, but he seemed to be regaining consciousness.

Gregory hurried over to see if he was okay. Patricia followed him, wincing from the pain in her arm. The rope was still tied around their uncle's chest, and Gregory pulled it off.

Uncle Steve shifted his position, and then mumbled again.

"What's he saying?" Gregory asked. "L-T?"

Patricia shrugged as she took off her scarf and pressed it against the blood on his chest. Her right arm wouldn't work at all, so she had to do it one-handed. "I don't know," she said, trying to stop the bleeding. "Maybe he thinks this happened at work, and his lieutenant is here."

Gregory used *his* scarf to pick up a small handful of snow. Then he used the damp scarf to wipe the blood away from Uncle Steve's face. Most of it came right off, and he saw that it had all come from a cut on his forehead. The gash didn't seem to be very deep, but he would definitely need stitches. There was a huge, dark bruise there, too.

Washing his face with the cold snow must have helped, because Uncle Steve's eyes opened partway, and he squinted at them. He tried to sit up, then groaned and fell back down.

"Call backup," he whispered. Then his hand went down to where his holster would have been, if he was on duty. "Where's my service revolver?"

Gregory and Patricia looked at each other uneasily. Did he have amnesia, maybe? That would be really bad. He might even think they were perpetrators! If he suddenly started giving them their Miranda rights, it would just be too weird.

"Well — I think it's in Massachusetts," Gregory answered.

Uncle Steve looked confused. He tried to get up again, but then collapsed.

"I don't think you should try to move," Patricia said. "You might be really hurt."

Uncle Steve stared up at her in sudden recognition. "Patricia?" he asked in a dazed voice. "What happened? Are you all right?" He managed to lift himself onto one elbow, and then looked around anxiously. "Hey! Where's the plane?"

Gregory and Patricia shrugged and pointed over the edge of the mountain.

Uncle Steve's mouth dropped open. "What?! How did we get out?"

Patricia pointed at Gregory, and Gregory pointed at Santa Paws.

Uncle Steve's mouth stayed open, as he tried to take all of this in. Then he started shaking his head. "I can't believe I got you kids into this," he said softly. "I am *so* sorry."

"You should just lie down," Patricia advised. "I don't think it's good for you to be, you know, agitated."

Uncle Steve narrowed his eyes, trying to piece together what was going on. He might not have amnesia, but he still seemed pretty out of it.

"Because you're *hurt*," she elaborated.

Uncle Steve nodded, looking — even though he was an adult — a little overwhelmed for a second. Then he gave his head a shake and put on a more confident expression.

"Okay," he said, sounding very sure of himself. "Don't worry, everything's going to be okay." He tried to sit up all the way, and winced. Noticing the makeshift scarf-bandage, he raised one edge to look underneath.

"I think you maybe have a sucking chest wound," Patricia said uneasily. "Or — a pneumothorax."

Uncle Steve stared at her, and then, unexpectedly, he grinned. "Oh. You think so, Doc?"

Patricia looked a little offended, but then she grinned, too. She turned to Gregory. "Get a CBC, Chem seven, type and cross for two units, chest films, and hang a dopamine drip, *stat*," she said crisply.

Gregory looked at her suspiciously.

"Now!" she barked. "He's in v-tach!"

Instead of just grinning, Uncle Steve laughed outright when he heard that. "You know what? I think your sister watches too much television," he said to Gregory.

Gregory nodded. Sometimes Patricia even referred to herself as "Queen of the Remote Control." "Yeah," he agreed. "And she's like, in *love* with that guy on that show."

Uncle Steve's face was tight with pain, but he laughed again. "Well, what would he do in this situation?" he asked.

"Well — call 911, probably," Patricia said logically. "I mean, he's an *actor*." She paused. "That is, after he kissed me hello."

All three of them laughed this time.

The dog wagged his tail, because everyone seemed happy now. Things must be okay. Maybe they would go ride in the car soon. That's what they *usually* did after they got out of the plane. He didn't really know where the car *was* right now — but they would know. They *always* knew. So he sat down in the snow to wait, watching them alertly.

"Don't worry," Uncle Steve said to Patricia. "I think it's just my collarbone. Looks like a compound fracture, that's all." He took a deep breath and started to sit up all the way, but then his face paled.

Patricia looked scared. "What?"

"And maybe my hip," he said in a faint voice. He tried to move again, and then sucked in his breath. "Oh, boy." He smiled feebly at them. "I, uh, might've wrenched my back a little, too."

Patricia and Gregory exchanged nervous glances.

"What do we do?" Gregory asked.

"Let me think for a minute, okay?" Uncle Steve said, speaking with an effort.

Gregory and Patricia waited nervously for him to open his eyes again. The dog moved into a worried crouch, since they all seemed to be up-

229

set again. He whimpered once, and Gregory automatically patted him.

"Okay," Uncle Steve said finally. His voice sounded a *little* stronger, but not much. "First things, first. Are either of you hurt?"

Gregory shook his head, but Patricia didn't answer.

"Patricia?" Uncle Steve asked more firmly.

"I kind of banged my arm," she muttered.

Since her right arm was just hanging uselessly at her side, it was pretty obvious that she had broken something.

"Okay," Uncle Steve said gently. "We're going to get a splint on you as soon as we can, and — it'll be okay. How bad's the pain?"

Patricia shrugged, avoiding his eyes.

"Okay," Uncle Steve said. "I hear you." He let out his breath. "Did either of you turn on the ELT?"

The ELT was the Emergency Locator Transmitter, which looked sort of like a walkie-talkie. ELTs sent out emergency signals, so that rescue planes would be able to find downed aircraft easily. And — they hadn't turned it on. In fact, neither of them had even *thought* of it. They had just assumed he meant "lieutenant." Patricia and Gregory both ducked their heads and looked guilty.

"Okay, no problem. Don't worry about it," Uncle Steve said calmly. He pulled in a deep breath.

"Where's the survival pack? I've got a handheld one in there."

Patricia and Gregory looked even more guilty. Then Gregory pointed miserably over the side of the mountain. After all of the times they had flown in the plane, the one time there was a *real* emergency, they hadn't remembered what to do. And now, it might cost them their lives.

Uncle Steve closed his eyes briefly, but then gave them a reassuring smile. "Okay. No problem," he said again. "I had to go a little off-course to get us down, but I filed a flight plan, so they'll know where to start looking. It just might take a little while."

"Will they be here today?" Gregory asked.

Uncle Steve glanced up at the sky. Ominous grey clouds had rolled in, and it was starting to get dark. "Probably in the morning," he answered.

So they were going to have to spend the night out here, alone, in the middle of the wilderness, in *December*.

"We're going to die," Gregory said grimly, "right?"

That was the *last* thing Patricia felt like hearing, and she couldn't help giving him a little shove.

Uncle Steve shook his head. "We are *not* going to die. We're going to stay really calm, set up some kind of shelter, and get a fire going. Okay?"

Thinking about sitting in front of a warm fire, Gregory and Patricia suddenly realized that their teeth were chattering. It was very windy on the mountain, and even Santa Paws seemed to be shivering.

"We'll all feel a lot better once we get warm," Uncle Steve promised.

At the moment, neither Gregory nor Patricia could imagine how they could feel much *worse*.

"I'm really sorry about the survival stuff," Gregory said. "I — I just forgot, I — "

Patricia interrupted him. "*I* should have remembered. I'm older than he is."

"And *I* should have figured out a way to land in the middle of some nice little town common somewhere," Uncle Steve said. "Look, we all got out of the plane in one piece, right? *That's* what's important."

"Yeah, but — " Patricia started.

"It's going to be dark soon," Uncle Steve said, cutting her off. "We need to move quickly here. Greg, take the dog, and go see how much firewood you can find." He looked around the mountain face, and then pointed to a spot surrounded by a thicket of pine trees. "See where those rocks are? And that fallen tree? That's where we'll settle in. We should be protected from the wind up there."

Gregory nodded, and climbed stiffly to his feet.

"Come on, Santa Paws," he said, giving him a short whistle.

The dog jumped up, relieved to be *doing* something. Maybe *now* they would go to the car. Sitting here in the wind was just too cold.

Patricia and Uncle Steve watched as Gregory and Santa Paws went trudging off through the foot-deep snow.

"So," Uncle Steve said wryly. "We having fun yet?"

Patricia tried to smile.

So far, her Christmas vacation had been anything but *fun*.

8

Patricia knew she should be doing something constructive, but she was too tired to think. It was easier just to rest for another minute. Uncle Steve looked even worse than she felt, but he motioned her over.

"Come here, honey, and let me look at you for a minute," he said.

Patricia got up, and moved to him. Uncle Steve held her chin gently so he could examine her face. Then he picked up the scarf Gregory had dropped, and used the end to blot away the blood below her nose and on her chin.

"Did you bite your lip?" he asked.

Patricia thought back, and then nodded. "When we crashed, I think."

"Okay," he said, and dabbed lightly at the cut. "You went right through. It looks like you had a little nosebleed, too. Do your teeth feel okay?"

Patricia ran her tongue around the inside of

her mouth to be sure, and then nodded. None of them seemed to be loose or anything.

"How about your head?" Uncle Steve asked, looking concerned. "Do you think you hit it?"

"Well — it doesn't hurt," Patricia said uncertainly.

"Good." Uncle Steve rolled some snow into the scarf, and then handed it to her. "Hold that against your lip, and let's see if we can get some of the swelling down."

Patricia nodded, and pressed the snow on the spot that hurt the most. "Do you think *you* have a concussion?" she asked, her voice muffled by the scarf.

"Who, me?" he asked cheerfully. "This is nothing. I used to play *football*, remember?" Then he indicated a couple of objects half-buried in the snow. "What're those?"

Patricia went over to see, surprised to find herself limping. Apparently, she had twisted her knee while trying to get free from the instrument panel. It hurt, but not nearly as much as her arm did. She bent down on her uninjured leg to examine the things that must have been knocked out of the plane during all of the confusion.

"My knapsack," she said. "And — I think this might be a life jacket."

Uncle Steve's eyes lit up. "*Good.* I've got some

MREs, and I forget what else, wrapped up in there."

MREs were Meals-Ready-to-Eat, which were Army rations. Patricia had never had one before, but *anything* would taste good right now. She was starting to get really hungry. Just in case, she kept poking through the snow with the toe of her oil-and-foam-stained boot to see what else she might find. Her knee felt swollen and clumsy, but she could still bend it a little.

"I see some stuff from the picnic basket, too," she said. "There's a Coke, and — I see the brownies!"

Uncle Steve nodded. *"Outstanding.* See if you can get all of it piled together, and then when Gregory gets back, he can carry everything."

While she was doing that, Uncle Steve dragged himself over to the edge of the cliff. It must have hurt a lot, because he groaned a few times, but he would just grit his teeth and keep going.

He studied the broken fir tree, and shook his head. "Was the plane caught on this?"

Patricia nodded.

Uncle Steve nodded, too, before shaking his head again. Then he peered down into the deep gorge. There was a sheer rock face on both sides, and the whole thing was coated with ice and snow. He stared at the wreckage down on the rocks, and then let out his breath.

"How close did we come to going over?" he asked.

Really close. "Um, about a second and a half," Patricia said.

Uncle Steve let out a low whistle.

Patricia glanced behind her to make sure that Gregory hadn't come back yet. "I, um, I pretty much panicked," she confessed. "I thought I was maybe even going to throw up or something. But Greg was *really* brave."

"I'm guessing you did fine," Uncle Steve said, and stared at the battered wreckage some more. "In fact, you kids are really something."

Patricia shrugged self-consciously. The only thing she could remember was how terrified she had been, every single second. Just being *scared* — which was how she felt right now — was definitely an improvement. "Do you think we can climb down there, and maybe get the ELT and all?" she asked.

Uncle Steve looked at her incredulously. "I don't think a team of fully-equipped *paratroopers* could climb down there," he answered.

Patricia nodded, and then couldn't help shivering. A couple of seconds either way, and she would have fallen onto those rocks. It made her dizzy to look down there, so she concentrated on gathering up the stray cargo, instead.

Across the clearing, Gregory was stomping around near the fallen tree with a huge armload of wood. He saw them watching, waved, and hiked back over. Santa Paws galloped playfully next to him, barking every so often.

Gregory's face was red from all of the exercise, but he was smiling. "There's a whole *bunch* of wood over there," he said. "Dead trees, and all. We found most of the wing, too. Can we maybe use it like a sled for you, Uncle Steve?"

"Let me see if I can get over there by myself, first," Uncle Steve suggested. "Then we'll use it to help build a shelter."

"Okay," Gregory said, sounding remarkably chipper. "We'll go get it. Come on, boy!" he called to Santa Paws, and they headed off again.

"Why don't you carry what you can," Uncle Steve said to Patricia, "and I'll catch up."

Patricia nodded and unzipped her knapsack. There was just enough room inside to pack in the few things she had found from the picnic basket. When she came across the plastic bag of carrot sticks her mother had cut up for them, she had to stop for a second so she wouldn't cry.

Did their parents know what had happened yet? Were they upset? What if she never saw them again? She squeezed her eyes shut and tried to remember the last thing she had said to both of them.

Her mother had been worried that she hadn't dressed warmly enough for the trip. And — her mother was *right*. Her father had stayed back at the house, because he was waiting for some overnight mail to come from New York. But he had given each of them a big hug before they left, the best kind where he lifted them right off the ground and spun around a couple of times.

"You all right?" Uncle Steve asked.

Patricia nodded and swung the knapsack over her good arm. That way, she could also carry the rolled-up life jacket in her hand and only have to make one trip. Then she started limping toward the rocks.

Watching Uncle Steve drag himself inch by inch through the snow made her want to cry all over again. His jaw was very tight, and he kept his eyes closed most of the time. He was breathing really hard, and every few feet, he would groan softly and suck in his breath.

"Um, maybe we *should* make a sled," she said hesitantly.

For a second, she thought he was going to yell at her. But then, he just shook his head.

"I'm fine," he panted. "Okay? It's just going to be slow."

Patricia nodded. Her father was always talking about how incredibly stubborn his little brother Steve was — and so, she wasn't about to argue. And, hey, *she* had been accused of being pretty stubborn, too.

About fifty feet away, she could see that Gregory had managed to tie the rope to the sheared-off wing. Now he and Santa Paws were pulling it toward them like an ungainly pair of Santa's reindeer.

A large branch was poking up out of the snow, and Uncle Steve paused long enough to tear off a thick twig. He stuck it between his teeth, and bit down *hard*. Then he resumed crawling. He had only made it about ten more feet, when Gregory and Santa Paws got to them.

"Taxi!" Gregory announced brightly.

Uncle Steve hesitated, but then gave up. Slowly, he eased himself up onto the metal wing. Once he was aboard, Gregory tugged on the rope, but the improvised sled didn't move.

"We pulled him before," he said to Santa Paws, "remember? We can do it again."

The dog cocked his head.

"*Pull*, boy," Gregory said. Then he yanked on the rope, using all of his weight.

Santa Paws joined in, ignoring the pain in his side, but it still didn't budge.

Uncle Steve swung his uninjured leg over the side and pushed powerfully against the snow. With that extra effort, the wing-sled squirted forward. Using the momentum, Gregory and Santa Paws started pulling the wing-sled across the drifts.

It seemed to take forever, but finally they all made it over to the fallen tree. Patricia and

Gregory sat heavily on top of a rock, while Uncle Steve stayed right where he was, trying to catch his breath. Even Santa Paws looked tired. It was dusk now, and they had to squint through the shadows to see each other.

Uncle Steve broke the silence. "Thanks, guys. Sorry to be so much trouble." He slid himself off the wing, his face grey from exhaustion and pain. "Greg, if you can lift the wide end up on the tree, and the other side onto that rock, we'll be in business."

"I can help," Patricia offered.

Uncle Steve shook his head. "No, why don't you get some more wood, while it's still light enough to see. But *don't go out of sight*." Then he felt around inside his right jacket pocket and frowned.

"Oh," Gregory said, and reached into his own pocket for the Swiss Army knife. "Are you looking for this?"

Uncle Steve nodded. "Thanks."

While Patricia gathered wood, and Gregory worked on the shelter, Uncle Steve began to cut pine boughs from some of the nearby trees with his good arm. Normally, of course, he would never have damaged trees that way — but, this wasn't exactly a normal situation. When survival was at stake, the rules changed.

For lack of a better idea, the dog followed Patricia around. He liked to carry things in his mouth, so when Patricia gave him a stick, he happily took it. She kept going back and forth with single armloads of kindling and thicker sticks. Each time, he would dance along next to her.

"Are you a good boy?" she asked him.

The dog barked, which made the stick fall out of his mouth. He grabbed it back up and shook his head playfully from side to side. If he was lucky, maybe she would throw it for him! Just because his ribs hurt, didn't mean that he couldn't still have fun!

"No, not now," Patricia said. Her hands and feet were so cold, and her arm was throbbing so much that the *last* thing she felt like doing was playing fetch. Besides that, her knee was beginning to ache more than ever. "Leave me alone, Santa Paws!"

The dog lowered his ears and stopped wagging his tail. Then he dropped the stick into the snow. Did she think he was a bad dog? She *must*.

Patricia sighed, ashamed of herself for having shouted at him. After all, only about an hour ago, he had helped save her *life*. "I'm sorry, you're very good, Santa Paws," she apologized. "It's just — right now, we have to work."

The dog still kept his head down, with his tail between his legs. He must have done *something* wrong, but he didn't know what it was. Now his side hurt even more than it had before.

Seeing him upset was more than she could take, and Patricia felt tears start down her cheeks. She let the sticks she was clutching fall, and then she sat down in the snow. It was cold, but she didn't care. She was *already* so cold that she couldn't think straight, anyway.

Her arm hurt so much that it felt like it was on fire. She hunched over it, rocking slightly. Gregory and Uncle Steve — and Santa Paws — were so brave, and she just wasn't making it, here. She buried her face in her sleeve and cried as quietly as she could. If they heard her, or came to look for her, she would feel even worse.

The dog *couldn't stand it* when he saw anyone cry. He hated it when people were sad. Especially *his* people. He sat down and nuzzled up next to her, trying to get as close as he could.

Patricia put her arm around him and hugged him tightly. His fur felt warm, and comforting. She had never been outside in the forest like this before, and she couldn't believe how *dark* it was. How frightening it seemed. The clouds were so thick that there weren't even any stars out.

Then she heard Gregory calling her name, his voice sharp with fear.

"Patricia!" he yelled. "Patricia, where are you?"

Santa Paws was already on his feet. Patricia hung onto his collar to help herself stand up faster. Then she stumbled through the snow in the direction of her brother's voice.

"What's wrong? I'm over here!" she yelled back.

"Come quick!" he said, sounding frantic. "I need help!"

9

It was hard to see in the dark, but Santa Paws was galloping ahead of her. Patricia just kept watching for a moving shape, and then she would race after it.

Then she ran into Gregory — *literally* — at the edge of the clearing.

"What's wrong?" she asked, out of breath. "Are you hurt?"

"Uncle Steve fainted or something," Gregory said, sounding very close to tears. "He was helping me make a fire pit, and then he just passed out. I didn't know what to do!"

Patricia put her hand on his shoulder to calm him down. "Just show me where he is, okay?"

Gregory nodded, and motioned for her to follow him.

When they got to the shelter, Patricia saw that Uncle Steve was lying on his back in the snow. She crouched down next to him, peering through the darkness. His breathing seemed nice and steady, but he was definitely unconscious.

"*Fix* him," Gregory said urgently. "I mean, you know all that medical stuff."

Patricia sighed. "I just know a bunch of words, Greg — I don't know how to *do* anything."

He stared at her accusingly. "But — I thought you *knew* stuff. You always act like you know *everything*."

"Give me a break, I'm only *twelve*!" she said.

They glared at each other until Patricia finally took a deep breath.

"Look," she said. "We're really cold, and we're really scared, and we don't know how to help him. Let's try to be nice to each other, okay?"

"Be sweet," Gregory muttered.

Patricia smiled a little. That was what their grandmother always said to them right before she hung up the telephone, instead of "good-bye." "Yeah," she said. "Exactly."

Watching them, the dog paced anxiously and whined deep in his throat.

Patricia slipped her glove off and tapped her uncle's face lightly with her hand. "Uncle Steve?" she asked tentatively.

There was no response.

Gregory and Santa Paws were waiting for her to make everything all right, so she tapped his face again. Then she nudged his arm.

Finally, his eyes opened. He shook his head to

clear it, squinted at them, and then sat up part-way.

"Sorry," he said hoarsely. "Got a little dizzy there." He rubbed his hand across his eyes and shook his head a few more times. "Okay." He frowned when he noticed Patricia's bare hand. "Hey, put your gloves on — it's cold out here."

If he was being authoritative, he must be okay. Or *better*, anyway. Patricia awkwardly wormed her hand back inside her glove. Just a couple of minutes of being exposed to the cold air had numbed her fingers pretty badly.

"Take it easy, I'm all right," Uncle Steve said to Gregory. "I overdid the lifting, that's all."

"You have to be careful," Gregory answered shakily. "That was way too scary."

Uncle Steve nodded. "I know. I'm sorry, pal."

While they were talking, Patricia glanced around the campsite. From what she could see, they had made a lot of progress. The wing was resting across the big tree trunk and a gigantic boulder to form the roof of a primitive triangular shelter. Someone — Gregory, presumably — had built up a snow wall to fill the open spot in the back. As a result, the shelter was fully en-closed, except for a wide opening in the front.

The snow had been trampled down to make a hard surface. Cushiony pine branches lined the bottom of the shelter to insulate it from the snow. In front of the opening, there was a neat semicircle made out of fairly big rocks and some jagged pieces of aluminum from the wing. They would form a firebreak. It would block the wind from the fire, and it would also help reflect the heat into their lean-to.

Smaller rocks were arranged together in front of the firebreak, as a base for their campfire. Otherwise, the heat from the coals would just melt all of the surrounding snow and the fire would go out right away.

"This is really *good*," Patricia said admiringly. "You're like, *nature guys*."

Uncle Steve's teeth flashed, so he must have smiled.

Gregory raised his fist in the air. "Airborne!" he said, trying to make his voice deep. Sometimes, he and his friend Oscar liked to pretend that they were in the Army, and they were always trying to chant infantry cadences.

"Okay, Airborne Ranger," Uncle Steve said, still smiling. "See if you can rip one more piece of metal off the end of the wing. We'll build the fire on it."

Gregory nodded, and climbed up on top of the fallen tree to work on the wing.

Uncle Steve shifted his position to one side and reached inside his jacket. His movements were extremely cautious. Finally, he came out with a small penlight. He flicked it on, and the bright beam cut through the darkness.

Now that they could see better, they all visibly relaxed. The campsite seemed friendlier, somehow. The black expanses of the wilderness were still surrounding them, but it felt as though they were in a safe haven.

Next, Uncle Steve dug painfully into one of the bellows pockets on his pants leg. He pulled out an ordinary plastic trash bag and then sliced open the two long sides with his Swiss Army knife.

"Here," he said, and handed it to Patricia. "Spread it out on the floor of the shelter. It'll help us stay dry."

Patricia nodded and carried the bag inside the shelter. Gregory had managed to tear another piece of fuselage from the wing, and he set it down on the bed of rocks.

Since everyone else had something to do, the dog looked at Uncle Steve expectantly.

"Santa Paws, why don't you just wag your tail and keep up morale?" Uncle Steve suggested.

The dog promptly lifted his right paw.

"Okay," Uncle Steve said agreeably. "That's good, too." Then he retrieved another garbage bag from his pocket. "Lay this one out on the ground, Patricia, and then we can inventory our supplies. And Greg, can you help me clear out my pockets?"

Gregory hesitated. "Will I hurt you?"

"No," Uncle Steve said, although it probably

wasn't true. "I just can't get to the ones on the left side very well."

Patricia watched as the two of them pulled out a surprising variety of objects. Between the flight jacket and the army pants, Uncle Steve had an *amazing* number of pockets.

"Are you maybe Mary Poppins in disguise?" she asked.

Uncle Steve nodded ironically. "Oh, yeah. I'm practically perfect in every way." He fumbled through the pile one-handed until he found a small plastic container of waterproof matches and a tube of fire-starter. "Here we go, Greg — it's show time."

Soon, a small blaze was glowing on the piece of fuselage. Following their uncle's instructions, Gregory carefully surrounded it with more kindling. Then, once the fire had caught pretty well, he added some thicker sticks. The wood crackled and snapped, and burned noisily away.

They all, including Santa Paws, gathered around the fire. No one spoke, so that they could just enjoy the luxury of starting to feel warm again. Or, at least, not quite as *cold*.

"Let's break out the brownies," Uncle Steve said finally. "I think we could all use a snack."

Patricia looked inside her knapsack until she found the foil-wrapped package. While she was at it, she took out the rest of the things from the picnic basket. There was a squashed meat loaf sandwich, the bag of carrot sticks, a can of Coke, a package of Santa Claus cocktail napkins, and a juice box. It might not be much, but it *seemed* like great riches.

There were six brownies in the package, and they each had one. Santa Paws gulped his down in one swallow, but the rest of them took their time. They wanted to savor every single bite. In the end, of course, Gregory ended up sharing the rest of his with Santa Paws, anyway.

"What else have you got in there?" Uncle Steve asked, indicating the knapsack.

"I don't know," Patricia said, and then she flushed self-consciously. "*Vogue.*"

Uncle Steve grinned. "Well, see," he said to Gregory, "things were looking mighty bleak, but now we're going to be able to sit here, and get up-to-speed on the spring collections. Life is *good.*"

The thought of them all sprawling in front of the fire, reading *Vogue*, was a pretty funny image, and Gregory laughed.

"I didn't know we were going to crash," Patricia said defensively. "So I just brought vacation stuff."

Gregory started pulling things out of the knapsack. His face lit up when he saw her notebook computer.

"Hey, whoa!" he said eagerly. "We can send *E-mail*! Then they'll come rescue us!"

Uncle Steve and Patricia just looked at him.

"It'll be great," Gregory went on. "I'll send some to Gram, and to Oscar, and — " He stopped. "Why aren't you guys happy?"

Patricia moved her jaw. "I'm going to say one word to you, Gregory."

"Plastics?" Uncle Steve guessed.

Patricia and Gregory looked at him, perplexed. He shook his head. "Never mind."

Patricia focused on Gregory. "*Modem*," she said. "The word is *modem*."

Gregory's face fell. "Oh. Right." To use the modem, they needed access to a wireless network or a telephone line — and if they were near either of those, they could just *call* for help.

"It was a good thought, though," Uncle Steve said kindly.

"Or we could just describe it as . . . a *thought*," Patricia said, and winked at Gregory.

After unloading the knapsack, Gregory emptied his own pockets. He also helped Patricia with hers, since she couldn't move her arm very well. Then he unstrapped the bright orange life jacket. Two dark brown sealed bags fell out, along with a metal cup with a sturdy handle and a cylinder that looked like a firecracker.

"What's that?" Patricia asked.

"It's a flare," Uncle Steve answered. "We can use it for a signal, if someone flies over. Greg, slice each of the MREs at one end, and we'll see what we have."

The two Meals-Ready-to-Eat had vacuum-sealed food packets inside. Some of the packets were pliable, and the others seemed to be shrink-wrapped. The first meal was corned beef hash, with a pack of dry fruit mix. There was also an oatmeal cookie bar, crackers, a packet of apple jelly, a brown plastic spoon, an envelope of cocoa powder, and some Beverage Base powder — which was like Tang or Kool-Aid. There was also something called Accessory Packet A. It contained two Chiclets, water-resistant matches, a tiny bottle of Tabasco sauce, a Wet-Nap for washing, some tissues, coffee, sugar, salt, and cream substitute.

The other meal was very much the same, except that the main course was escalloped potatoes with ham, and it had a chocolate covered brownie, some applesauce, and a package of caramels to go along with its accessory packet.

"Fill the two bags with snow, and put them near the fire," Uncle Steve said. "Close enough so it'll start melting. Then we'll be able to heat up some water for cocoa."

It turned out that Uncle Steve had been carrying all sorts of useful things in his many pockets. There was an emergency space blanket, a squat white candle, a black watch cap, some

Chap Stick, his wallet, car keys, some stamps, a half-eaten roll of Tums, and a box of cough drops. He had also unearthed a nail clipper, a handkerchief, a notepad, two pens, another garbage bag, two packages of pocket heaters, needle-nose pliers, a roll of duct tape, and — of course — his Swiss Army knife.

"Adults have a lot of baggage, huh?" Patricia remarked.

"So I hear," Uncle Steve said dryly.

Along with *Vogue*, Patricia had brought the latest issue of *Entertainment Weekly*, the most recent J. Crew catalog, and a copy of *Wuthering Heights*. She had also packed extra sunglasses, her Walkman, some cassettes, her favorite pink sweatshirt, a Magic Marker, a hairbrush, some Lauren perfume, a blue ponytail holder, and vanilla-flavored lip gloss.

"It's good to look and smell your best when you're in a plane crash," Uncle Steve observed.

"Uh-huh," Patricia said. Dryly.

The only things Gregory had in his pockets were six more Milk-Bones, forty-two cents, half a candy cane, a cheap harmonica he didn't know how to play, an old ticket stub from a Bruins game, some sea shells, and a battered tennis ball.

Santa Paws had been overjoyed to see the tennis ball — to say nothing of the Milk-Bones.

Gregory shook his head. "Not now," he told

him as he zipped them back into his jacket pocket. "Maybe later."

Disappointed, the dog flopped back down by the fire. So Gregory relented and gave him a small piece of Milk-Bone. The dog wagged his tail and started crunching.

"Are you warm enough now to take your jacket off for a minute?" Uncle Steve asked Patricia. "I want Gregory to put a splint on that arm."

Patricia nodded, and awkwardly unzipped it. She was able to slip the jacket off her left side with no trouble, but the right side was a different story. The second she jarred her arm, she gasped and her eyes filled with tears.

Hearing the distress in her voice, the dog scrambled up. He watched her intently, his forehead furrowed with worry. He had never felt so helpless before!

"Okay, okay," Uncle Steve said quickly. "Greg's just going to ease it off for you. Hold my hand, and squeeze as hard as you want, okay?"

Patricia held his good hand with *her* good hand.

Gregory slowly peeled her jacket off. He *really* didn't want to hurt her. His sister had her eyes shut the whole time, but he could feel that she was shaking.

"You want to wear my down vest?" he asked.

"I've got way more layers on than you."

Patricia opened her eyes. "Won't you be cold?"

"Not as cold as *you* are," Gregory said. He took off his jacket, and unsnapped the down vest he was wearing underneath. Then he guided the right side over her broken arm, and helped her stick her left arm in, too. It was terrible to see her shivering so much, and he quickly fastened all of the snaps.

"From now on, long underwear," Patricia vowed. "Even in August."

Gregory had to laugh as he pictured her lounging on Crane's Beach in her bathing suit, sunglasses — and long underwear.

"Take her glove off, and feel her hand," Uncle Steve said, "I want to make sure she's getting enough circulation."

"It's nice and warm," Gregory reported.

"Now press one of her fingernails and release it," Uncle Steve told him.

"Her nail turned white, and then back to pink."

"Good. Now cut *Vogue* in half," Uncle Steve said. "Just go right down the binding. Then hold the pieces against her other arm to see if they'll fit. I think they're going to be too long, so you can just cut them down to size."

The magazine *was* too long, and Gregory sawed about three inches off. He rolled one half around her upper arm and taped it in place with some of the duct tape. Then he did the same

256

thing to her forearm. He had to be very careful with the tape, so that the splints wouldn't be too tight.

The last step was making a sling. First, he wrapped his scarf just below her elbow, and then tied it around her neck. After that, he looped his belt around her wrist and fastened it around her neck, too. The most important part was for her wrist to be higher than her elbow. Gregory turned the penlight back on, and flashed it up and down her arm to make sure everything looked okay.

Patricia kept her eyes closed and held onto Uncle Steve's hand the whole time.

"How does it feel?" Uncle Steve asked.

Patricia managed a weak smile. "Like I have a broken arm."

Uncle Steve nodded, and gave her hand a sympathetic squeeze. "You did a good job, Greg," he said.

Gregory zipped her jacket back up, trying not to jostle her arm. Patricia mouthed the word, "Thanks," and he nodded.

Now it was Uncle Steve's turn!

10

Uncle Steve was so badly hurt that there wasn't really very much that Gregory could do to help him. They didn't have any bandages, so he pressed the whole package of Santa Claus cocktail napkins against the torn part of his shoulder. Then he tied it in place with Patricia's scarf and used Uncle Steve's belt for a sling.

Splinting his broken hip was even more complicated. Gregory searched through their woodpile until he found a stick long enough to reach from the outside of his uncle's ankle, all the way up to his rib cage. Then he selected another one to fit against the inside of his leg.

Next, he sliced the sleeves off Patricia's pink sweatshirt and set them aside. The Swiss Army knife was pretty much worth its weight in *gold*. After that, he cut the body of the sweatshirt into two pieces. He rolled each piece around one of the sticks for padding and started lightly taping them into place.

"Is that too tight?" he asked nervously.

Uncle Steve shook his head, gritting his teeth against the pain.

Gregory taped the two sticks, so that Uncle Steve's hip was immobilized as much as possible. Then he rezipped his flight jacket and tied his scarf for him. Finally, he used the Swiss Army knife to cut the discarded sweatshirt sleeves in half. He stopped before he reached the cuffs, so that they would hold together. Now he and Patricia would be able to use the sleeves as improvised scarves.

When all of that was done, Gregory let out an exhausted breath. He felt as though he could fall down right where he was and sleep for a *week*.

"Have another brownie, Dr. Callahan," Uncle Steve said, with a weary smile. "I think you've earned it."

Gregory was starving, but he hesitated. "Don't we have to ration them and all?"

"Right now, I think you need the energy more," Uncle Steve said.

Gregory glanced at his sister for confirmation. "Patty?"

"Fine with me," she said, sounding very tired.

Gregory was too hungry to argue, although he saved one bite for Santa Paws.

The dog snapped it down, and then leaned over to lick Gregory's face in thanks. The dog's stomach was rumbling, and he hoped that they would be able to eat some more food soon. It was way past his supper time! He remembered that when he had been on his own, living outside, he had *always* been hungry. So far, this situation was terrible in the same way. He wasn't sure why any of it was happening, but he knew that he would do whatever he could to help and protect his owners. His ribs still ached, and he moved around to try to find a more comfortable position.

Uncle Steve poured some half-melted snow from one of the MRE bags into the metal cup. While he boiled it over the fire, Gregory and Patricia took turns going behind the nearest boulder to go to the bathroom. It was scary to leave their warm shelter — even to walk just a few feet away — but they felt better knowing that their uncle and Santa Paws were right nearby.

Back at the shelter, Gregory unwrapped the emergency space blanket. The package was almost as small as his hand, but the blanket was surprisingly large. It looked like a huge, paper-thin piece of aluminum foil. The blanket seemed pretty flimsy, but it would help keep them warm during the night. When it was time to go to sleep, Uncle Steve wanted the two of them to snuggle up at the back of the shelter with Santa Paws. In the meantime, he would lie by the woodpile, so he could keep the fire going throughout the night.

After the water had boiled for a few minutes, Gregory stirred in one of the cocoa packets from the MREs. It wasn't safe to drink water from the woods without boiling, or purifying, it first. Fresh snow was safer than water from streams, but they still had to be careful.

Since they only had one cup, they took turns sipping the hot drink. For the first time in hours, Gregory and Patricia could feel themselves warming up inside. When the cocoa was gone, Uncle Steve melted some more water and let Santa Paws drink it up.

The dog finished the cup and then wagged his tail.

The only sounds were the crackling of the fire, and the whistling wind. The temperature had dropped at least fifteen degrees, and it felt like it might snow.

"It's so quiet out here," Gregory whispered.

"I could play some music," Patricia offered. Her Walkman was also a tape recorder. If she disconnected her headphones, they would all be able to hear.

"Don't tell me," Uncle Steve said. "All you have is Frank Sinatra."

Gregory and Patricia smiled, although it made them sad to think about their parents. By now, they had probably arrived in Vermont — and gotten the bad news.

Gregory poked through the small pile of cassettes among their supplies. "The BoDeans," he read aloud. "Memphis Slim, Nina Simone, Harry Connick, Jr., and — the Chipmunks?"

"Nothing personal, but that is a *really* weird mix," Uncle Steve commented.

As far as Patricia was concerned, when it came to music, variety was a good thing. "There's a Joshua Redman tape, too," she said.

Gregory made a face. "Can't we just listen to the Chipmunks?"

Uncle Steve and Patricia shrugged, instead of disagreeing. The Chipmunks tape was full of Christmas carols, and they sat close together to listen to them.

Santa Paws was very intrigued by the tape recorder. He sniffed it a few times, trying to figure out where the music was coming from. Once he even poked it with his paw.

"It's okay, boy," Gregory said, and put his arm around him.

The dog wagged his tail and sat down next to him.

Listening to the Christmas carols made Gregory and Patricia feel very homesick. Right now, they were supposed to be safe in their grandparents' cabin, surrounded by the whole family.

Uncle Steve probably felt pretty lonely and afraid, too, but he didn't say anything.

"Are the planes going to come find us tomorrow?" Gregory asked.

Uncle Steve didn't answer right away. "I hope so, Greg," he said finally. "I *really* hope so."

Gregory and Patricia were too exhausted to stay awake much longer. So they crawled under the space blanket, with Santa Paws snuggling up in between them. They were both wearing their makeshift scarves wrapped across the lower half of their faces. They had also pulled their hats down over their ears so that only their eyes showed. Their jackets were zipped, their gloves were on, and they were fully dressed. Despite all of that, they were *still* cold.

"Does your arm hurt a whole lot?" Gregory asked, right before they went to sleep.

Patricia nodded. It was throbbing horribly, but she didn't want to complain. She knew that Uncle Steve was in much worse shape than she was.

"They're going to rescue us tomorrow," Gregory said confidently. "I *know* they are."

Patricia nodded again.

Then they both closed their eyes.

It was a long, bone-chilling night, and Patricia kept having nightmares. Every time she woke up, she wasn't sure where she was — or why she was so cold. Then she would see Uncle Steve keeping watch over the fire, and remember what had happened. Thinking about it only made things worse, so she just made herself go back to sleep.

She woke up for good just after dawn. When she moved, Santa Paws opened his eyes. He wagged his tail under the space blanket, and rested his muzzle on her shoulder.

She reached up to scratch his ears, and his tail wagged harder.

"Good boy," she said softly. "Don't wake Greg up."

The dog wagged his tail, and lowered his head so she would scratch his ears some more. Since his ribs still really hurt, he was glad that she hadn't patted his side.

The wind seemed stronger, and she poked her head out from underneath the blanket to see that it was snowing. *Hard.* At least four or five inches had already fallen.

She heard low coughing, and quickly turned her head toward her uncle. He was lying next to the much-smaller pile of wood, looking even worse than he had the day before. His eyes were half-closed, and his face was brightly flushed. His wallet was open, and he was staring at a picture of his wife and baby.

Patricia crawled out from underneath the

space blanket, being careful not to wake Gregory up. She motioned for Santa Paws to stay. He wagged his tail, nestled closer to Gregory, and went back to sleep.

"Uncle Steve?" she whispered.

He looked up dully, and tried to smile at her. "Morning," he said, and then coughed some more.

She didn't ask him how he felt, because she was afraid of what the answer would be. So she looked out at the whirling snowstorm, instead. In the meantime, Uncle Steve closed his wallet and tucked it inside his jacket.

The storm wasn't quite a blizzard, but the flakes were coming down fast. There was almost no visibility, and the winds were gusting forcefully.

"They won't be able to fly in this, will they," Patricia said.

Uncle Steve shook his head.

"Do you think it's going to stop soon?" she asked.

He shook his head.

That meant that they weren't going to be rescued anytime soon. Definitely not today, and maybe not tomorrow, either.

"If it takes them a few days, will we be able to make it that long?" she asked.

Uncle Steve glanced over to make sure that Gregory was still asleep. "We're, um — " He hesitated. "The truth is, we're in kind of a tight spot here, Patricia."

In other words, *no*. Patricia nodded.

He reached over to take her hand. "I'm sorry. I wish I could do a better job of taking care of things here."

"It's not your fault you're *hurt*," she said.

"No," he conceded. "But I'm not exactly much help, either. Look, don't worry. When the storm stops, we'll put some signals out there, and — " He let out his breath unhappily. "We'll just do our best, okay?"

It didn't even seem possible that this was the way that they were going to celebrate Christmas Eve. It seemed even less possible that they could actually *die* out here. "Do you know where we are?" she asked.

He shrugged, and then winced from the effort. "I got a little disoriented by the crash, but — yeah, more or less." He looked around, and then pointed. "If I'm right, there should be a road about five or ten miles that way."

Only five or ten miles? "That's not far," Patricia said, feeling a flash of hope for the first time since the crash. "When Rachel and I were in the Walkathon last year, we went *twenty* miles."

Uncle Steve smiled sadly at her. "Those are pretty rugged mountains out there, honey. It would be a tough haul even without all of this snow."

Maybe so, but what choice did they have? "How much longer do you think you can hold out?" she asked. "If we wait until a plane *maybe* comes, it might be — " She didn't want to say "too late," so she stopped. "I don't want to just sit here. I think we have to *do* something."

Uncle Steve nodded reluctantly, and they looked over at Gregory and Santa Paws, who were still sleeping soundly beneath the space blanket.

"I don't want to leave you here, but I don't want to send my little brother out into the forest by himself, either," Patricia said quietly.

"No, we can't do that," Uncle Steve agreed. "Even with the dog, it's too dangerous for him to go alone." He indicated her sling. "Are you in good enough shape to walk? Tell me the truth, okay?"

Patricia wasn't sure, but she nodded. "It's not so bad. I'll just be really careful."

"It's going to be even tougher than you'd imagine," he warned. "You're really going to be tired, and cold, and — "

"Do you have a better idea?" she asked.

"No," Uncle Steve said, and then he sighed. "I wish I did."

11

Once the decision had been made, there were a lot of things they had to do to get ready. Patricia woke Gregory up, and they all shared the icy can of Coke. His eyes got very big when he heard that they were going to try to hike out.

"Is it safe?" he asked.

"Our plane crashed, Greg. *None* of this is safe," Patricia pointed out.

Since that was true, Gregory nodded amiably. If she and Uncle Steve wanted him to hike, he would hike. No problem.

The first thing they had to do, was to make sure that Uncle Steve had plenty of wood to keep the fire going until help arrived. He wouldn't be strong enough to crawl around on his own, and if he ran out of wood, he would freeze.

The driving snow made it that much harder to find wood, but at least there were a lot of dead trees around. They broke off as many branches as they could reach. Other branches had fallen down during the storm, and they dragged them back to the shelter to snap into more manageable pieces.

They also tied the rope to Santa Paws' harness again, so that he could help them retrieve some of the biggest branches. To try and keep the wood dry, they stacked most of it at the far end of the shelter where it would be under cover.

While they were working, Uncle Steve had been boiling water. He heated enough to fill the two empty MRE envelopes, and then divided an envelope of the orange-flavored beverage powder between them. The resulting, diluted orange drink tasted kind of weird, but it was nice and *hot*.

Then Uncle Steve melted more water in the empty metal cup and let Santa Paws drink from it.

The dog lapped down the lukewarm water gratefully. He was *very* thirsty, and eating mouthfuls of snow only made things worse. His side hurt so much, that he was having trouble breathing, too. He drank the water so fast, that Uncle Steve refilled it two more times to make sure that he had had enough.

When Santa Paws was finished, Gregory wiped out the cup with a handful of snow. "You aren't going to make any cracks about dog germs?" he asked Patricia.

"Don't worry, I'm *thinking* them," she assured him.

While Uncle Steve gave them last-minute advice, they shared the meat loaf sandwich, some of the carrot sticks, and the last brownie. Santa Paws also had half of a Milk-Bone.

"Okay," Uncle Steve said, after drawing a crude map on his notepad. "This is approximately where we are. As nearly as I can figure, you want to head south, or southwest. There's a little compass on top of the case where the matches are."

Gregory examined the top of the little plastic tube. "The, um, needle points north?" he asked, just to be sure.

Uncle Steve nodded. "That's not going to be perfectly accurate, but it'll give you a general idea. Whenever you pass a distinctive landmark, you can write it down in the notepad. Or, if you want, you can even draw it."

Some of the advice he gave them was very complicated, and some of it was just common sense. For example, he told them that ice melted much more quickly than snow. So if they wanted to heat water, to save time, they should collect any icicles they could find. Another way to get water was to pack some snow into one of the garbage bags and put it inside their jackets.

While they walked, their body heat would start melting the snow. Then they could boil it, without wasting too much firewood.

"If you get too tired or cold, *stop*," Uncle Steve said, between bouts of coughing. "Find someplace out of the wind, light a fire if you can, and get your strength back. You want to stop *before* you get frostbitten, not the other way around."

Gregory and Patricia nodded solemnly. There was so much to remember that it was hard to keep track.

Uncle Steve wanted them to pack all of the remaining food into Patricia's knapsack, but they flat-out refused. He was going to need to keep *his* strength up, too. Finally, he agreed to keep the coffee, sugar, and cream substitute, one packet of crackers and jelly, the fruit mix, the tiny Tabasco bottle, the cough drops, and one of the packets of gum. He would also keep the empty Coke can to heat water in, while they brought the metal cup along.

They agreed that Uncle Steve would hold onto the penlight, while Gregory and Patricia kept the candle. Then Gregory wandered around the nearby trees until he found a really long sapling. He brought it back and strapped the orange life jacket to the end, so that Uncle Steve could wave it as a signal to any planes that might go by. In the meantime, he and Patricia would pack the flare.

"You kids bring the space blanket and the pocket heaters, too," Uncle Steve said. "The heaters only last a few hours, so save them until you *really* need them."

Gregory and Patricia exchanged glances, wondering if they should refuse. Wouldn't he need them more than they would?

"*End* of discussion," Uncle Steve said in a firm "hold it right there!" cop-voice.

"Yeah, but — " Patricia started.

Uncle Steve cut her off. "I have a nice, insulated shelter, and a fire going," he said. "I'll be *fine*. You two — excuse me, Santa Paws — you *three* are going to be out in the middle of it. What are you going to do, build a lean-to every time you need a break?"

The dog looked up alertly when he heard his name. They had all been talking so seriously that he thought they had forgotten him.

"How about my harmonica?" Gregory offered. "You could teach yourself to play."

"And you can read *Entertainment Weekly*. It's really good," Patricia said. "*Wuthering Heights*, too."

Uncle Steve laughed. "Okay. If you kids agree to take the Walkman, it's a deal."

Gregory packed the supplies they were bringing into Patricia's knapsack. It wasn't very heavy, and he didn't think he would have much trouble carrying it. He and Uncle Steve both put on extra pairs of Patricia's sunglasses to protect their eyes from snow blindness. Then Uncle Steve checked through the knapsack one last time, to see if they had everything they needed.

"Okay," he said, and put on a smile. "I guess that's it."

It was hard to say good-bye, and they all avoided each other's eyes. Santa Paws knew that something was happening and instinctively, he raised one paw in the point position.

"It's going to be fine," Uncle Steve said, sounding more confident than he looked.

Gregory and Patricia nodded, and kicked at the snow.

"Look, I'm going to be sitting here, and reading *Entertainment Weekly*, and having a grand old time," Uncle Steve said.

Gregory and Patricia nodded again. Patricia could feel tears in her eyes, and she quickly rubbed her glove underneath her sunglasses. Gregory just kept shifting his weight and blinking a lot.

"Come here," Uncle Steve said. He gave Gregory a quick, one-armed hug, and squeezed Patricia's good hand. "You're great kids, and I *really* love you."

"We love you, too," Patricia answered, her voice quavering a little.

"We'll go really fast, so help'll come right away," Gregory promised.

"Just be careful," Uncle Steve said. Then he reached up to pat Santa Paws. "Take care of them, boy. I'm counting on you."

The dog wagged his tail, and then barked.

"Hang onto the rope and let him break the trail for you," Uncle Steve told them. "And trust his instincts. He has better hearing, a stronger sense of smell — you name it. So, follow his lead."

With that, they all looked at each other again.

"See you soon," Uncle Steve said.

Gregory and Patricia nodded.

It was time to go.

The first few hundred yards were pretty easy. It was all downhill, and the trees protected them somewhat from the wind and snow. Santa Paws plowed along up ahead of them, the snow coming almost all the way up to his chest. His ribs felt like they were burning, but he forced himself to keep walking. Gregory and Patricia followed directly in his tracks.

With their sweatshirt-scarves wrapped across their faces, it was hard to talk. It didn't really matter, though, because they wanted to save their energy for walking. Every so often, they would pause long enough for Gregory to stick a small piece of duct tape on a tree. They wanted to mark their trail, so that any rescuers would be able to find Uncle Steve.

The ground suddenly got steeper, and they had to walk more slowly. Even though they were trying to be careful, they both kept slipping and sliding. Then Santa Paws stopped short.

"What is it?" Patricia asked.

Gregory waded forward through the snow to stand next to him, and saw that there was a ten-foot drop in front of them. There was enough snow down there so that it might be safe to jump — but it also might *not* be.

"What do you think?" he asked, when Patricia came up to join them.

She shook her head vehemently. "No way."

"It's going to take forever, if we go around," Gregory warned her.

"It's *really* going to take forever, if we both break our legs," Patricia said.

The dog waited patiently for them to decide what to do. This wasn't a very nice place to go on a walk, but if that's what they wanted, he was happy to cooperate. Even so, he would much rather be in their nice, warm house, napping underneath Mr. Callahan's desk.

His fur was covered with snow, and he shook violently to knock some of it off. The pain in his side sharpened, and he yelped once. A big chunk of snow had blown into his ear and he turned his head from side to side to try and dislodge it. His paws were also caked with snow. He lifted each one in turn and shook the icy particles away.

It was so windy on this exposed ledge that Patricia and Gregory were having trouble keeping their balance. The snow was swirling around them, and they couldn't see more than a few feet in any direction.

"Let's just keep going!" she yelled, and pointed off to the left, where the terrain appeared to slope more gently. "That way looks easier."

Gregory nodded, and turned Santa Paws in that direction.

"Come on, boy," he urged him.

The dog cocked his head, not sure where he was supposed to go.

"Find the car," Gregory told him. "Let's go find the car!" He had taught that phrase to Santa Paws to help him locate his parents' station wagon in crowded parking lots. But he could also use it here, because if Santa Paws couldn't find their *actual* car, he would always search until he found *any* car. If he knew that they were looking for the car right now, maybe he would be able to lead them to a road.

The dog sniffed the cold air and then looked at him, baffled. There definitely weren't any cars anywhere *near* here. The only scents he was picking up were things like pine trees and deer and decomposing timber. And — wait — a rabbit, maybe. Yeah, he could definitely smell a rabbit.

"Come on, Santa Paws," Gregory said. "Find the car. You can do it."

The dog wanted to make him happy, so he started making his way down the slope. The footing was very tricky, and he hesitated before each step. Gregory and Patricia were just as cautious. Sometimes, the going was so treacherous that they had to hang onto trees to keep from falling.

After a long time, they made it to the bottom of the mountain. They were in a valley now, and the ground was fairly level. But surprisingly, compared to stumbling downhill, it seemed like more work to navigate the flat terrain. Before, at least they had had gravity on their side.

It felt as though they had been walking forever. But when Gregory stopped to look at his watch after marking yet another tree with tape, they found out that it had only been an hour and a half.

"How far do you think we've gone?" Gregory asked, his breath warm against his scarf.

"Not very," Patricia answered grimly.

Gregory nodded. That was about what he had figured. He glanced up at the sky, but the snow was still coming down just as hard as ever.

Then he took out the match container and checked the little compass to see where north was. He wasn't still completely sure how it worked, but they *seemed* to be doing all right.

"We going in the right direction?" Patricia asked.

"I think so," Gregory said uncertainly. "Maybe a little bit too much east."

Patricia nodded. Either way, they were going to be heading *up*hill soon. This valley was pretty small, and mountains rose up all around them.

"Go for another half hour, and then we'll rest?" Gregory suggested. Uncle Steve had said that it was really important to pace themselves.

The thought of that was exhausting, but Patricia nodded. Somehow, they had to make it as far as they could before it got dark.

Their lives — and Uncle Steve's life — depended on it!

12

It was snowing so hard that most of the time, they couldn't really see where they were going. But Santa Paws kept plunging forward into the storm. They hung on tightly to the rope and let him lead them through the forest.

"Do you think he knows where he's going?" Gregory yelled.

"I hope so!" Patricia yelled back.

They forged on and on, through endless drifts. Sometimes the snow only came up to the tops of their boots. Other times, it was waist-deep. On top of which, they kept tripping over buried rocks and logs.

Except for the sounds of their labored breathing and the icy pellets of snow landing all around them, the woods were utterly silent. They hadn't even seen any *wildlife*.

After a while, Patricia was so cold that she was starting to stagger. Since she knew that she couldn't make it much further, she yanked on the rope to get her brother's attention.

"Greg, I have to stop for a while," she said weakly.

He was concentrating so hard on walking that the concept of doing something *else* seemed confusing.

"Just for a minute," she said. "Please?"

"Oh. Right." He looked around the dense forest, swaying slightly on his feet. "Do we just sit down where we are?"

Patricia gestured a few feet away. "Under that tree, maybe."

Gregory nodded and lurched over there.

Feeling the tug on his harness, the dog turned around. Gregory was going a different way now, so he reversed his direction and followed him. He loved his owners, but this was the *worst* walk he had ever been on. Too cold, too windy, too *everything*. And they still weren't anywhere *near* a car.

Gregory's hands were clumsy from the cold, but he unzipped the knapsack. He took out the space blanket and spread it on the ground. That way, they wouldn't have to sit directly on the snow. He started to flop down, but Patricia shook her head.

"Let's get some of this snow off first," she said.

Gregory nodded and started brushing her off.

He felt very uncoordinated and had to remind himself not to brush too hard where her arm was broken. Patricia used her free hand to knock most of the snow off him, too.

Bundled up with her face completely covered, his sister was unrecognizable. "You look like a really fat one-armed snowman," Gregory observed.

"*You* look like Charlie Brown's long-lost Canadian cousin," Patricia said, and paused significantly. "The *disturbed* one."

Maybe they were getting punchy, but they laughed a lot harder than either joke deserved. Then they stamped their feet over and over, trying to clear their snow-encrusted boots.

Just to be sociable, the dog shook a few times, sending a spray of snow in all directions.

Gregory and Patricia sat down on one end of the space blanket and Santa Paws squirmed in between them. Then Gregory pulled the ends of the blanket up around them. Now they were sheltered from the blowing snow, and might be able to warm up.

"I don't like nature anymore," Patricia said.

Gregory nodded. "If we make it out of this, I'm like, staying inside with Dad from now on."

They sat under the blanket, shivering. Santa Paws seemed pretty comfortable, and they both leaned close to him.

"Should we make a fire?" Gregory asked.

Patricia sighed. "That would mean we'd have to go look for wood, and figure out where to build it and all."

Right now, that sounded like *way* too much work.

"Next time we stop?" Gregory said, and Patricia nodded.

Santa Paws yawned and curled up into a tight circle. He was *really* tired. There wasn't much room, and he had to drape himself across their legs. Gregory and Patricia watched enviously as he drifted into a nap.

"He's lucky," Gregory said.

"Yeah," Patricia agreed. "We're going to have to take turns, if we sleep. Otherwise, we might freeze to death."

Gregory shuddered. After surviving all of this, that would be too awful.

Patricia changed the subject. "Let's drink our juice box. It might make us feel better."

Gregory lowered his scarf enough to grin at her. "When we sing 'My Favorite Things,' we *always* feel better."

Patricia looked right back at him. "I don't care if we *are* in the middle of nowhere. *Nothing* would convince me to sing 'My Favorite Things.'"

"I'm going to tell people you kept running down the mountains with your arms out, pretending you were Maria," Gregory said mischievously.

Patricia laughed. "Hey, if we make it out of this, you can tell people anything you want."

Gregory had been carrying the juice box inside the pocket of his hooded sweatshirt so that it wouldn't freeze. He poked the little straw inside, and they passed the box back and forth. The juice was actually fruit punch, and it was good and sweet.

"Can we listen to the Chipmunks for a minute?" Gregory asked.

Patricia nodded and fumbled for her Walkman. The batteries would probably run out pretty soon, but they might as well enjoy it until then.

They huddled under the space blanket, listening to music, and savoring every single sip of fruit punch. They weren't really warm, but at least they had stopped shivering.

Their hands and feet were so cold, that they broke down and opened one of the pocket heaters. The heaters looked like tiny white beanbags, and there were two in each package. They were about an inch and a half wide, and three inches long. The little bags were filled with some sort of minerals, which were activated when the bag was exposed to air.

Patricia put her heater inside her one exposed glove, while Gregory immediately dropped his into his left hiking boot. After a few minutes, he switched his heater to the other boot. Patricia also transferred hers to one of her boots. When that foot had warmed up, she changed it to the other one.

She couldn't retie her boots with one hand, so Gregory had to do it for her.

"We can stop again in a while, and switch them," he said.

"Okay," Patricia agreed, wishing that they had a *hundred* little heaters and didn't have to conserve them. "Are your hands warm enough?"

Gregory nodded. "They're all right. They just feel, I don't know, kind of *thick*."

"Take them out and blow on them a little," Patricia suggested. "Or put them under your arms for a minute. That might help."

Gregory did just that until he could move his fingers pretty well again. Patting Santa Paws made them feel warmer, too. The dog opened his eyes and thumped his tail a few times.

"Ready to go back out there?" Patricia asked finally.

Gregory put his gloves back on. "Guess we don't have much choice," he said.

Patricia nodded, and they climbed out of the space blanket to face the storm again.

They walked, and walked, and walked. Slipped, stumbled, and slid. Limped, and staggered, and limped some more. Sometimes they would make it partway up on a slope, only to fall back down and have to start all over again.

Then they heard a strange rumbling sound somewhere up above them.

Gregory squinted up into the falling snow. "What's that noise?" he asked.

Patricia shrugged, too tired to pay much attention. "I don't know. Sounds like some kind of engine or something, or — " Realizing what she had just said, she stared at her brother. "Greg! It's a plane!"

He stared back at her. "What? Are you sure?"

"They're searching for us!" she said. "We're saved!" Then she began looking around frantically, trying to locate the sound. "Where are they?! Greg, come on, we have to make sure they see us!"

They were surrounded by a thick cluster of trees, and it was hard to know which way to run. This might be their only chance for survival, and they had to guess right!

"This way!" Gregory shouted.

"No, *this* way!" Patricia said, pointing uphill. "Hurry! Before they leave!"

They scrambled through the snow as fast as they could, stumbling over rocks and branches. Sensing their excitement, Santa Paws barked loudly and raced up ahead of them.

As they ran, Gregory dug the signal flare out of the knapsack, and gripped it tightly in one hand.

"Should I set it off?" he yelled. "So they'll see us?"

"Set it off *where*?" Patricia yelled back. "We have to figure out where the plane is, first!"

The vibrating sound seemed to be louder now, and Santa Paws was staring up at the sky as intently as they were.

"Come on!" Patricia said urgently. "We need to get out in the open!"

There were trees everywhere, and no sign of a clearing or lake or any other open area. The plane's engine seemed to be off to the right, and they ran in that direction. The thought of being rescued gave them so much energy that they leaped over drifts that would have exhausted them a few minutes earlier. If they fell down, they would just pick themselves up and keep running.

They still hadn't seen anything, and now, the sound of the engine seemed to be fading away. One minute, it was there; the next minute, they could only hear the wind blowing.

"Wait!" Gregory yelled. "Come back!"

They both yelled, and waved, and jumped up and down, while Santa Paws barked wildly and ran around in circles. If someone really was out searching for them, why weren't they looking more carefully? Didn't the rescue people *want* to find them?

Patricia was the first one to give up. She sank

down into the snow, trying not to cry. Not only had they not been rescued, but now that the plane had searched this area, it probably wouldn't come back.

"Down here!" Gregory kept shouting into the storm. "We're down here!" He set off the flare, and peered hopefully into the driving snow. "Come back!"

Santa Paws barked some more, and threw in a couple of howls for good measure.

"Greg," Patricia said quietly. "Take it easy. Don't waste your energy."

"But — " He glanced down at her, still waving his arms to try and get the pilot's attention. "I mean — "

Patricia shook her head. "It's too late. They didn't see us."

Gregory slowly let his arms drop, so disappointed that he almost burst into tears. Then he slumped down miserably next to her in the snow.

The plane — if there had even *been* one up there — was gone.

The afternoon crawled by. It was still snowing, although maybe not quite as hard as it had been earlier. They were both so disappointed that the search plane hadn't seen them, that they barely spoke as they slogged through the drifts. Santa Paws seemed tired, too, and his tail dragged behind him.

After a while, they stopped to crouch under the space blanket and nibble on an MRE oatmeal cookie.

"I really thought that plane was going to come save us," Gregory said miserably.

Patricia reached over to put her arm around him for a minute. "If they didn't find us, maybe they'll find Uncle Steve. At least now, we know that they're looking."

Gregory was too depressed to find much consolation in that, but he nodded.

"You want to light a fire?" Patricia asked.

"Let's just wait until we set up camp for the night," Gregory said.

Patricia was too tired to argue, so she just shrugged and ate her share of the oatmeal cookie.

Then Gregory noticed that there were ice crystals caked all around the pads on Santa Paws' feet. He took his gloves off and gently cleaned the dog's paws out. Then he rubbed his hands together and stuck them inside his jacket to try and rewarm them.

Santa Paws thumped his tail against the space blanket. His paws were cold and sore, and it was a relief to be able to rest for a while. Resting helped ease the pain in his ribs a little, too. But it still hurt to breathe, and he had to take very shallow breaths.

They sat long enough to let their body heat fill

the enclosed blanket and listen to a few Nina Simone songs. Gregory and Patricia were both
yawning, and they had to fight to stay awake.
Santa Paws was already dozing.

"We're going to have to set up for the night
soon, Greg," Patricia said. "Put aside some time
to find wood and all."

Gregory lifted his jacket cuff enough to peer
at his watch. It was almost two-thirty, so they
probably had about two hours of light left. "One
more hour?" he proposed. "See if we can get over
this stupid mountain?"

They had been climbing for a couple of hours
straight now, and Patricia didn't feel as though
they had made any progress.

"Okay," she said, trying to sound confident.
"Let's do it."

Then they staggered back to their feet and
pushed on. The ground was so steep that Gregory and Patricia were gasping for breath and
their legs trembled from the effort of climbing.
Santa Paws was still in the lead, but he seemed
to be very tired. His ears were drooping, and
every few feet, he would stop and look back at
them plaintively.

"He's really losing it," Gregory said. "I'll go up
front and break the trail for a while."

Patricia nodded. "Okay. We can switch off
every fifteen minutes."

Gregory bent down to hug Santa Paws and

then lead him back behind Patricia. Walking in the rear would take the least energy, since he could just step in their boot prints. The dog was so exhausted that he wagged his tail forlornly and was content to follow them for now. His paws were aching, his side was throbbing, and he was weak from hunger.

The snow came up to Gregory's knees. It took so much effort to plow through the untouched drifts that he was perspiring heavily after only a few minutes.

"You all right?" Patricia asked, when she saw him start to weave a little.

Gregory nodded, too tired to respond. They were approaching a ridge running along the side of the mountain, and the wind was picking up. So much snow was pelting his face that he could barely see an arm's length away.

The snow felt crusty under his feet. Because it was so much colder on the open ridge, a sheen of ice had formed quickly on the surface of the snow. Each time he took a step, his foot crunched through and it took a lot of effort to pull it free. No wonder Santa Paws had gotten so tired!

"Can you see anything on the other side?" Patricia yelled.

Gregory couldn't really see anything at *all*. "Snow," he yelled back. "Trees."

"No gas station?" Patricia asked. "No McDonald's?"

No *anything*.

Instead of going all the way up the mountain, Gregory decided it would make more sense just to cross over the ridge and start down the other side.

There was a wide slab of snow in front of him, and he climbed up on top of it. He was just turning to tell Patricia that everything looked safe, when suddenly, the entire slab gave way under his weight.

Then, he disappeared in an avalanche of snow!

13

"Greg!" Patricia shouted, completely horri-fied.

Before she had time to move, Santa Paws had already bolted past her. He galloped over the side and plunged down into the gigantic pile of snow below.

When Patricia made it to the top of the ridge, she saw no sign of Gregory anywhere below. Santa Paws was about thirty feet down the slope, digging frantically through the snow with his front paws.

Realizing that her brother had been buried by what might be tons of snow, Patricia almost screamed. As she ran to help Santa Paws, she fell halfway and started sliding. She rolled right past him and had to race back up.

Being able to use only one arm to dig made her cry in frustration. She kicked at the snow with her boots, too, but Gregory was nowhere in sight.

The dog's paws were a blur of motion and snow flew behind him as he burrowed deeper and deeper. Hoping desperately that he had found the right place, Patricia dug right next to him.

If they didn't hurry, he would suffocate!

The first thing they saw was a snow-soaked jeans leg.

"There he is, Santa Paws!" Patricia shouted. "His head! We have to clear his head!"

The dog scraped the snow away from Gregory's back, trying to dig him free. He was lying face down and very still.

"I see his hat!" Patricia said. "Right there!"

Santa Paws dug so hard that he pulled the hat right off. Seeing her brother's hair, Patricia reached into the snow pit to brush the last bits from his face. Then, while Santa Paws tugged on his sweatshirt hood from behind, she used her arm and both legs to try to push him over.

Working together, they managed to move him onto his back. Gregory's face was chalky-white and his lips looked blue. Patricia was terrified that he might have been smothered, but he moved one arm feebly. Then he started coughing and spitting out snow. Some of the color was coming back into his cheeks, and Patricia breathed a sigh of relief.

"Gregory?" she asked shakily. "Can you hear me?"

"I'm really cold," he whispered, his teeth chattering so much that he could barely form the words.

She was going to have to get him out of the wind and in front of a fire, *fast*. She scanned the slope rapidly. Snow, and trees, and more snow. A good ways down the side of the mountain, she could see what looked like a formation of rocks through the trees. It looked like their best chance.

Gregory was trying to sit up now. He moved his arms and legs experimentally, and shrugged his shoulders a few times. Santa Paws came over and licked his face joyfully, and Gregory did his best to give him a clumsy pat on the head.

"Be careful. Did you hurt anything?" Patricia asked.

"B-b-bruises and stuff," he said, stuttering from the cold.

"Okay." She was so glad to see him alive and talking that she hugged him with her good arm. "Rest here for a minute, and I'll go down to the rocks and see if I can make a shelter."

Gregory nodded, and leaned against Santa Paws to recover himself. Then, he sat bolt upright and the color drained from his face.

"What?" Patricia asked, scared all over again.

"The knapsack," he whispered, and looked around at the mammoth pile of snow around. "It's gone!"

* * *

Without the knapsack, they were in big trouble. Patricia started searching, but soon realized that it was a lost cause. Because the compass was attached to the top of the match container, Gregory had been carrying the matches in his jacket pocket. The only other things he had in his pockets were the Swiss Army knife and two Milk-Bones.

"I'm sorry, Patty," he said, shivering uncontrollably. "I didn't mean to — "

She hugged him again. "We'll be fine, Greg. We have the matches, so we can still build a fire. It's going to be okay." Then she held her hand out to help him to his feet.

When Gregory tried to put weight on his left ankle, his leg gave out. He gasped, and fell back into the snow.

"Is it broken?" Patricia asked, dreading his response.

"I think it's just twisted," he said weakly.

They looked at each other, both on the verge of bursting into hysterical tears.

Patricia didn't speak until she was pretty sure she could keep her voice steady. "Lift your arm around me, so I can help you down to those rocks," she said.

Gregory leaned on her heavily, unable to put much weight on his injured ankle. Then they started down the slope. Their progress was so slow that *snails* could have made it down

295

there and back in the same amount of time.

Santa Paws moved ahead of them, thrusting his body through the snow to break a trail. Having a path to follow made it much easier to walk. Or, in Gregory's case, *limp*. Actually, Patricia was limping, too — and Santa Paws' gait wasn't all that steady, either.

Once they were inside the rock formation, the wind seemed to die down. Patricia swept the snow away from a small boulder. Then she eased Gregory onto it, so he could rest. He pulled his hood up over his head, wrapped his arms around himself, and tried to stop shivering.

Santa Paws was already climbing around the rocks and sniffing various crevices, his sides heaving from the effort of breaking their trail. He stopped in front of one and started barking.

Patricia walked over to see what he wanted to show her. She crouched down to peer into the crevice. It wasn't exactly a cave, but there seemed to be enough room for them to crawl inside. A few inches of snow had been blown through the opening, but much less than she would have expected.

"Good dog!" she praised him. "What a good boy!"

Santa Paws wagged his tail.

Gregory limped over to see what was going on.

"What do you think?" Patricia asked. "It looks safe."

Gregory nodded, shaking too hard to speak.

Patricia crawled inside first to clear aside as much of the snow as possible. It would be a tight fit in here with all three of them, but maybe they would be warmer that way.

There was a large crack at the furthest end of the crevice, and she kicked some snow over to block it. Once she was finished, she crawled back out.

"Go in out of the wind, okay?" she said to Gregory.

He was so cold that he didn't even try to argue.

Patricia decided to collect firewood first. Once Gregory was warmer, she would find some pine boughs for them to lie on. Doing everything one-handed took twice as long, but Santa Paws helped her by dragging the branches she tied to his harness. She even found a small, dead evergreen tree, and Santa Paws swiftly pulled it over to the rocks for her.

It wouldn't be safe to light the fire inside their shelter, because it would use up all of their oxygen. So Patricia doggedly kicked away the snow just outside until she reached bare rock. It wasn't very windy here, so she didn't take the time to build a firebreak.

Most of the wood was very damp, and she wasted three matches without even managing to light the tiniest twig.

"P-pine needles," Gregory said.

That was a good idea, and Patricia reached as far inside the dead evergreen tree as she could. She pulled out a thick handful of dusty needles, and scattered them around the twigs. Then, remembering the notepad Uncle Steve had given them, she reached into her inside jacket pocket.

The pages were nice and dry, and she crumpled several into tight balls of paper.

Gregory dragged himself over to the opening. "L-let me t-try," he said. "I can use both hands." His hands were shaking so much that he had trouble striking the match. But when it caught, he held the little flame to one of the wadded-up pieces of paper.

It immediately flared up, and then another one began burning. Patricia blew gently on the pine needles, hoping to make them ignite, too. At the same time, Gregory fed more wads of notepad paper into the blaze.

It took a while, but soon they had a small, steady fire.

"Can you keep it going, while I go find branches for us to sleep on?" Patricia asked.

Gregory nodded as he warmed his hands. He was still trembling, but not quite as badly as he had been before.

Patricia was in the middle of getting branches, when she realized that Santa Paws hadn't followed her.

"Santa Paws!" she called. "Come here, boy!"

When he didn't come bounding over, she assumed that he was in the cave with Gregory and went back to what she was doing. She had just dumped her second load of boughs outside the crevice, when Gregory poked his head out.

"Where's Santa Paws?" he asked, looking worried.

Patricia frowned. "I thought he was with *you*."

Gregory shook his head, and they stared at each other.

"What if he's hurt?" Gregory asked. "Maybe he fell down, or got lost, or — " Instead of finishing the sentence, he hauled himself outside. "Santa Paws! Where are you, Santa Paws!?"

They both shouted his name over and over and whistled for him. Any second, they expected him to appear, but he seemed to have vanished.

"Look, stay here," Patricia said, trying not to panic. "I'll go look for him, and — "

"If anything's happened to him — " Gregory started at the same time.

Just then, they heard the familiar sound of license tags jingling. A snow-covered shape trotted into the rock formation, his tail waving triumphantly. There was a canvas strap in his mouth, and he was dragging a bulky object through the snow.

Santa Paws had found the knapsack!

They patted, and hugged, and praised Santa Paws for a long time. Delighted by all of the attention, Santa Paws wagged his tail furiously and rolled over onto his back so they would rub his stomach.

It was getting dark now, and they were happy to be warm and safe inside their rock shelter. They sat with the space blanket draped over their shoulders, thankful to be alive — and together.

Patricia had placed a garbage bag with snow inside her jacket while she was gathering wood, and by now, most of it had melted. So Gregory took out their metal cup and began boiling water. They only had one packet of cocoa left, so they only used half of it. The thin chocolate liquid tasted delicious.

When the cocoa was gone, they heated more water in the cup. Then they squeezed the bag of escalloped potatoes and ham inside and boiled it for a while. When Gregory sliced the top of the bag open, the wonderful smell of hot food billowed out.

They waited for their supper to cool a little, and then spooned out Santa Paws' share. The dog gobbled the steaming food up. Then he wagged his tail to show how glad he was to have gotten something to eat.

The ham and potatoes tasted pretty salty, but Gregory and Patricia enjoyed every bite. Having some food in their stomachs made all the difference in the world.

"You think Uncle Steve's okay?" Gregory asked.

"Sure," Patricia said, making her voice sound more confident than she felt. "We got him all of that firewood, and — he's fine. And we'll be able to get him help tomorrow, I just know it."

Gregory nodded, although he knew she was just trying to make him feel better. Santa Paws seemed to be breathing a little funny, and Gregory frowned. "Is he okay?" he asked. "Do you think he's hurt?"

Patricia watched his side rise and fall erratically. "Maybe he's just tired," she said uneasily. "He had to work really hard today."

Gregory reached forward and patted the dog gently. "Are you okay, boy?"

Santa Paws opened his eyes for a few seconds, wagged his tail, and then went back to sleep. Gregory looked at Patricia, who shrugged, and then they both settled back uneasily.

For a long time, it was quiet.

Then Patricia let out her breath. "I can't believe it's Christmas Eve," she said in a low voice.

Gregory nodded unhappily, but then suddenly

turned to look at her. "Hey! What did you get me for a present?"

She grinned at him. "I'll give you one guess."

"Sunglasses," he said without hesitating.

Patricia's grin broadened, so he knew he was right. And he *liked* sunglasses, so that was fine. He had gotten *her* a blue felt hat with a little feather in the brim.

With luck, they would get to *open* those presents sometime.

Before lying down on their pine boughs, they listened to the Chipmunks tape of Christmas carols twice, until the Walkman batteries finally wore down. After that, it was quiet again, except for the crackle of their small fire.

The wind was blowing, and somewhere off in the distance, they heard the faint howl of an eastern coyote. Santa Paws was instantly on his feet, barking. Gregory and Patricia felt scared for a minute, but they knew that Santa Paws would protect them. After a while, he settled back down underneath the space blanket, and they knew that the coyote was gone.

They tried to take turns staying awake, but sometime during the night, they both fell asleep. When they woke up in the morning, the fire had gone out. But they were still pretty warm, because Santa Paws had moved to cover them with his body when the temperature started dropping.

It had finally stopped snowing outside. Under better circumstances, the landscape would have looked like a winter wonderland. The sky was bright and clear, and all of the branches on the trees glistened with snow.

"Well," Gregory said, and sighed. "Merry Christmas."

"Yeah." Patricia tried to smile. "You, too."

By poking through the ashes of the fire with a stick, they found some glowing embers. So they got the fire going again, and made another thin cup of cocoa. They ate some crackers and apple jelly, and fed Santa Paws one of the last two Milk-Bones. Then they melted enough water for him to drink, too.

Before leaving their shelter, they put the fire out. Patricia covered the ashes with snow, just to be extra sure. Then she found a crooked stick for Gregory to lean on while he walked. His ankle was better, but he was still limping badly.

They started downhill, with Santa Paws leading the way. Refreshed from getting some sleep, they made pretty good time. Then again, walking through deep snow in the sunshine was a lot simpler than trying to make their way through a near-blizzard.

When they got to the bottom of the mountain, the ground leveled off, and they could walk without stumbling. Santa Paws stopped every so often, and sniffed the air before going on.

Sometimes he would start off in one direction, only to turn and lead them a different way. Gregory and Patricia just followed him, no matter what he did.

There seemed to be more room to walk between the trees now. Before, they had been climbing over rocks and everything. But now, the way seemed fairly clear, although the snow was still knee-deep in most places.

Patricia glanced up to her right as they were walking, and then stopped short. "Gregory, look!" she said.

Gregory followed her gaze, and saw a wooden, official-looking sign nailed to a tree. It said RESTRICTED USE AREA, and the sign had been posted by the Appalachian Mountain Club and the United States Forest Service.

"Whoa," he said nervously. "Does that mean we're trespassing?"

Patricia shook her head as a huge grin spread across her face. *Now* she understood why the path seemed easier to follow. "No. It means we're on a *trail*," she answered.

14

"So, like, we'll be in a town soon?" Gregory asked eagerly. He was so excited that he even forgot to limp for a minute.

Being on a trail meant that *some* kind of civilization had to be nearby. "I don't know," Patricia admitted. "But it has to lead to a road — or a cabin, or — I don't know. But — it's good!"

There weren't any tracks in the snow, so no one else had walked on this trail recently. Then again, December wasn't exactly the prime hiking season.

Santa Paws forced himself forward through the chest-deep snow, doing his best to make a path for Gregory and Patricia. His ribs were hurting so much now that he was panting heavily, and sometimes he coughed, too. Each step was an effort, but he just kept putting one paw in front of the other.

Gregory and Patricia were so exhausted themselves that they didn't notice how much Santa

Paws was struggling. As they all waded end-lessly through the drifts, they began to pass more small painted signs. There were arrows pointing them to different trails, and showing them how to get *back* to the mountains. Then they saw a sign that read KANCAMAGUS HWY., 1.2 MILES.

They were just over a mile away from the highway!

"Oh, boy," Gregory said, and put his arms around Santa Paws. "What a good dog!" He took the last Milk-Bone out of his pocket and gave it to him.

The dog wagged his tail and crunched his treat, still panting weakly. He wasn't sure what he had done that was so good, but the biscuit made his stomach hurt less. *Nothing* helped his ribs. He had started to catch slight whiffs of gasoline as they trudged along, but no matter how hard he tried, he *still* hadn't found the car.

When Santa Paws had finished his biscuit, he wagged his tail at Gregory and Patricia. Then he resumed his panting, unsteady trot down the snowy trail.

"Maybe we should take a turn," Patricia suggested, looking worried. "Let him rest for a while."

"Yeah," Gregory agreed. "He seems *really* tired."

First, Gregory tried to get up in front, and then Patricia tried. But each time, Santa Paws would gallop around the side until he was in the lead again.

"I guess he wants to go first," Gregory said, out of breath.

Patricia nodded, breathing too hard to answer. It certainly *seemed* that way.

They were all so exhausted that sometimes they would stumble off the trail. Then they would have to flounder around in the drifts until they stumbled back onto it. After a while, they found themselves in front of a wide area where the snow seemed somewhat grey and caved in. Santa Paws instantly stopped, and lifted one paw in the air.

"What's wrong with him?" Gregory asked.

"I don't know." Patricia limped forward to check. "Maybe he lost the trail, or — "

Before she could finish her sentence, there was a terrible cracking sound and the wet snow gave way beneath her feet! They had walked right on top of a snow-covered, partially frozen stream, and she had fallen through the ice!

The current beneath the thin crust of ice was very swift, and Patricia fought to stay afloat. Within seconds, she was so cold that her teeth were chattering and her legs and good arm were numb. Every time she tried to climb out, the surrounding ice would break away. The current was so strong that it was going to pull her underwater soon!

"Hang on, Patricia!" Gregory yelled. He started toward her, but then heard an ominous cracking underneath his boots. He froze where he was, and looked down at the ice sagging beneath his weight.

"Don't!" Patricia ordered through chattering teeth. "You'll fall through, too!"

Remembering that you were supposed to lie down and spread your weight evenly on thin ice, Gregory quickly flattened on the snow.

"Don't worry, I'm coming!" he promised.

Without hesitating, Santa Paws leaped over him and dove right into the freezing water. He swam over next to Patricia and dog-paddled in place. Patricia grabbed onto the seat belt loop on his harness, and hung on as tightly as she could. But her hand was so numb that she lost her grip and slipped underwater for a few seconds.

Santa Paws grabbed her jacket collar between his teeth and tugged her head up above the surface of the water. Patricia coughed and spluttered and gasped for air.

Gregory reached his arm out as far as he could. "Come here, boy!" he called. "You can do it!"

Santa Paws swam in his direction, dragging Patricia along behind him. She was still coughing

and gasping, but she managed to grasp his harness again. Since she was hanging on now, Santa
Paws released her jacket and just concentrated
on swimming.

"S-s-sticks," Patricia gasped at Gregory, her
voice shaking from the cold. "G-get some sticks!"

The ice sagged more as Gregory propelled
himself backwards, pushing with both hands.
Once the creaking sounds had stopped, he
jumped up and ran toward the nearest tree. He
ripped off several branches and carried them
back to the ice. Then he spread them out, so that
Patricia and Santa Paws would be able to grip
onto something when they climbed out.

Santa Paws dog-paddled in a small circle so
that Patricia would be closest to the edge of the
ice. Then he pressed his body against hers, trying to push her to safety.

"Roll, Patty!" Gregory yelled. "Roll yourself
up!"

Patricia tried, but she was so cold that she
kept slipping back into the swirling water.

"Grab the end of a branch!" Gregory shouted.
"Then I can pull you!"

With Santa Paws keeping her afloat, Patricia
gathered up just enough strength for one last
lunge. She was too weak to hang on, but she
managed to wedge her arm around one of the
branches. With Santa Paws pushing and Gregory

pulling, she was able to crawl to safety. Then she lay where she was, struggling to catch her breath.

"Stay really flat!" Gregory warned her.

Patricia nodded, shivering so hard that she couldn't speak.

Santa Paws was trying to climb out of the stream, but his paws kept sliding on the ice and he would slip back into the water.

Quickly, Gregory swung one of the branches toward him. "Play tug, boy!" he yelled. "Come on!"

Santa Paws grabbed the end of the branch with his teeth in a viselike grip. Then Gregory pulled as hard as he could, until Santa Paws was able to scramble up onto the ice. He shook violently, but most of the water on his fur had already frozen into tiny icicles.

Patricia was so cold that she was having trouble standing up. Gregory helped her to her feet, and then guided her over to the nearest large tree.

"Sit down out of the wind, okay?" he said. "I'll make a fire really fast! Come here, boy! You stay, too."

Patricia nodded, hunching down into her jacket and shivering uncontrollably. Santa Paws was shivering almost as hard, and he leaned up against her. Patricia hugged him closer, trying to get warm.

Gregory piled up the driest branches he could find, and then squirted what was left of their tube of fire-starter onto the stack. There were only two matches in the match container, and the first one wouldn't light.

"What if this one doesn't work?" Gregory asked uneasily, looking at their last match.

Patricia didn't want to think about that, so she just shook her head.

Gregory took a deep breath, and then struck the match. After a tense second, it flared up and he cupped his hand around the flame so that the wind wouldn't blow it out. He brought it carefully to one of the globs of fire-starter, which sputtered, but then also started burning.

As soon as the fire was burning steadily, he began to heat a cupful of water. They didn't have any cocoa left, but he knew that it was a lot more important for Patricia to drink something *hot*, than it was for the water to taste good.

The fire was giving off a lot of heat now, but Patricia's face was very pale and she was still shivering.

"You'll feel better when you drink this," Gregory said, doing his best not to panic. "I *know* you will."

Patricia nodded feebly, and kept shivering.

Gregory was paying more attention to Patricia than he was to the tin cup, and by accident, he let his arm stray too close to the fire. His sleeve burst into flames and he looked down at it in stunned horror.

"Help, what do I do?" he yelled, close to hysteria. "I'm burning!"

Patricia and Santa Paws both lunged forward weakly and knocked him down into the snow. The flames went out right away from the lack of oxygen, but Patricia and Santa Paws stayed on top of him for a minute just to be sure.

"Y-you okay?" Patricia asked through her chattering teeth.

"I think so," Gregory whispered, his heart pounding so loud in his ears that he couldn't really hear. "Th-thanks." He sat up with an effort, and examined what was left of his sleeve. The fire had burned all the way through his layers and down to his forearm, leaving a red shiny spot behind. It hurt a lot, and he pressed a thick handful of snow against it to cool the burn.

The water from the cup had spilled and put their campfire out, too. The wet branches were steaming a little, and there was smoke everywhere.

Patricia and Gregory stared at each other in a daze.

"We don't have any matches left," Gregory said, trying not to cry.

Patricia nodded, feeling a few tears of her own trickle down her cheeks.

Santa Paws whined deep in his throat, and

started pacing back and forth. Then he paused, held his paw up, and sniffed the air curiously.

"With our luck, it's p-probably a grizzly bear or something," Patricia said grimly.

Santa Paws stood very still, his head cocked to one side. Then, suddenly, he galloped away from them.

"Santa Paws, come back!" Gregory shouted after him. "You'll get lost!"

Santa Paws kept running, until he had disappeared around a curve in the trail.

Patricia grabbed a low branch on the tree and used it to pull herself to her feet. "C-come on," she said. "We'd better go find him."

Gregory nodded, and lifted her good arm around his shoulders so that he could help her walk. They followed the trail of paw prints, stumbling along as quickly as they could. Santa Paws' tracks led right out of the woods and into an unplowed parking lot. There was a small, wooden information booth, but it was closed for the season.

Just beyond the parking lot, they could see the Kancamagus Highway. Only one lane had been cleared, but it appeared to be passable.

"He did it," Gregory breathed. "He saved us!"

Patricia nodded weakly, and sank down onto a snowy picnic bench to rest.

From somewhere up on the highway, they could hear frantic barking.

"Take it easy, boy," a deep male voice was saying. "Come here, okay? I'm not going to hurt you."

Santa Paws just kept barking and racing back and forth. After all their hours of walking, he had *finally* smelled a car! Now he just had to lead the driver back to Gregory and Patricia.

Realizing that Santa Paws had found help, Gregory and Patricia staggered over to the edge of the road. They could see a snowplow idling in the middle of the highway, and a burly man with a thick blond beard hurrying after Santa Paws. He was wearing a thick blue parka and a Lincoln Sanitation Department baseball cap.

Gregory sagged against Patricia, his legs so weak that he almost fell. "We made it," he whispered, hugging her as tightly as he could.

"I know," she whispered back.

Then, they both burst into tears!

After that, everything happened fast. The snowplow driver, whose name was Andy, helped them up into the warm cab of his truck and wrapped them up in a heavy wool blanket. He had a thermos of hot coffee and Gregory and Patricia took turns drinking from the plastic cup. They were both still crying, and shivering so much that they spilled almost as much coffee as they managed to drink.

First, the local police came, followed by some

state troopers and a paramedic. Gregory and Patricia told them everything, especially where they had left Uncle Steve and how they *had* to go search for him *right away*. They both talked so fast that they kept interrupting each other, and Officer Jeffreys, the state trooper who was in charge, had to keep telling them to slow down.

Soon, they were bundled up in the back of the state trooper's four-wheel-drive Jeep. It had been arranged that their parents were going to meet them at the hospital up in Littleton. They had left as soon as they got the call, and would be there as soon as possible.

The police officers were all very nice to them, and explained that rescue planes had already been up searching all morning. Now, at least, they knew *where* to look. Gregory and Patricia just prayed that their uncle was still okay.

The ride up to Littleton seemed to take forever. Trooper Jeffreys drove, and the paramedic rode in the passenger's seat. Gregory and Patricia were too exhausted to talk anymore, and Santa Paws fell asleep across their laps.

By the time they got to the hospital, Trooper Jeffreys had to wake all of them up. There were a lot of reporters in front of the emergency room, and plenty of television camerapeople, too. As soon as the paramedic opened the back door of the Jeep, the reporters started shouting questions. Bright lights on top of the cameras were flashing, and everyone started crowding around them.

"Tell us about your ordeal!" a reporter cried out.

"Did you ever think all hope was lost?" another wanted to know.

"Where's the hero dog?" a third demanded.

There were so many people that Gregory and Patricia hung back inside the car for a minute.

"Let's clear the way!" Trooper Jeffreys said in a commanding voice. "Back off now!"

Other police officers moved forward to control the crowd, and open a path to the emergency room entrance.

Santa Paws was the first one to get out of the car. He took one tentative step forward, and suddenly collapsed. He coughed weakly, and then closed his eyes.

"Santa Paws!" Gregory gasped, and rushed forward to help him.

The paramedic scooped Santa Paws up from the ground and rushed into the emergency room with him in her arms.

"The dog went down!" she shouted. "I think he's critical!"

"Bring him into Trauma One!" one of the doctors ordered. "And I want both kids in Trauma Two!"

"We can't leave Santa Paws!" Patricia said frantically. "We have to stay with him!"

"It's all right," another doctor said, in a very soothing voice. "It's going to be fine. They're taking very good care of him."

There was a curtain between the two trauma rooms, and Gregory and Patricia could hear voices yelling about "IVs *stat*" and "Taking chest films" and that someone should call in a veterinarian, *fast*.

Gregory and Patricia refused treatment until they were sure that Santa Paws was going to be okay. The X rays showed that he had broken several ribs in the crash, and that his right lung had collapsed. He was also badly dehydrated, and suffering from hypothermia.

"Is he all right?" Gregory asked repeatedly. "Is he going to be all right?"

"He's in intensive care now," one of the nurses explained. "Don't worry, he's a good, strong dog. He'll pull through."

But Gregory and Patricia *were* worried. All those hours, Santa Paws had been hurt, and they hadn't even *realized* it. But there was nothing that they could do about that now, so they just held hands tightly, and waited for news about him.

Then, they heard two very familiar, worried voices in the front of the emergency room. Their parents had arrived!

"Where are they?" Mrs. Callahan was asking. "Please, where are our children?"

"Right this way," a nurse answered, and led them to Trauma Two.

As soon as they saw their parents, Gregory and Patricia started crying again. Their parents were crying, too, and hugged them over and over. Aunt Emily had come along with them, and she was smiling bravely, but her lips kept quivering.

"Santa Paws is hurt," Gregory said through his tears, as Patricia was asking if the planes had found Uncle Steve yet. "Is Santa Paws okay?"

Unfortunately, there was nothing they could do now but *wait*.

It turned out that Gregory had torn some ligaments in his ankle. The doctors made him a soft cast, and he would need crutches for about six weeks. He also had a second-degree burn on his arm, and some minor frostbite.

Patricia was also slightly frostbitten, and she was still shivering from her fall through the ice. Her knee was sprained, and she had broken her arm in *two* places. The huge cast went all the way from her fingertips to her shoulder. It hurt so much that she just kept holding on to her mother's hand the whole time she was in the trauma room. The doctors had given her a painkiller, but the only thing it had accomplished so far was to make her very sleepy.

"We really didn't want to leave him," she whispered to her mother, struggling not to cry as they waited to hear about Uncle Steve. "But I didn't know what else to do."

Mrs. Callahan kissed her gently on the forehead. "You did the only thing you *could* have done, Patricia," she said, and kissed her again. "We're *very* proud of you. Both of you."

Just then, Gregory came swinging into the room on his crutches with a big grin on his face. Mr. Callahan walked next to him, resting his hand on his son's shoulder.

"Dad and I just went to see Santa Paws," Gregory said. "He's going to be okay! He wagged his tail and everything!"

Hearing that, Patricia started crying again and hugged her mother gratefully.

As a precaution, the doctors wanted all three of them to stay in the hospital overnight. Gregory and Patricia protested, but their parents insisted. In the end, they were put together in the same room in the pediatrics ward. Santa Paws was still in intensive care downstairs, being watched by a team of local veterinarians.

The nurses brought the family a late lunch, but none of them could eat it. They were too busy worrying. Gregory and Patricia's grandparents were driving down with Miranda, and could arrive at any time.

Then, at about three-thirty, the word came in that a rescue chopper had found Uncle Steve. He was very weak, but still alive, and they were air-lifting him directly to the hospital.

Aunt Emily went downstairs to the Emergency Room to wait for him. Soon, she sent word up that he was conscious, and talking, and wanted to know how *they* were.

For the first time since the plane had crashed, Gregory and Patricia relaxed. Uncle Steve was okay! They were *all* okay!

"I'm *really* tired," Patricia said to her parents. Over in the next bed, Gregory was already asleep.

They slept until about nine o'clock that night, with their parents watching over them the whole time. When they woke up, they drank juice and ate chicken soup and chocolate pudding.

"How's Uncle Steve?" Patricia asked. "Can we go see him? And Santa Paws, too?"

"Let me find out," Mr. Callahan answered. He went out to the nurses' station, and returned with a big smile on his face. "He's awake now, and they said it would be fine."

Gregory and Patricia rode down the hallway in wheelchairs, because it was a hospital policy. But since their parents were the ones pushing them, they didn't really mind.

In addition to his collarbone, Uncle Steve had fractured his pelvis and badly strained his back. He also had some frostbite and a severe case of bronchitis. The doctors had him on lots of antibiotics, so that it wouldn't turn into pneumonia.

Gregory and Patricia's grandparents were already in the room, with Aunt Emily and Miranda. The hospital dieticians had cooked a special holiday meal for everyone, and the nurses had set up a beautiful Christmas tree in the corner of the room. It was decorated with red and green bulbs and a string of brightly twinkling lights. Someone had also found a CD player, and Christmas carols were playing in the background.

When Uncle Steve saw them come in, he put down his spoonful of Jell-O and gave them a big grin. He looked tired and frail, but he also looked extremely glad to see them.

"Well, if it isn't two of my favorite heroes!" he said.

There was a lot of noise as they all tried to talk at once, and Miranda yelled, "Yay, Daddy!" over and over. Then there was a familiar low woof, and they all turned to look at the door.

It was Santa Paws, riding on a gurney!

Gregory and Patricia both limped over to hug him, and Santa Paws wagged his tail. He was still wearing an IV in his front paw, but he looked happy and alert. He would be back to normal in no time!

"*Here's* the hero," Gregory said proudly. "All we did was follow him."

Patricia nodded. "No matter what happened, he always took care of us."

Then Gregory laughed. "Yeah. We told him to find the car, and — he found the car!"

Everyone was still laughing, and talking at once, and Santa Paws took advantage of the confusion to bark some more. Hearing all of the noise, other patients from the floor had gathered around to share in the excitement. There were also nurses and doctors everywhere, and when Santa Paws barked again, they all clapped.

"Merry Christmas!" someone yelled.

"And a Happy New Year!" someone else added.

Santa Paws kept barking and wagging his tail as hard as he could. He was overjoyed to be together with the whole family again. Somehow, in spite of their grueling adventure, they were all warm, and happy, and *safe*.

It had turned out to be a *very* Merry Christmas, after all!

Get your paws on more great animal books!

How can one Pet cause so much Trouble?

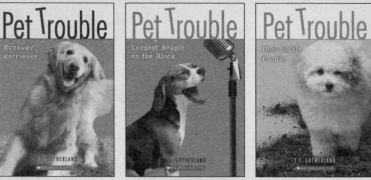

Runaway Retriever

Loudest Beagle on the Block

Mud-Puddle Poodle

Bulldog Won't Budge

Oh No, Newf!

Smarty-Pants Sheltie

Bad to the Bone Boxer

Dachshund Disaster

Read the series and find out!

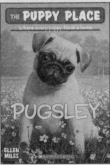

You belong at

WILDWOOD STABLES

Friendship, rivalry, and the amazing place that
brings them together . . . Read them all!

#1: Daring to Dream

#2: Playing for Keeps

#3: Racing Against Time

#4: Learning to Fly

#5: Stealing the Prize

For more magical fun, be sure to
check out these tails of enchantment!

READ ALL ABOUT IT!

More canine adventures with Bruce and Andi!